OLD HABITS DIE HARD

Also by
LaJill Hunt

Drama Queen

No More Drama

Shoulda, Woulda, Coulda

Old Habits Die Hard

Anthology:

Around the Way Girls

Around the Way Girls 2

A Dollar and a Dream

OLD HABITS DIE HARD

LAJILL HUNT

www.urbanbooks.net

Urban Books LLC
1199 Straight Path
West Babylon, NY 11704

Copyright © 2007 LaJill Hunt

ISBN-13 978-1-60162-023-1
ISBN-10 1-60162-023-3

First Printing November 2007
Printed in the United States of America

10 9 8 7 6 5 4 3 2 1

Submit Wholesale Orders to:
Kensington Publishing Corp.
C/O Penguin Group (USA) Inc.
Attention: Order Processing
405 Murray Hill Parkway
East Rutherford, NJ 07073-2316
Phone: 1-800-526-0275
Fax: 1-800-227-9604

This book is dedicated to my parents, Charles W. Smith and Martha J. Smith. You have always been in my corner and supported me whether I was down on my luck or on top of the world. I love and appreciate you both, dearly.

Also, to my aunt, Joycelyn W. Hunt.
Your selfless spirit, continual giving of yourself, your time, and your talents are to be admired. Thank you for all that you do and I love you so very much. You are truly a blessing and a Godsend and please know that I appreciate your being a constant presence in our family.

Acknowledgments

First and foremost, to the most high God, for again, blessing me with another story to tell and the opportunity to tell it.

To my pastor, Dr. K. W. Brown and First Lady Elder Valerie Brown for your love, support, advice, and leadership. I aspire to become what you encourage me to be. It's just gonna take me a little time to get there, lol.

To the Mt. Lebanon Missionary Baptist Church family, thank you for all of your love and support.

To Alyx, Kam, and Ken. I now realize that my opportunities are not even about me, it's about you and I pray that you all reap all the rewards and benefits. I LOVE YOU!!

To LaToya, Chaz, Braxton, Uncle Pie, Karis, Ashley, Gloria, Corey, Kendall, and Blanket . . . family is everything, even if it's dysfunctional!!

To Carl and Martha Weber, my publisher extraordinaire and my editor unparalleled. Thank you for all you have done for me and allowing me on this journey. My success is greatly due to your teamwork and talents.

My best friends: Joy, Shan, Saundra, Yvette, Tonya, Roxanne, and my Cherie Amore. Through the years, the tears, the laughter, the pain, the ups and downs, thank you for always being in my corner.

My VZ family: Angela B, Andrea J, Jodina F, Chenay C, Donna G, Chris "CTY" Y, Yolanda S, Robin L, and Danita M . . . you are the bomb, and I love you.

To Omedia Cutler, Toye Farrar, and Milly Avent, for being my best critics and my biggest cheering section. Whoo-hoo!!

To my literary twin, Dwayne S. Joseph, for always being there for me and your constant encouragement. You are the most talented, deserving person I know and nothing but good things are gonna happen for you.

To my brothers Roy Glenn and K. Elliott, Torrance Oxendine, and Norrell Smith, thanks for always having my back.

To the fans, the book clubs, the bookstores, and anyone who took the time to read my book, thank you for giving me the opportunity to entertain you and thanks for the support.

In the famous words of my friend Erick S. Gray, author of *Ghetto Heaven*:

Live It! Write It! Be About It!

Hit me up at MsLajaka@AOL.com or www.myspace.com/LaJillHunt

Blessings!!

Prologue

Camille walked inside After Effex, the salon where she worked. "Lincoln! Where are you?"

There was no answer. Yaya, her boss, told her that Lincoln, the contractor, would be there doing some work, but he was nowhere to be found.

He must've had to run out for a second. She walked past the large empty box, which used to house the new princess chair he was installing. She went into Yaya's office and began searching for the contract. It was nowhere to be found.

Just as she was about to call and let her know, she spotted a piece of paper lying on the floor. She leaned down to pick it up and then she heard voices.

"Why the hell are you following me around? What the hell do you want from me?" she heard Lincoln say

"I want you to act like you know me, for starters. You can't just think that this is over. I'm telling you right now," a woman replied.

Camille remained behind the desk, listening.

"It was never anything to begin with. Okay, we kicked it

and I hit it. So what? You act like we were together or something."

"You act like we weren't together," the female snapped.

"Look, I don't even know why you're trying to play yourself out like this. I don't even know you and it's obvious you don't know me—you're straight bananas, chick!"

"You know me well enough to screw me a few weeks ago when we left Ochie's. Don't even try to fake like you don't remember. You told me I gave the best head ever while I was going down on you in your van. You weren't that drunk."

"That doesn't say much about you, now does it? Look, if we did do anything I can guarantee you two things—one, I used a condom because I always do; and two, it didn't mean anything to me. And if you thought otherwise, I'm sorry. So, if you think that by harassing the hell outta me is gonna get me to believe this bullshit, you're crazy."

"You don't have to believe me, Lincoln. The paternity suit I plan on hitting you with will be proof enough. I heard you talking to Jarrod next door the other day, about how you've decided to change and you're thinking really hard about getting with that bitch Taryn, because now you see how much she means to you. Ha! Well, guess what—when she finds out I'm carrying your seed, she ain't gonna have nothing to do with you. And I, for one, am glad. Not that it matters, anyway. Actually, the only thing that matters is the fact that you're gonna take care of me, and you're taking care of this baby—I mean that."

"Girl, you'd better stop playing with me," Lincoln said laughing.

"You think this is a joke? But don't worry; I'm sure it'll be correct on those checks you'll be stroking out to me every month for the next eighteen years. Go ahead and laugh now. Because when push comes to shove, I'm taking you down and everyone down with you."

Camille peeked above the desk to see who Lincoln was

talking to. She looked up just in time to see the familiar girl storm out the back door, right on Lincoln's heels. She was so nervous, she almost peed on herself. *Lincoln got this chick pregnant? There's no way! Taryn is going to kill her and him!*

She knew for a fact that withdrawing from school was the best thing for her; now, seeing all this unfold right before her eyes, she had no doubt, her life at the salon was about to get interesting. Once she was sure the girl was gone, she stood up. She stared at the paper in her hand and realized it was the contract that she was searching for. She didn't waste any time faxing it and was hurrying to get back to her niece's soccer game where her family was.

Camille was so busy rushing out the door that she didn't see the tall gentleman outside the door. She ran smack into him, surprising both him and her.

"Whoa, are you a'ight?" he asked.

"Yes, I'm fine," she told him. "Sorry."

"It's okay. Hey, you work in there? I need to get something right quick," the man told her. He was so tall that Camille had to look up to talk to him.

"Yeah, but we're closed," she answered.

"I know, but can you please just help a brother out, cutie" he said, giving her a salacious grin.

Already agitated, her nerves were on edge and she really didn't feel like dealing with him. She was feeling hot and sticky, a combination of the late summer heat and her own PMS issues. The last thing she needed at that moment was some dude trying to mack her.

"I'm sorry." She shrugged and started to walk off. She was stopped by his hand on her shoulder. She snatched away and frowned at him. "Get your hands off me."

"My bad. Look, I just need to get a gift card right quick, that's it. It won't even take you two minutes," he pleaded. "This is really important. It's for my—"

"You're gonna have to come back Monday morning," she

4 LaJill Hunt

told him and rushed away. She started her SUV and glanced at him before she pulled off. For a second, she felt bad but figured if it was that important, he would return Monday morning as she suggested.

Camille drove down the street; thinking about whether she should say anything about Lincoln's supposed baby mama to Yaya or Taryn, the other owner of the salon and Yaya's best friend who had been the person who hired Camille, even when Yaya didn't want to. It was a well-known fact that Taryn had a thing for Lincoln for some time now. Camille didn't know what to do. She reached in her pocket for her cell phone to let her family know she was on the way back to the park, but it wasn't there. She looked in the seat beside her and noticed her purse wasn't there, either. *Damn, I left my phone and my purse at the salon.* She made a U-turn in the middle of the street and pushed hard on the gas pedal, rushing to retrieve her belongings. So focused on the drive back, Camille almost didn't see the flashing lights in her rearview mirror.

"Oh, hell naw," she said out loud. She pulled her truck over to the side of the road and rolled her window down. The officer walked up and she asked him, "Is there a problem?"

"Ma'am, you made an illegal U-turn and you were speeding. License and registration please," he said, his face void of any emotion.

She tossed her head back and exhaled. "I don't have my license. I left my purse at work and I'm on my way back to get it right now."

"I need your name and Social Security number, ma'am," he told her. She gave him the information he requested and sat back and waited. *I can't believe this is happening to me. I've never gotten a ticket a day in my life. He only pulled me over because I'm black, I know it.* She leaned back in her seat, praying no one she knew drove by and saw her.

A few minutes later, the police officer returned, and told

her, "Ma'am, I'm going to need for you to get out of the vehicle."

"Excuse me?" Camille said, confused by what he was saying. She thought he would return with a ticket and a court date.

"You're gonna have to get out the car, slowly," he said. She noticed him place his hand on his gun and she started to panic. Tears filled her eyes and she was afraid to move. "Ma'am, I'm asking you, get out of the car."

She decided to follow the officer's instructions and she slowly opened the door and got out. Her vision was blurred and she wiped the tears to see clearly. "What's wrong?"

"You have two warrants for your arrest," he said. "Turn around and put your hands on the vehicle."

"How? For what?" she asked him.

"Turn around, ma'am. Hands on the vehicle," he said again.

Camille looked at his uniform and made a mental note of his name and badge number, in case she needed it later. She was dazed as if caught in a bad dream. *Wake up so it can be over with. You've gotta be sleeping.* She put her hands on the side of her truck and waited as the officer frisked her.

"You have any weapons on you?"

"No, I don't," she said, sniffling. She turned her head and saw a silver Chrysler slow down as it passed. She caught the eyes of the driver and saw that it was the same guy who tried to stop her outside the salon. She closed her eyes, regretting that she didn't help him. He looked at her and kept going. *I shoulda helped him. He's probably thinking karma is a bitch.*

Just as the officer was reading her rights, she could hear someone saying, "Is there a problem?"

"Sir, you need to return to your vehicle. This is a police matter," the officer warned him.

"I'm just trying to see what's going on, officer. This young lady is a friend of mine and I just need to make sure she's okay," the guy said. Camille turned to see that the guy had indeed turned around and was walking toward her. She didn't know what she felt more of, guilt or relief.

"She's fine, sir. I'm going to have to take Ms. Davis downtown now and you can meet us down there if you like. But you're gonna have to leave, now!"

Camille could see the concern in the guy's face. Clearly in a last attempt to help her he asked, "Can I just bring her downtown?"

"Back in the car, sir," the police officer's voice got louder.

"Wait!" the guy said. "What about her vehicle?"

The officer paused and then asked her, "You want your friend to take care of your truck for you? If not, I'm gonna have to have it impounded."

Camille tried to think. *Should I trust a complete stranger with the safekeeping of my truck or have it impounded?* She didn't know what to do.

"Let me get her keys and get it back to the salon where she works." The guy walked over to them.

"Is that what you wanna do, ma'am?" the officer asked.

Camille nodded and the officer tossed the keys to the perfect stranger. God, please don't let him steal my truck.

"I'll be downtown as soon as I get the truck to the salon, Ms. Davis," he told her. "Don't worry about anything."

"That's fine, sir," the officer said. "She'll be at the magistrate's office."

Sitting in the back of the squad car, Camille cried. She didn't know what the hell was happening. She had never been in trouble in her life. Just as it seemed as if things were turning around and her life was getting better, it all shifted in an instant. Now, she was on her way to jail, a complete stranger had taken possession of her car and she could feel her period coming on. Life couldn't get any worse.

Chapter 1

"Okay, this is getting ridiculous," Taryn said as she walked into Yaya's office.

Looking up from her computer and seeing the bouquet of yellow roses Taryn was carrying, Yaya smiled. "For me? I wonder who they're from?"

"The same damn person that sent the ones you got day before yesterday, that's who from." Taryn pushed the vase of flowers that were already sitting on Yaya's desk over and placed the vase she was holding next to it. "Why the hell don't you take some of these damn flowers home? It's starting to look like a funeral home in here."

"I keep forgetting to take them. Besides, they make my office look nice." Yaya reached into the bouquet and took out the small card. "Fitz is so sweet."

"He's so whipped." Taryn faked a gag.

"Yaya, your three o'clock is here," Monya's voice came through the intercom system.

"He can't be whipped, T, I haven't even given him any," Yaya snapped back and laughed.

"Stop lying." Taryn shook her head.

"I'm serious. We haven't done anything other than kiss." Yaya shrugged as they walked into the main area of the salon. Business was steady and she was glad. After Effex was a dream that she and Taryn came up with a long time ago and now, with the help of Yaya's brother Quincy, the salon was now a reality. It wasn't in the high-class area that Yaya wanted it to be in, but she was working on that happening in the near future. For now, elite clientele had to come to the hood for the one-of-a-kind facials, esthetics, and makeup artistry that she and Taryn provided along with the awesome manicures and pedicures and nail tricks, courtesy of Monya. The three formed a dynamic team and were in high demand in and out of the salon. And now that she had discovered a formidable protégé in Camille, her plans for her business to grow seemed to be inevitable. She really couldn't take credit for hiring Camille. Taryn had been the one to give the girl a chance. To be honest, Yaya really didn't want to hire her. Quincy was dating Paige, whom Yaya didn't like at first. Camille lived with Paige. Yaya quickly got over her issues with Paige and found that Camille was a dynamic employee who had a bright future in front of her.

"So, you've only kissed him and he's sent you roses every other day for the past two weeks?" Taryn continued. Yaya looked over at her best friend and business partner. At five foot nine, Taryn was tall and looked nowhere near the two hundred ten pounds she weighed. She was a full-figured diva and wherever she walked, heads turned, both men and women. Not only was she beautiful, but her fly sense of style enabled her to play up her thick hips and considerable cleavage. Taryn had the ability to make a *Jet* "Beauty of the Week" jealous. Her confidence commanded all attention on her and she got it. Even in the After Effex long-sleeved T-shirt, jeans, and black boots she wore, she looked more like a supermodel than a makeup artist/nail tech. Yaya looked down at the outfit she had on and somehow knew that Taryn's still looked more appealing in hers, although they wore the same thing.

"Come on, T. You know that if we did do anything, I would tell you," Yaya commented.

"You must be doing something, because roses ain't cheap," Monya said giggling.

"You don't even know what we're talking about, Monya, be quiet," Yaya replied. She knew that Monya knew exactly what they were talking about. Her newfound relationship with Fitzgerald had been the talk of the salon. Everyone was glad that she had finally gotten rid of her ex-boyfriend Jason and decided to give Fitz a chance—something she had been hesitant to do. Not only was he a blue-collar worker, employed by UPS, drove a Honda Accord station wagon, of all vehicles, had dreadlocks, a style she was hardly attracted to, but he had a son. Dating a man with a child was something she had promised herself she would never, ever do. It seemed that although Fitz did not fit the mold of what she thought was going to be her ideal mate, he did possess some things that could not help but appeal to her: the man was fine as hell, no doubt about that. Every time she looked at him, the hairs on her neck stood up and she had to catch her breath. Not only was he fine, but he was cute. He was a gentleman, he was charming, and he was her protector; he had proved his loyalty by knocking Jason out a few weeks ago when he attempted to disrespect Yaya at the salon. Seeing the way Fitz defended her made her step out the box where she usually remained when it came to dating. There was also the fact that she noticed that Quincy had stepped out of his box and found his soul mate, Paige. Now maybe, she had found hers.

"I know that they must be some powerful kisses for him to be sending you flowers like that," Taryn teased.

"Maybe it's *where* she's kissing him," Monya added.

The salon erupted with laughter and Yaya stood speechless. She looked over at her three o'clock client who was near tears from laughing so hard. "Ha-ha-ha, see if it's that funny when I pluck that uni-brow of yours."

The door opened and Camille walked in. Yaya felt sorry for her young employee. Camille had been going through a lot over the past couple of months with her mother, brother, and sister-in-law and Yaya could see that it was beginning to take its toll on the girl, mentally and physically. The Camille who walked through the door was a far cry from the vibrant, eager-to-learn young woman who had proved herself worthy of a position at After Effex. Her eyes were troubled and she wore a somber look on her face. Yaya knew how it felt to be at the end of your rope, and she knew that was where Camille was at this point. She had to do something and do something quick. As soon as she heard about Camille being arrested, Yaya didn't hesitate calling a lawyer friend of hers, Jamison Grossman, and he agreed to represent Camille.

"Hey, Cam, you okay?" She walked over and put her arms around Camille's shoulders.

"Yeah, I'm good." She sighed. "Hey everyone."

"What's up, girl?"

"Hey Camille."

Camille was greeted by the patrons and employees simultaneously.

"You have a couple of messages waiting for you," Taryn said to Camille.

"For me?" Camille looked surprised.

"Yeah, girl, some dude's called like three times." Monya gave her an impressed look. "Terrance."

"Oh, yeah," Camille said, shrugging, "He's the guy that was there when the *situation* happened the other day."

"And he's calling already? What did you do? *Kiss* him?" Taryn looked over at Yaya, who was leading her client into the Zen room, where they gave facials. Everyone other than Yaya and Camille began laughing.

"Huh?" Camille was confused.

"Shut up," Yaya snapped as she walked out. "Ignore them, Camille, they're all ignorant."

Not wanting to even think about what they were talking about nor any of her other increasing list of problems, Camille took a seat behind the counter located on the side of the salon and began her receptionist duties. She was so busy taking calls, making appointments, and acting as cashier, that she didn't notice the limousine that had pulled up outside the salon almost an hour later.

"Oh, no, this can't be happening," Taryn groaned.

"Who's that?" One of Monya's clients leaned over so she could get a closer look.

"It's probably Yaya's boyfriend, Fitz. He's been doing all sorts of romantic stuff to impress her," Taryn said. "Yaya, your man is out here in a limo for you."

"What?" Yaya walked out of the Zen room with her client behind her, looking refreshed and revived, her brows done and her face glowing.

She stared out the window as the limo driver got out and opened the door. Instead of Fitz stepping out as Taryn had predicted, an extremely tall guy got out and reached back inside. A hand grabbed his and he assisted an older woman out. He leaned over and kissed her on the cheek then put his arm through hers. The two smiled as they walked through the door.

"Hello, welcome to After Effex," Yaya greeted them.

"Hi, I'm Terrance Oxford, this is my mother, Irene, and today's her birthday," he said, smiling.

"Happy birthday!" they all said in unison.

"Thank you, thank you. I told Tuff he didn't have to go through all this trouble, but he is making such a fuss." Mrs. Oxford smiled.

"Nonsense, Ma, you only turn fifty once and you deserve all this fuss!" He shook his head.

"Terrance Alouiscious Oxford, I can't believe you just stood there and told my age!"

"I'm sorry, Ma, I'm just so proud of how good you look at this age. I didn't mean to," Terrance apologized.

"Alouiscious?" Camille giggled. He looked over and smiled. She couldn't believe he had actually been telling the truth about his needing a gift for someone special. She owed him big-time and she knew it. Looking down at the day's appointments, she was relieved to see that she would be able to fit Mrs. Oxford into everyone's schedule.

"That's okay, Mrs. Oxford, your son's right, you look wonderful and you do deserve the star treatment." Yaya nodded. "So, not that you need it, but what will we be doing for you today?"

"The works," Terrance said.

"The works?" His mother repeated. "What is that?"

"Manicure, pedicure, facial, and makeup application," Yaya answered.

"Tuff, that's too much. I don't need all that."

"Nobody said you needed it, Ma. You're getting it," he told her. "Camille has everything taken care of for you, right, Camille?"

"Sure do, Mrs. Oxford, and we're all ready for you." Camille nodded.

"If you'll just follow me," Yaya took Mrs. Oxford by the arm. "We are going to start with a facial."

"Whoo, I've never had one of those. I'm so excited, and please call me Irene," she told her.

"I'm glad to see you made it to work," Terrance told her.

"Thanks," she said.

"You look so familiar," one of the clients said to him. "Where do I know you from?"

"I'm the weekend sports anchor on channel forty-three," he said, smiling.

"Yeah, the *Tuff Love Report*," she said, nodding, and told

the woman sitting next to her, "I told you. You tried to make me think I was crazy."

"All righty now, another TV star in the house. Monya, get the camera and add him to the wall of fame," Taryn announced.

Terrance walked over to the board of photos already hanging, which included shots of Taryn, Monya, and Yaya posing with their clients, famous and not so famous. There were pictures of them with R&B singers, rappers, NBA and NFL players, even strippers.

He whistled and said, "Uh, I don't think so. These are real stars up here. Is that Usher?"

"Yeah, that's him," Monya said as she walked up with the camera. "Say cheese."

"I'm not a client, my mother is," he told her, covering his face with his arm.

"You may need to make an appointment with me, from the looks of those nails," Monya told him. He looked down at his hands.

Taryn continued, "And if the hands look like that, there's no telling how the feet look. I can work that out for you."

"Damn, y'all really know how to make a brother feel good about himself, huh? I'm glad I have a great grade of hair or you would be sending me next door to see Jarrod," One of the barbers from the shop next door. He laughed and then turned to Camille. "And what's your specialty?"

"I'm just the receptionist." She shrugged. Something about the way he was looking at her made her feel self-conscious. She began fidgeting with things on the counter.

"Don't even try it, Cam," Taryn responded. "Ms. Camille here is the most talented makeup artist in training on this side of the planet. The girl is fierce and she's had no formal training."

"True that," Monya added, as if she was Taryn's personal amen corner.

"Cool," he said. "So, I'm going to get out of here and perpetrate in the limo for a while. You wanna hang out with me until my mom gets done?"

"Uh, I don't think so. I'm at work." She giggled, shaking her head.

"I figured you were gonna say that. It was worth a try though," he told her. "Maybe I can get a rain check?"

"Maybe," she told him.

"So, what time do I need to come back?" He smiled.

"I said maybe," she told him, surprised at his determination.

"I was talking about picking up my mother," he said, laughing. If there was ever a time she wanted the floor to open up and swallow her, it was now. She could hear the snickers from the other women in the room.

"Well, I think she'll be done in about two hours," she told him without looking up. "Would you like to pay now or when you return?"

"I can take care of it now," he said, passing her his credit card. She took his payment and passed him the slip to sign. He left a generous tip and said, "Thank you for hooking my mom up."

"It's the least I can do after what you did for me," she told him. "I really owe you big-time."

"It's all good. You don't owe me a thing. I'll be back in a couple hours."

"Okay," she said, smiling at him. She couldn't help be amused by his charm and sincerity. Terrance Oxford was a true gentleman, something she had yet to experience in her twenty years of living.

Chapter 2

"I see Lincoln finished the Zen room, it looks nice."
"Yeah, he came last night and got it done," Yaya said to Fitzgerald. They had met for dinner and while they were eating, she realized she had forgotten her makeup case at the salon and had to come back and get it. "You know I called your bootleg brother and threatened him."

"He told me," Fitz answered. His older brother was a contractor and actually helped design the salon. Picking up Yaya's large makeup bag and putting it on his shoulder, he looked around her office and asked, "You taking any of these flowers home?"

"Maybe I should. I think the girls are beginning to get a little jealous. One of my clients showed up in a limo today and Taryn thought it was you."

"Tell Taryn stop hating. I'll have Lincoln send her some flowers so she can feel special tomorrow."

It was no secret that Taryn had a thing for Lincoln. It was still unclear, though, whether Lincoln felt the same about Taryn.

"Your brother better wise up and get with Taryn before

another man comes along and snatches her up," Yaya said, matter-of-factly.

"Hey, what can I say? He's a slow learner. I know a good thing when I find it."

"Is that why you send me flowers? Because I'm a good *thing?*" She put her hands on her hip and waited for him to answer.

"No, I send you flowers because I love you." He walked over and kissed her tenderly on the lips. "And because they're beautiful like you."

"Good answer." She winked and fought the urge to reach under his shirt and caress his chest. She had decided to take things slow with Fitz. In her past relationships, there were times she found herself so caught up in the sex that she couldn't see the stupidity of her boyfriends and before she knew it, she was asking herself how the hell she wound up with another fool. The fact that Fitz was fine as hell didn't help her horniness, but she was determined to wait until she was sure that Fitzgerald was more than a rebound guy that she got with since she was no longer with Jason.

"Damn, you smell good," he said as he pulled her body to his.

"Naw, that's just the flowers my man sent me to make me feel special," she said, laughing, hoping comedy would relieve the sexual tension in the room. Luckily, Busta Rhymes's "Touch It" began blasting from her jacket pocket.

"My sentiments exactly, Busta," Fitz said aloud.

"Be quiet," she said and took the phone out. "Hello."

"Hey, Yaya, what's going on?" Jamison's voice greeted her.

"What's up, Jimmy Jam? You gonna be able to help my girl out?"

"I'ma damn sure try. Someone has really got her in a bind. Have you talked to her?"

"Not yet. We were slammed today and I didn't get a chance to. What the hell is going on?" Yaya released herself from Fitz's grasp so she could focus on what Jamison was telling her.

"Well, basically, it's a hellified case of identity theft," Jamison replied.

"Identity theft?"

"Yeah, someone has stolen her identity. She has three bench warrants out for failure to appear. Two on traffic violations and one for check writing. It's a mess."

"Damn," Yaya said, sighing. She couldn't believe it.

"Not only that, but her credit is ruined, Yaya. They got credit cards that are maxed out and several store accounts. It's a huge mess."

"So, what is she—no, what are *we* gonna do?"

"Well, for starters, shut down the accounts that are still open in her name and dispute the ones that are maxed out. I've already contacted all the credit bureaus and the DMV but it's gonna take a minute to get all this squared away," he answered. "I just wanna find the bastard that's doing this to her, and when I do . . ."

"I'm going to kick their ass," Yaya finished his sentence for him. "Look Jimmy, I appreciate you helping her out like this. I'll take care of your fee. Just let me know what it is."

"Don't worry about that right now. You know me and you go way back, Yaya. I'm just worried about Camille. She's a nice girl, reminds me a lot of you with her sexy ass."

"Don't go there, Jamison," Yaya warned.

"You know that girl's too young for me. Besides, she's a client. I would never go there. Now with you on the other hand . . ." he teased.

Yaya looked over at Fitz and prayed he couldn't hear Jamison through the phone. "I gotta go, Jimmy. Thanks a lot, and please keep me updated."

"I will. I'll probably come by there sometime this week and check your new salon out. I hear you're doing big things over there. I'm proud of you, girl."

"Thanks, I'll see you then," Yaya said and ended the call.

"Jimmy Jam?"

"Yeah, that's my friend Jamison. The one I told you is handling Camille's case. We graduated from high school together."

"He says he's gonna to be able to get Camille straight?"

"Yeah, someone's stolen her identity, from what he said," she told him. "I feel really bad for her. She's a good kid."

"I can't believe you're reaching out and helping someone. I guess what people say about you is wrong," he said, smiling.

"And what do they say about me?"

"That you're selfish and can be a real—"

"A real what?" Yaya snapped. She knew people thought that she was self-centered, snobbish, and maybe even a bitch, but she was changing her ways. She had been spoiled most of her life by her brother, her uncle, and mainly all the men she had dated. But she had seen the error of her ways and was trying to become a better person. No longer did she see things as her way or no way, but she was still not concerned about what people thought or felt about what she did. "And I don't care what people say about me anyway. I like Camille. She's a good person and if I help her out, it's my business."

"See, there you go, assuming what I was about to say."

"And what were you about to say?"

"A real good person when you stop trying to front like you're so damn hard-core." He laughed. "But I love all of you, even the hard-core parts of you. As a matter of fact, there's a hard-core part of me I think you should check out yourself."

Again, she found herself wrapped in his strong embrace, kissing passionately while fighting the urge to have him bend her over her desk and take her from behind, something she had fantasized about on more than one occasion. "Don't worry, I'm sure I'll be checking out that part of you soon enough. Just not right now," she told him when she was able to tear her mouth away from his.

"And I can't wait." He caressed the back of her neck. Waiting was the right thing to do, but damn it was gonna be hard.

"Don't worry, Cam, we're gonna get you the best attorney and get all this mess straightened out. There's no way someone is gonna get away with this, believe that."

Camille looked at Paige, who was the closest thing she had to a sister. Paige had always been there for her from the moment she started dating Marlon, her brother. And although Lucille, their mother, treated Paige like crap, Paige continued to maintain a true relationship with Camille and hold on to Marlon. Finally, two children and seven years of dealing with Lucille's psychotic behavior and Marlon's inability to be a man and marry her, Paige packed up, lock, stock, and barrel and left him. When Camille heard Paige was gone, she felt like she was alone in the world. She and her mother never had a true maternal bond and Marlon was so caught up in his own drama after finding out the woman he had cheated with, Kasey, was now pregnant. Her brother tried to be there when he could, but their conversations were few and far between and most times ended in an argument. When Camille found out that their father was alive and not dead as their mother told them for years, Paige was the only person Camille knew she could turn to. And being the genuine person that she was, Paige stood right by her and supported her through the entire ordeal. When she finished her freshman year of college and needed somewhere to stay for the summer, it was Paige's house that she moved into. That house was now her home, and she hoped once she found out Camille decided to turn down her scholarship and not return to school, Paige continued to be there for her.

"I already have a lawyer. His name is Jamison Grossman and he's a friend of Yaya's," Camille told her.

"He's probably expensive if he's a friend of Yaya's," Paige replied. "You know all her friends are ballers."

"You're right." Camille laughed. "And did I mention how fine he was?"

"Yeah, those are the two requirements she has in order to associate with you. Money and good looks," Paige said, sighing.

"Yaya is not that bad once you get to know her."

Camille knew that Paige didn't care too much for Yaya due to the fact that Yaya tried everything in her power to break Paige and Quincy up and almost succeeded in doing so until she realized that Paige truly was a great person and good for her brother.

"I'll just take your word for it," Paige said, nodding, "As long as you feel like Jamison Grossman can help you, then that's all that matters. And you know I got your back. I just hope you can get all this cleared before you leave for school in a couple of weeks."

She started to confess to Paige that she wasn't returning to school, but chickened out at the last second. She decided to change the subject instead. "Did you call Meeko and ask her about Celeste?"

Celeste and Meeko were both Paige's cousins. Celeste, the girl who Camille overheard announcing to Lincoln that she was having his baby, had been the troublemaker of the family for years. She was constantly starting drama and running, blaming others and claiming to be the victim whenever she got caught. Meeko was Paige's cousin who kept up with all the family gossip, didn't bite her tongue for anyone and didn't have a hard time putting anyone in their place. She had recently gotten married and had a baby, living a fairy-tale life. Unlike the relationship she had with Celeste, Paige and Meeko were as close as sisters.

Paige nodded her head. "Yeah, I did. She said exactly what I did. No one has mentioned anything about Celeste being pregnant and she's probably lying. The girl doesn't have anything going for her, no job, no friends, and no life, so she has to create trouble in order to get attention. If Lincoln knows anything like I know, he'll get a restraining order."

"He didn't even remember her name," Camille said, laughing. She tried to feel sorry for Celeste, but she couldn't. The girl was desperate for love, but she went about it the wrong way. She slept with any man who looked in her general direction, and fell in love with any man who showed her the slightest bit of attention. She had been engaged twice, both times to convicted felons serving life sentences. She had schemed and plotted on men her entire life, and still wound up all alone. She was truly the epitome of desperation and pathetic. Now, here she was claiming to be pregnant by a man who didn't even remember who she was, let alone recalled sleeping with her.

"You didn't say anything at work, did you?"

"No, I wouldn't dare tell Lincoln's business like that. Besides, Taryn would go ballistic," Camille replied. Her cell began ringing and she saw her brother's name on the screen. She quickly asked Paige, "You didn't tell Marlon what happened yesterday, did you?"

"No, I didn't say anything to him," Paige said as she got up from the sofa. "I'm gone to bed. Good night."

"Hello," Camille flipped the phone open and answered it.

"Hey kiddo, what's going on?" her brother greeted her.

"Nothing much. What's going on with you?"

"Uh, what you got planned for Sunday afternoon?"

From the tone of his voice, she knew Marlon wanted something. "Why?"

"I need for you to meet me at the house at around four-thirty," he told her.

"What house?" she asked quickly, hoping he wasn't talking about his old house where their mother now lived with Kasey, because that wasn't about to happen. For some reason, Lucille and Kasey took an instant liking to each other. When Lucille's house went into foreclosure, she wasted no time moving in with Kasey and Marlon. Soon after, unable to take living with his alcoholic mother and trifling, new pregnant wife, Marlon surprised them all by moving out. Neither woman really cared, though, because he continued to pay the bills and take care of them.

"My house, Camille. Well, my old house where Mama and Kasey stay."

"I don't think so. What do you need me to meet you there for?" She frowned. She knew Marlon had to be smoking something in order to call and ask her something like that.

"Look, Kasey's baby shower is there on Sunday and I need for you to go with me. I also need for you to bring Myla and Savannah," he told her. "But don't tell Paige where you're taking them."

Camille didn't even hesitate before she replied, "Hell no! Marlon, have you lost your mind? You know that ain't even happening. First of all, I hate that woman you married and I don't even want to be bothered with Mama. Second, there's no way I'm going to even bring those girls anywhere near either one of them. And third, Paige would kill me and so would Rachel. You know they would find out. Why would you even want to go to her shower?"

Rachel was the mother of Marlon's other daughter, Savannah, who was fourteen. Marlon had found out last year that he even had a daughter because when Rachel came to the house to tell him she was pregnant, at the tender age of fifteen, Lucille had run her off and she had never returned. Rachel was a sweetheart, just as Paige was, and the two women got along great. It was Kasey who tried to cause damaging drama, even going so far as to give the girls a DNA test to prove that Marlon wasn't the father of either one of them. The test, however, proved that he did father both girls. From that point on, both Paige and Rachel forbade Marlon to have the girls anywhere near his mother or wife and Camille didn't blame them.

"Because it's my baby she's carrying and I wanna show my support," he told her. "And I don't care how much you hate her, that's your niece or nephew."

"I'm not going," she told him. She could see her alcoholic mother causing a scene as she always had and Camille refused to be around when that happened. She decided a long time ago, that once she became an adult, she would stay as far away from her mother as she could. She no longer had to endure the drunken rage and embarrassing outbursts as she had growing up. She loved her brother and there wasn't anything she wouldn't do for him, but this was too much for him to even ask.

"Camille, I'm begging you. I am always there for you, no matter what. There hasn't been not one time you've needed me and I wasn't there for you, was it?"

He's trying to make you feel guilty; be strong, she told herself. She paused and then answered, "Yeah."

"I never ask you for anything in return because you're my sister and I don't expect anything from you and it's my job to take care of you. But Camille, you're the only person in my life that I can count on. I'm not saying you gotta stay and enjoy the shower, but I need for you to come just to support me in this. This ain't easy for me, either."

Camille could hear the stress in his voice. She wanted to tell him no one told him to go cheat on Paige, knock the ugly woman up and then marry her, but instead, she told him, "Look, I don't wanna go, but I will. I'm only gonna make an appearance and then I'm out. But there's no way in hell I'm bringing those girls. That ain't even right and you know it."

"Kasey asked if they could attend and I told her only if you brought them." He sighed. "I wanted to see them too."

"Then you call their mothers and make plans to see them that doesn't include that heifer-looking wife of yours or Lucille. Are you trying to piss Paige and Rachel off, Marlon?"

"No, I'm not," he told her. "Okay, I'll see you Sunday. I'll meet you in front of the house at four-thirty. Thanks, kiddo, I really appreciate this. Hey, what day are you leaving for school?"

"Uh, I haven't decided yet," she told him. "I'll see you Sunday."

"Okay, love you."

"Love you too," she said.

She closed her eyes and leaned back on the sofa. She knew in her heart that being a makeup artist was what she was born to do and working for Yaya and Taryn was an opportunity of a lifetime. She just prayed that Paige and Marlon would understand the decision she made without even telling them.

Chapter 3

The gift to enhance a person's beauty and transform their outer appearances was not one Yaya and Taryn took for granted and they constantly did everything within their power to improve and elevate their craft. They were both licensed estheticians and made sure to attend workshops, seminars, and classes that allowed them to grow, learn, and more importantly, network. This was the first thing that had come to mind when Camille walked into Yaya's office, once the salon had closed for the day and told her she had decided to work full-time at the salon instead of returning to school.

"Are you sure this is what you want to do?" she asked her, glancing over at Taryn who had yet to say anything.

"Yes, I'm sure." Camille nodded. "I've prayed about it and I know this is what I wanna do. It's what makes me happy."

"You know this isn't an easy career, right?" Yaya told her. "And you're gonna have to be certified."

"Certified?" Camille frowned.

"Yeah, certified," Taryn repeated. "Either way you look at it, you gotta go to school, girlfriend."

"I don't have a problem with that, I mean, I like school," Camille said, shrugging.

"And I'm sure you'll do well," Yaya told her. She had called and made the arrangements the beginning of the week when Camille told her she had decided to become a makeup artist a few weeks ago. She had a feeling that this was the decision Camille would be making. "Here's the name and number you need to call. They're expecting you, but you need to take care of it now. Classes start in about two weeks."

"I'll call first thing in the morning." Camille took the slip of paper from Yaya's hand and walked out of the office.

"This has to be déjà vu for you, Yaya," Taryn said, laughing.

"What are you talking about?"

"Being young and ambitious and dropping out of college to follow your dreams," Taryn replied.

Yaya looked at her friend. "Disappointing my family who told me I was crazy and going to end up broke."

"But you showed *them,* didn't you?" They both laughed and began going over the monthly budget for the salon. Things were really going well for them since opening six months ago. They were already beginning to see a profit.

"I really wanna talk to Quincy about opening a new salon in the Galleria next to his shop," Yaya told her, referring to the mall where one of her brother's barbershops were located. "The craft store that used to be there is moving."

"You really think we're ready for another salon so soon, Yaya? I mean, we're doing well right now, but I don't know if we're ready for a second location."

"Come on, T. This place is booming. A lot of our clients aren't even from this side of town. They just drive over here to be serviced, you know that. And that's a much nicer area."

"I just don't want to grow too fast too soon," Taryn said sighing, looking at the figures on the sheet in front of her. "One of the reasons we're doing well right now is because we don't have the overhead. We don't have rent to pay. Thank

God for your brother not charging us because the building is paid for."

"The rent in the Galleria isn't that bad, Taryn. I've already been checking it out. Come on, we got in this to make After Effex an empire. Don't chicken out on me now," Yaya said. She hoped Taryn wasn't becoming complacent. Yaya wanted to build on the success of the business and not settle and she needed for her partner to feel the same way.

"And let's say we do decide to open a second location in the Galleria to service high-end clients. Who's gonna fill the void in the shop when those clients stop coming to the downtown location?"

Yaya didn't respond, she just stared at Taryn, unable to think of an answer.

"I do want to build the empire, Yaya, but we've gotta be smart about it. Between the salon and maintaining clients outside the salon, we're already wearing ourselves thin. You were just complaining about not feeling well last week."

"That's because my reflux was acting up. You know Monya can run this shop with her eyes closed, especially now that we have two more nail techs. Let's just go see it. Okay?"

Taryn stared at her best friend and saw the determination in her eyes. Yaya was the most driven person she knew and creating the After Effex empire they had planned years ago was in her sights. There was no way Taryn could deny her partner the support she needed. She just hoped right now was the right time. "I guess going to see it wouldn't hurt."

Yaya ran and gave her friend a big hug. She knew Taryn had her back and they were in this together.

"Uh, am I interrupting something?"

They jumped back, startled, and laughed as they saw Lincoln standing in the doorway.

"Hey Lincoln," Yaya spoke as she walked past him.

"What's up, Yaya. Hi there, Ms. Green, you're looking fine as ever." He smiled and put his arm around her. Taryn couldn't help smiling. Lincoln was fine as hell and her attraction to him was not a secret. At six foot four, two hundred-forty-five pounds, he had the build of a male underwear model.

"Why thank you, Mr. Webster, and to what do I owe the pleasure of this visit?"

"I wanted to know if you wanted to hang out with me tonight. I'm going to check out that new Will Smith movie."

Taryn sighed, wondering if he was asking her because he truly wanted to spend time with her, or because none of his little chicken heads were available. She decided that she had wanted to check the movie out herself and she did enjoy hanging out with Lincoln, so she told him, "Sounds good. Give me a minute to get my things from out my office."

"Cool." He smiled and followed her down the hallway to her office.

"You ready to get outta here?" Yaya asked when she walked into the salon. Camille looked up from the receipts she was tallying. Everyone else had already left and the salon was locked up. Yaya cut the front lights off and hung the *closed* sign in the window.

"Yeah, as soon as I finish with the deposit for the bank," Camille told her.

Yaya saw the worried look on her face. "What's wrong? The money's not right?"

"No, the money's fine. I'm just thinking about this whole school thing. If classes start in two weeks, then it's probably too late to apply for financial aid, and with this whole identity theft thing, I'm not gonna be able to get a loan." She could no longer stop the tears she had been fighting and they fell from her eyes.

"I'm sure Paige and your brother will help you, Camille." Yaya walked over and touched her hand.

"They don't even know that I'm not going back to school." Camille shook her head. "I haven't even told them yet."

"I know how you feel, Camille. I was in the exact position you're in now. Hey, you said you've prayed about it and you know this is what you wanna do. If that's the decision you've made, then you've gotta have faith that it's the right one and don't let anything stop you from succeeding. Not your family, not financial aid, nothing. You're gonna have to work for it and make it happen." She reached and grabbed a tissue and passed it to her.

"I know, and I'm willing to do that." Camille took the tissue and dabbled at her eyes.

"Look at you ruining that great mascara," Yaya teased. She was glad when she saw a slight smile on Camille's face. "Don't worry about money for school. You'll get it. You can always apply for the After Effex Empire Scholarship."

"I didn't know there was one available," Camille told her.

"There wasn't one until a few minutes ago." Yaya laughed. "But it does cover tuition, books, and supplies and it's only given to the elite applicants. Which means, you qualify."

Yaya saw so much of herself in Camille that it was uncanny. It wasn't that long ago that Yaya herself had turned down a full scholarship to pursue a career as a makeup artist. Quincy stopped talking to her for months, saying how disappointed he was in her choice. Her uncle, who raised them, told her she was going to regret her decision. The only person that supported her was Taryn. The two women worked hard and became each other's backbones and to her family's surprise, soon Yaya was making a six-figure income. Now, she was given the opportunity to do for Camille, what her own family didn't do for her. It was her opportunity to pay it forward and she didn't hesitate doing so.

"Thanks, Yaya." Camille smiled and gave her a hug.

Again, Lincoln's voice startled them. "Does my brother know about all this girl-on-girl action you got going on here, Yaya?"

"Shut up, Lincoln, you're just mad because you can't get any action," Yaya told him.

"Is that true, Ms. Green?" Lincoln looked over at Taryn. "I can't get any action?"

Before Taryn could answer, there was a knock on the door. They all looked to see who it was.

"Who is that? They can't read the *closed* sign on the door?" Yaya asked.

"It's a lady," Lincoln announced, walking toward the door. He yelled through the glass, "We're closed!"

The woman knocked and gestured for him to open the door. He turned the lock and held it wide enough to hear what she was saying.

"I'm looking for Camille. Her truck is still out here. Is she in there?" the woman told him.

He turned around and told Camille, "It's some lady looking for you."

Confused, Camille walked to the door to see who it was. As she got closer and recognized her, she stopped in her tracks. "Damn, what the hell does she want?"

"Who is it?" Yaya asked.

"It's Kasey, the woman Marlon married," Camille answered.

"So, that would be your sister-in-law?" Taryn asked.

"No, it would be the woman Marlon married," Camille said, matter-of-factly. There was no way in hell she would ever consider Kasey any relative of hers. She walked over; her arms folded and asked, "What do you want?"

"Hi, Camille, I just wanted a few minutes of your time. I've been calling your cell phone for the past week, leaving messages and you haven't responded." Kasey's syrupy voice made her cringe. She looked at the plump woman with the thick lips that made her bucked teeth even bigger. There was nothing attractive about the woman, not even her light-colored eyes. To Camille, they made her look demonic.

"Let her in," Yaya said and Camille gave her an evil look.

"We don't want people to think we're open," Yaya said, shrugging.

Lincoln opened the door and Kasey stepped inside. "I wanted to invite you to my baby shower on Sunday. It starts at three-thirty."

"You drove almost an hour to tell me about your baby shower?" Camille couldn't believe her. "I already know about your shower; Marlon told me the other day."

"Well, the invitation I sent came back return to sender, so I figured I had the wrong address," Kasey told her.

Camille had received the invitation the beginning of the week, and had written *return to sender* on it without even opening it. "Well, I already know about it."

"Will you be attending?" Kasey asked.

"I hadn't planned on it," she lied. She didn't dare give Kasey the satisfaction of even thinking she would be there on Sunday.

"Look, I know you don't really care for me, Camille, but the fact of the matter is that I'm carrying your brother's child. All I'm asking you for is a little support . . . after all, we are family."

Camille felt her anger rising and took a step back for fear of hitting the pregnant woman. "We are NOT family. My brother may have been stupid enough to knock you up, but I didn't have anything to do with that. I'm not obligated to you in any way. Now, you said what you had to say, you can leave."

"This baby is just as much your blood relative as Myla and Savannah are. There's no denying that!"

"Uh, this isn't the time or place for this." Taryn walked and stood behind Camille.

"Well, considering you gave Myla and Savannah a blood test without their parents' consent, maybe we should hold off on that thought until someone gives your baby one!"

"Lady, I think you should go before things get outta hand and someone gets hurt," Lincoln said to Kasey.

"Lincoln, lock the door behind her please," Yaya snapped.

A strange look came over Kasey's face and her stare went

from Camille to Lincoln. She smiled wickedly. "Oh, so you're Lincoln. I guess congratulations are in order."

"What the hell are you talking about?" He looked at her like she was crazy.

Camille's heart began pounding and she realized that Kasey knew. Celeste and Kasey forged a disgusting friendship, hoping to make Paige's life miserable as a team. Celeste and her mother had even stayed with Kasey and Lucille for a while after Celeste's mom was going through dialysis. Kasey was probably the first person Celeste told when she got the news herself. "Get the hell out, Kasey. NOW!"

"Are you excited? I know she is. I'm soooo happy for you," Kasey continued.

"She's crazy." Yaya shook her head.

"I don't know what the hell you're talking about," Lincoln said frowning. "You need to leave."

"You haven't told them that Celeste is pregnant with your baby?" Kasey yelled just as Lincoln closed the door and locked it.

A deafening silence filled the room and no one moved as the reality of what Kasey yelled out sunk in.

"That bitch is crazy." Lincoln looked from one woman to another.

"I told you that," Camille said, furious at Kasey. She looked over at Taryn who was still looking shocked.

"T, you all right?" Yaya asked.

"What the hell did she mean Celeste is pregnant with your baby? Did you sleep with Celeste, Lincoln?" Taryn asked.

"Hell no, I ain't sleep with her. I don't even know who she is," Lincoln replied.

"Celeste, the big frumpy girl with the glasses, she worked here for about two weeks when we first opened. Always complaining," Taryn told him.

"No, I did not sleep with her. I barely remember who you're talking about," Lincoln replied. He walked over and looked Taryn in the eye. "Taryn, I promise, whoever she is, she ain't carrying my baby."

Taryn stared back at him and more than anything, hoped he was telling the truth.

"I hope you had better taste than that, Lincoln," Yaya said, laughing. "That girl is nothing but trouble and she ain't even all that cute."

Camille thought about the way Celeste confronted Lincoln about her pregnancy. Camille didn't know if the baby Celeste claimed to be carrying was Lincoln's, but Celeste seemed determined to make him pay in some way.

Chapter 4

"So, you're really gonna go to this baby shower rather than hang out with me?" Terrance asked.

Camille smiled and held her cell phone to her ear with her shoulder as she looked for her Pussycat Dolls CD. "I promised my brother. I swear, if I hadn't promised him I would go, I would hang out with you this evening."

She would rather be spending time with Terrance. They had been talking on the phone more and more frequently and he had even taken her to lunch the day before. He was intelligent and he made her laugh. She learned a lot about him. He was a high school and college basketball star who majored in broadcasting. He played ball overseas for two years once he graduated from college and returned back to the States where he was now working his first job as a weekend sports reporter. His goal was to become an anchor on ESPN. He had the looks and the personality and even though he was slightly older—she was twenty and he was twenty-four—they seemed to be on the same page, career-wise. They both had discovered something they loved and were determined to succeed in their field. The better she got to know him, the more time she wanted to spend with him.

"From what you've told me about this woman, I can't imagine even going. Did you get a gift?" he asked.

"I got a gift card to Wal-Mart." She laughed. "She can spend that twenty-five dollars any way she chooses to."

"That's crazy," he said, laughing. "So, are you gonna spill the beans to your brother today?"

"I don't think today would be the right time," she told him and settled in for the forty-five-minute drive to what used to be Marlon and Paige's house.

"Still procrastinating, huh? They think you're leaving in a few days, you better hurry up and come clean. Don't tell me you're scared," he teased.

"I'm not scared," she told him. "I'm just waiting for the right time."

They continued talking until she pulled up in front of the house. There were a few cars out front and blue balloons were tied to the mailbox. She spotted Marlon sitting in his car on his cell phone and tooted her horn. He looked up and waved.

"Well, I'm here. I will call you in about thirty minutes when I'm leaving," she said, not wanting to get off the phone.

"Wow, a whole thirty minutes. The ride there took longer than that."

"I doubt if I'll even be able to tolerate my mother for that long," she said, sighing. "I'll call you in a little while."

"Okay," he said. "Be nice."

"I will," she told him and she realized she had shared more of her life with him over the past week than she had anyone else, other than Paige. She rarely opened up to anyone, especially guys, but there was something about Terrance that made her feel comfortable. She could talk to him. She got out of her SUV and Marlon stood in front of the house waiting for her.

"What's up, kiddo?" He kissed her on her forehead, something he had done all of her life.

"Hey, you, you coulda went in without me. You do own this house, you know."

"I don't live here, though," he replied and then added, "Besides, I thought it would be better if we went in together."

"Chicken," she told him. "But I'm glad you planned for us to be an hour late."

They walked to the front door and rang the bell. She felt weird doing so because when he and Paige lived here together, she had a key and would let herself in. A few moments later, the door opened and there was Celeste, smiling at them.

"Well, look who arrived. I'm surprised to see both of you. Come on in," she said and stood back so they could pass. Camille couldn't help glancing at Celeste's stomach to see if it showed any signs of carrying a baby. She didn't see anything but the usual bulge it had.

"Hey Celeste." Camille forced herself to speak.

"Camille." Celeste gave her a nasty look then gushed, "Hi, Marlon. I'm so glad you could make it. Everyone's in the den. You know where that is," she said, laughing.

Camille followed her brother down the hall. She looked at what once used to be a wonderful home. It now held cheap furniture and seemed dingier than when Paige and Marlon lived there. And there was a funny odor, which made Camille's stomach turn. They arrived in the den where Kasey and her guests were all laughing and eating.

"Look, it's my husband and my sister-in-law, everyone!" Kasey wobbled her fat body and grabbed Marlon, pulling him to her. She tried to kiss him but he turned away. She then turned her attention to Camille. She gave her a look that said, *walk over here with that BS if you want to and see what happens*. Kasey got the point and gave a modest wave. "Thanks for coming, Camille."

"Did someone say my children got here?"

Camille cringed and turned to see her mother. It had been a while since she had seen her and she still looked the same. Decked out in a T-shirt that read *#1 Grandma* and a pair of denim capris, her outfit was made complete by the cigarette dangling from her mouth and the drink in her hand. Compared to her mother and the other guests, Camille and Marlon were overdressed. Her red-and-black kimono-style dress and heels and his dark slacks and dress shirt would have probably been more appropriate had it been a shower for anyone else.

"Hey Mama." Marlon walked over and kissed his mother on the forehead.

"Hey there son," she said, smiling.

"Hi Mama," Camille said. She didn't even make an effort to hug her.

"Camille, you look skinny as hell. That wench ain't feeding you?" Lucille scowled, referring to Paige.

"I'm the same size I always was, Mama, and I'm eating better than ever," she snapped.

Marlon gave her a warning look and she looked around for an empty seat. She spotted one near the gift table, and headed for it. She reached in her pocket and tossed the unsigned gift card she bought on the way over on it and plopped down. A woman who introduced herself as Kasey's sister sat down next to her and tried to make small talk but Camille was not in the mood. Her stomach began growling and she realized she was hungry. She excused herself and walked over to the bar where the food was. Nothing looked appetizing except for the chips and salsa so that was the only thing she put on her plate.

She was about to go and take her seat when she heard Celeste announce, "Okay, time for the cake."

The guests *oooooohed* and *ahhhhhhhed* as she walked in carrying a large blue-and-white decorated sheet cake and placed it in the middle of the coffee table. Camille glanced at it and then did a double take. She stared at the writing on it and made sure she was not mistaken. Her stomach began churning and she felt as if she was about to vomit at any moment.

"Are you all right, sweetie?" Kasey's sister asked.

"I gotta get outta here," Camille answered and scanned the small crowd for her brother. The sight of Kasey cutting into the cake made her even more nauseous. She spotted Marlon in the corner of her eye and headed toward him. "I'm gone."

"What's wrong?" he asked.

"I can't believe this. Of all the low-down, spiteful, mean things in the world, this has to be the worst," she told him. She could feel tears filling her eyes as she talked.

"What the hell is going on?" Marlon asked again, still confused.

"Did you see the cake?" Camille asked him.

"I saw Celeste bring it in." He shrugged. "What's wrong with it?"

"Did you read the cake, Marlon?" She pointed at it. Kasey looked up and gave her a sickening look and she knew that she was no doubt as evil as they come.

"No, what did it say?" he asked.

"You go and read it," she told him. Camille watched as her brother walked over to the table and looked at the cake. She could see the pain in his face as he read the words written on it.

"What the hell? Why would you do this, Kasey? What the hell is wrong with you?" His voice was a whole octave higher than normal.

"Marlon, calm down, you're embarrassing me." Kasey tried to play it off. The guests became quiet as they watched the expectant parents argue.

"I can't believe you would do such a thing!" Marlon screamed at her.

"Marlon Davis! You watch your tone right now!" Lucille yelled at him.

"I can't believe *you* would let her do *this*," he turned to his mother and told her.

"I think what she's doing is right," Lucille snapped.

"How?" Marlon asked her. "What would possess you to even agree to this?"

"Let's just go, Marlon." Camille walked over and grabbed her brother's hand.

"I really don't see what the problem is." Kasey folded her arms. "And this isn't something that should be discussed right now."

"Come *on*, Marlon." This time Camille yanked his arm to the point that his body moved along with her. She pulled him all the way out the front door and when they finally made it outside, she held her brother tight and they cried together. The loss of his son with Paige was the most painful thing she had seen her brother go through. It was the hardest moment in their lives and she knew he was still dealing with it. Camille closed her eyes and the sight of the cake flashed before her again with the words clearly written: *Welcome Baby Myles M. Davis*. It was the same name of his deceased son.

Chapter 5

Taryn poured herself a glass of wine and opened her freezer as she debated whether to go out for Sunday dinner or create a meal from what she had at home. She had a taste for eggplant Parmesan, but there was no way she was going to fix that. So, she either had to go to her favorite Greek spot and get it or settle for Banquet fried chicken and oodles of noodles. It was the first time in almost two months that she found herself with a free weekend. She and Yaya had limited themselves to traveling out of town on jobs to only two weekends out of the month but she had been so booked up on the Saturdays that she was in town that it barely felt as if she had a break. Camille oticed this and didn't book any clients for her, which gave her a much-needed free weekend.

"This sucks," she said out loud to no one. She shut the refrigerator door, grabbed the glass of wine and walked into her living room. She grabbed the remote and clicked on the flat screen TV hanging on the wall. Nothing on television caught her interest, and Taryn realized that she was frustrated. She and Lincoln played pool at a local bar for most of the night before. Again, the chemistry between them was apparent, especially as he continually pressed his body against hers to show her how to make a good shot. Taryn mastered the art of flirtation a long time ago and she played right along with him. At the end of the night, both of them were feeling nice from the shots of Jack Daniel's they were taking between pool shots. He drove her home and they sat in her driveway and talked. He was still adamant about not sleeping with Celeste and she had no reason not to believe him. From the short time she had known Celeste, she knew the girl was a conniving liar. Yaya made the mistake of hiring Celeste when the salon first opened, hoping Celeste would give some type of insight on Paige and her hidden agendas for dating Quincy, which turned out to be none. Yaya's suspicions turned out to be worthless and Celeste had caused more chaos than what she was worth. She was quickly fired, which was a relief to Taryn because she disliked the girl from day one.

"Wow, it's late as hell," she told him as she looked down at her watch and realized that they had been sitting there for a whole hour. "Why don't you just come in."

"Naw, I'm good," he said to her as he ran his hand along hers.

"Why not? I can make us another drink," she suggested. He never wanted to come inside her home, although she invited him several times.

"I promise, I won't bite," she said, laughing.

"That's why I don't wanna come in," he said, smiling. The whiteness of his teeth seemed to sparkle against his smooth, mahogany skin.

"If you're scared, say you're scared." She winked at him and licked her lips.

"Don't play," he warned. "A brother will pull your hold card and then what?"

"Please, I'm a big girl, I can handle myself." Her voice was husky and the sexual tension filled the car.

Lincoln leaned over and his face was in front of hers. Taryn could smell the faint odor of liquor on his breath as she stared into his eyes. This was the moment she had been waiting for. The kiss she had desired for months. Her heart began pounding and she closed her eyes and parted her lips ever so slightly. His hand was under her chin and he tilted her head. Then, she felt his soft lips on her cheek.

"I'll call you tomorrow," he whispered.

Her eyes opened and she frowned. Confused and stunned by what had just happened, her only response was, "Okay."

She walked into her house and watched out the window while he sat in the driveway for a few more minutes and then finally, drove away. He still hadn't called, and she wasn't about to call him. Whatever type of game Lincoln was playing, Taryn was no longer going to be a part of. *Girl, you don't have time for games.*

You are a beautiful, intelligent, prosperous woman and any man in his right mind would realize how lucky he was to have your affection. Forget him. Taryn's inner voice began speaking.

"You're right," she said and quickly got up off the sofa. "I don't have time to be waiting around for a man who can't make up his mind whether he likes me or not."

Thirty minutes later, she was cruising downtown toward Jasper's, one of her favorite hot spots where she knew she could find some great food, great music, and enjoy her Sunday afternoon. The restaurant wasn't as crowded as she thought it would be. The jazz band was playing and she sat alone. The owner of the club, Uncle Jay, came and sat with her for a few minutes as she ate.

"You know if I was a few years younger, Taryn, girl, you would be the woman for me." He winked at her.

"And Uncle Jay, if I were a few years older—" she started.

"He would be old as hell," her friend, Jamison Grossman interrupted them. She was glad to see him and he was looking as fine as ever in a gray, four-button suit. He and Yaya graduated from high school together and Taryn had always found him attractive.

"Stop hating, Jimmy," Taryn said as Jamison leaned over and hugged her.

"He's just jealous, that's all," Uncle Jay said and rose to leave the table, "and he's married."

"Oh no you didn't. Weren't you round here passing out cigars not too long ago, proud papa?"

"But I ain't married," Uncle Jay said, laughing.

"Don't worry, Uncle Jay. He knows better than that, right Jimmy?"

Jimmy made sure Uncle Jay was out of listening distance and told her, "Yeah, but damn, if I wasn't married, I would be trying to get at you for real. You are one fly woman, you know that?"

Taryn shook her head at her friend. "Boy, please, ask me something I don't know the answer to."

As they sat and talked, Taryn noticed Yaya's ex-boyfriend, Jason, walk in with his best friend, Travis. She really didn't like either one of them, especially Travis who always took it upon himself to make a comment about her breasts whenever he saw her. She hoped they didn't notice her as they walked by.

"Hey," Jason said as they walked by. "Taryn, how are you?"

"I'm fine, Jason," she said. She was still pissed at him for causing a fight with Fitz a couple of weeks ago at the salon when he and Yaya broke up. She decided to be polite and speak to Travis. "Hello, Travis."

"Hello, beautiful," Travis said without trying to hide the fact that he was staring at her breasts. "You're looking lovely, as usual. All of you."

"And you're being an asshole today, as usual." She cut her eyes at him. They walked off without saying another word and she saw Jimmy's failed attempt not to smile. "Can you believe him?"

"He likes you."

"You've lost your mind. Travis and I can't stand each other." She looked at Jimmy as if he was crazy.

"I'm a man, and I know when another man is feeling a woman," Jimmy told her.

"He only looks at my breasts when he's around me. Now, if you said he liked those, you would be correct," she said, sighing.

"Can't blame him for that one." Jimmy laughed and nodded toward her noticeable double D's.

Taryn folded her arms across her chest. "And I thought you were one of the good guys."

"I am one of the good ones." He smiled at her. "What are you drinking?"

"Vodka and cranberry," she told him.

"Be right back," he said and walked over to the bar.

Damn, he is fine. But his ass is married, she reminded herself, knowing that there was no way she would even think about getting with a married man. Feeling someone staring at her, Taryn turned and saw Travis smiling. She rolled her eyes and turned away.

"Where's Bianca?" she asked Jamison when he returned with her drink. She had met his wife a few times and she seemed very sweet.

"At home," he answered as he sat back in his chair and shrugged. "I tried to get her to come with me, but she declined."

"You should've stayed home with her," Taryn told him. "Spent some quality time at the crib. I know with all the hours you work, you all don't get much of that."

"Yeah, you're right, but I also don't get to go out much, either. And staying at home is definitely not my thing. You know that," he told her.

"Speaking of work, Yaya told me you're gonna take Camille's

case. Thanks a lot. We appreciate that," she said sincerely. "That girl's been through a lot."

"Who? Yaya or Camille?" he teased.

"Both," she said, laughing.

"Camille reminds me so much of Yaya," he said, nodding.

"I told her the same thing," Taryn agreed. "That was one of the reasons—"

Her attention was drawn across the room where Lincoln was coming in the restaurant followed by Fitz and another woman. For a split second, a twinge of jealousy hit her. She couldn't help notice the smile on his face as he talked to the woman. *He ain't your man, so don't even start tripping,* she reminded herself.

"What's wrong?" Jimmy asked her.

Realizing she stopped talking in mid-sentence, she tried to remember what she was about to say, but couldn't. "Nothing. It's getting late and I need to be getting out of here. You know a girl has to get her beauty rest."

"As beautiful as you are, you can miss a whole lot of nights," he teased as they both got up from the table. Taryn reached for her bill, but Jimmy stopped her.

"I got it," he told her.

"I appreciate it, Mr. Grossman, but I don't think so."

"Why, what's wrong? I had a great time sitting here talking and the least I can do is pay for your meal," he said, frowning.

"I had a great time too," she admitted. "But having a married man pay for my dinner and a drink doesn't sit well with me. I wouldn't want you to get the wrong idea."

"Uh, the only idea I had was to use it as a tax deduction considering we did discuss a pending case of mine. So, this was a business dinner."

Taryn had to laugh. She looked at the receipt in her hand and passed it to him. "Damn, if I woulda known that, I woulda got dessert."

Jamison laughed as he reached in his pocket and took out his credit card. They walked over to the cashier and were paying when she heard Lincoln calling her name. She tried to ignore him by digging in her purse to find her keys.

"That ain't gonna work, he's on his way over here," Jimmy leaned over and whispered in her ear.

"Hey, Taryn, what's going on?" Lincoln walked up and spoke.

"Oh, hey Lincoln, what's going on?" She smiled at him.

"Nothing much. Me and Fitz decided to come hang out with some friends for a little while, that's all," Lincoln said. Taryn couldn't help notice his glance at Jamison.

"That's nice," she said.

"Yeah, you leaving? You should come have a drink with us." Lincoln stepped closer to her.

"Naw, we've been here a minute and I need to get going." She gestured toward Jimmy. "Jimmy, this is Lincoln Webster. He's the contractor who designed the shop for us."

"Nice to meet you, Lincoln." Jimmy extended his hand and Lincoln shook it.

"Yeah, same here," Lincoln said.

"Lincoln, what are you drinking?" the woman who had come in with them walked over and asked.

"Hennessy, a double," he said then added, "Yo, Sonya, this is Taryn, the friend Fitz and I were telling you about. Sonya just moved to town. She lives in the condo across from me and Fitz."

The girl smiled. "Oh, hi Taryn, the guys were telling me about your salon. It sounds really nice. I can't wait to come and see it."

Taryn reached into her purse and handed Sonya a card. "Just call and make an appointment. We can hook you right up."

"Thanks," Sonya said and turned to Lincoln. "Hennessy, double shot."

"Well, I'll see you later, Lincoln," Taryn said. "You ready, Jimmy?"

"Yeah, nice meeting you, Lincoln." Jimmy held the door open for Taryn. Lincoln didn't respond as they walked out.

"Thank you, Mr. Grossman," she said when they arrived at her ivory Acura TL in the parking lot.

"You are a trip, you know that? Old boy is heated."

"So, he ain't my man," she said, shrugging, and unlocked her door.

"Maybe my being married is a good thing after all. Hell, from the way things transpired tonight between the breast man and the contractor, I would have to fight to prove my love every night," he joked.

"Believe me, sweetie, I got enough to feed the needy, isn't that what Biggie said. Go home to your wife before you get into trouble."

"I will, thanks, Taryn. And tell Yaya I'll call her later this week."

Taryn smiled to herself as she drove home. She was glad that she decided to come out rather than stay at home. All she wanted to do now was take a long hot bath and climb into bed. As soon as she pulled into her driveway, her cell phone began ringing. She saw that it was Lincoln and decided to ignore it, deciding it was pointless to talk to him, especially since he was welcoming Sonya to the neighborhood. Jamison had confirmed something she already knew, she had it going on.

DING DONG, DING DONG!!

Taryn had just fallen asleep when the constant ringing of her door-bell woke her. She slowly climbed out of bed, grabbing her short robe and pulling it tight around her.

"This can't be nobody but Yaya," she said aloud. Her best friend was the only one who rang her bell like that. She turned her living room lights on and snatched open the door. "What, girl?"

"I take it you were expecting someone else?"

"Lincoln, what are you doing here? It's after midnight." She closed the robe even tighter. She was glad she had on her cute lavender pajama set rather than the raggedy gray sweats she wasn't able to wear because they were in the dirty clothes.

"I just decided to swing by, that's all." He smiled at her, almost causing her to melt. "You got company?"

She frowned at him. "If I do, it's none of your business. Is that why you came over here to see if someone was here?"

"Naw, it ain't like that at all. I'm saying, I really wanna talk to you."

"About what?" she said, folding her arms.

"Can I come in?" The door widened as she pushed it open with her arm. He followed her into the living room. "Nice place."

"Thanks," she said, sighing.

"So . . ." He looked uncomfortable.

"What?"

"I was kinda surprised to see you out with that guy," he said, shrugging.

"Why? I do date, don't you?" she snapped.

"I'm just saying, you never mentioned dating anyone else, I guess."

"I wasn't aware that I had to mention it to you." Taryn couldn't even feel bad about letting Lincoln think she was on a date with Jimmy. "Do you tell me when you're out dating, Lincoln?"

"I don't date, you know that," he said.

"And that's your choice. But even if you did, it would be none of my business." She sat down on the sofa. "Is this what you wanted to talk about?"

Lincoln seemed to be agitated. "No, it's not." He ran his

hand over his head and exhaled. Taryn didn't know whether to be pissed, concerned or worried.

"What's on your mind, Lincoln?"

Lincoln looked into her eyes and sat down beside her. "You are."

"What are you . . ."

"Look, I've wanted to tell you this for a while. But, I'm not good at saying the right thing when it comes to situations like this. You are so beautiful and smart and funny and I like you." He sighed.

Here we go again. Taryn shook her head. She had heard this speech so many times before and she really didn't feel like hearing it again for the hundredth time. It was the same way since high school. *"I like you, Taryn, but not in that way. You're like a sister to me."* Contrary to popular belief, it wasn't always the unattractive girls who got the "just be friends" speech. She was definitely considered a dime piece, and had no trouble catching a man's attention, but her ability to make men feel comfortable whenever they were around her was a curse. Maybe it was her humor, her honesty, her ability to hang with the fellows. Sometimes she felt as if she was more inclined to being man's best friend more than dogs were.

"I like you too Lincoln." She rolled her eyes. "If you've come over here for me to give you advice about how to get with Sonya, I can't help you."

"Sonya? I didn't come over here to talk about her. And for the record, I don't need your help getting with a girl." He laughed. "I can't believe you."

"Lincoln . . ."

Before she could say anything else, his mouth covered hers and she became lost in his kiss. He parted her lips with his tongue and she savored his taste. A moan escaped from her lips and his arms slipped around her waist. They explored each other's mouths for what seemed like eternity, neither one of them wanting to release.

Finally, Taryn pulled away and leaned her head back against the sofa. "Damn."

Lincoln pressed his forehead against hers and she could sense his relief. He smiled and again, stared into her eyes and told her, "I've wanted to do that for so long."

"Why did you decide to do it tonight? Because you saw me with someone else?"

"That has nothing to do with it. I know what I feel and the fact that I saw you with another guy is insignificant. I don't feel threatened by any man."

"And just how do you feel, Lincoln?" She sat back and waited for his answer.

"I'm in love with you, Taryn."

Chapter 6

"*Daddy's home, daddy's home to stay*," Taryn sang as she walked into the salon carrying a box of bagels she picked up from Panera Bread on her way to work. Yaya, Monya, and Camille all looked at her as if she was crazy. She smiled at them and said, "Good morning, ladies!"

"What the hell?" Monya asked.

"Looks like someone had a wonderful weekend," Camille said, laughing.

Taryn replied, trying to sound as calm as possible, "Why can't I just be in a good mood?"

"Uh, because it's Monday and you're never in a good mood on Mondays," Camille answered.

"And you never buy bagels unless it's someone's birthday," Monya added.

"And Fitz already told me they saw you out with a nice-looking dude last night at Jasper's." Yaya walked over and stood in front of her, giving an accusing look. "Dish."

"Dish about what?" Taryn shook her head.

"Who you were with?" Monya answered.

"And what the hell he did for you to make you come in here singing like that," Yaya said.

"You all are making a big deal out of nothing," Taryn said, laughing, "He saw me with Jimmy, that's all."

"Jam?" Yaya and Monya both said at the same time.

"Yes." Taryn sighed and put the box on the counter.

"The producer?" Camille squealed. "Wow!"

"No, fool, your attorney," Yaya told her. "Jamison Grossman, we call him Jimmy Jam."

"Oh, I thought he was married." Camille was confused.

"He's not with Bianca anymore? What happened?" Monya asked as she opened the box and checked out the contents.

"He's still with Bianca," Taryn told her.

"T, don't tell me you're sleeping with a married man," Yaya snapped. "And you know his wife too. That's just wrong."

"Shut up, Yaya, you know I wouldn't do nothing like that," Taryn replied, offended that her best friend would think she would do something of that nature. "I was having dinner alone, when Jimmy came over to join me. We were having a drink and talking when Fitz and Lincoln walked in with some girl."

"What girl?" Yaya frowned. "Fitz told me they took their new neighbor across the hall out for drinks. He didn't mention a girl."

"The girl was the neighbor, her name is Sonya," Taryn said, taking out an onion bagel and reaching for the cream cheese.

"Mmmmm, welcome to the neighborhood," Monya giggled.

"So, Lincoln saw you with Jimmy? I guess that didn't look right at all." Camille reached for her bagel. "Did he say anything?"

"Who cares what it looked like to Lincoln? He ain't her man. He's had all this time to make a move and didn't. I hope he didn't say anything," Monya commented.

"Naw, he didn't say anything," Taryn said, sighing.

"Good," Monya said.

"He showed up at my doorstep around eleven last night," Taryn confessed.

"Oh no he didn't," Yaya responded

"He's so typical." Monya shook her head.

"Awww, that's so sweet," Camille whined. "How romantic."

"You are too gullible, Camille," Yaya told her. "The only reason he came over her house was to see if Jimmy was there. I hope you didn't answer the door."

"Oh." Camille shrugged.

"He was leaning on my doorbell so hard, that I thought it was you and opened the door without even asking who it was. And that's not why he came over."

"Then tell us, T, why did he come over?" Yaya winked at the other two girls.

"He came over to tell me he was in love with me." Taryn tried not to blush. The girls began squealing and they formed a group hug. She knew that they were happy for her. It had been a long time coming, but it looked as if Taryn had finally found love.

"Enough about me, how was Dallas and the hair show?" Taryn asked when they had calmed down.

"It was off the chain as usual. I had a ball," Yaya said. She told them all about the productive weekend she had in Dallas where she was the head makeup artist for the largest hair show of the year. "And guess who I met?"

"Who?" they all asked at the same time.

"Geneva Johnson," she said with pride. Geneva Johnson was the first African American female golf pro. She was only nineteen years old and making headlines with her golf game, easily becoming the female Tiger Woods.

"The golf star?" Camille asked.

"Yep, the one and only. We had brunch yesterday morning and she is actually about to go on a promotional tour for Nike," Yaya replied.

"Yaya, don't even try it." Taryn knew what her friend was about to say next.

"T, hold on," Yaya said.

"We agreed, Yaya, and you know with everything going on around here, you can't do this." Taryn sat down.

"Yaya, we're just getting the shop off the ground," Monya added.

"I know, I know," Yaya answered. "Don't you think I know the commitment I made when we opened the salon? I'm not crazy," she told them. "But I did agree to do her shoot for the promotional tour."

"What? You're kidding? I can't believe that!" Again, squeals erupted in the salon.

Yaya knew that they would be excited. It was the biggest opportunity she had ever been given and she would've been a fool to turn it down. Not only did it mean even more exposure for her, but for After Effex. Now all she had to do was figure out how to get her partners to agree to let her go on tour with Geneva for two weeks; and by their initial reactions, that wasn't gonna be an easy task.

"So, did you go to the shower?" Taryn asked.

"God, unfortunately I did. I don't know why I even agreed to do that. I knew that it was going to be nothing but drama," Camille answered, her voice full of frustration.

"Oh no, what happened?" Monya positioned herself to hear Camille's story.

"Well, it seems that Kasey has decided to name the baby Myles," she told them.

"I like the name Myles," Taryn said.

"I love the name Myles. The problem is that it's the name of my brother's first son," Camille replied.

"I didn't know you had a nephew. I thought you only had two nieces." Yaya frowned.

"Marlon and Paige had a son, Myles."

"Okay, now I'm really confused," Yaya said. "Where is he?"

"He died the day he was born." Camille could feel the tears forming in her eyes and she blinked.

"Damn, I didn't know," Yaya said.

"I'm sorry," Monya told her.

"It's okay. It was almost three years ago," Camille said shrugging. She almost added that she felt it was one of the reasons Marlon and Paige broke up, but decided that would be too much information, especially due to the fact that Paige was now dating Yaya's brother.

"You mean to tell me that Kasey knows this and she's still giving her baby that name?" Monya shook her head. "That's messed up!"

"Oh hell no, I know Marlon can't let her get away with something like that," Taryn told her. "What did he say?"

"He really didn't say anything. He was in shock."

"I can imagine. She is really crazy," Yaya said. "What did your mother say?"

"My mother thinks Kasey is the greatest thing that's ever happened."

"From what you've told us about your mother, any woman that drew Marlon's attention away from Paige is the greatest, not to mention the fact that Kasey is someone else that she can control."

Camille nodded and had to wonder if the fact that she could control Kasey was the only reason her mother liked her. The woman was hardly attractive, ignorant as hell, beyond ghetto and as fake as a $20 hooker in a Miss America pageant. She was just glad that Marlon had realized it and hauled ass when he did.

"Hey there, ladies."

Camille looked over at the door and saw Paige walking in. She was surprised because Paige hadn't mentioned stopping by the salon this morning and she didn't have an appointment.

"Hey Paige. How are you?" they all spoke.

"What's up?" Camille walked over and asked, hoping nothing was wrong.

"We need to talk," Paige said. Something in her voice made Camille nervous. Her thoughts turned to Marlon and she hoped that her brother hadn't gone and done anything stupid after what happened at the shower yesterday.

"Uh, okay," Camille said, looking around nervously.

"You all can use my office," Yaya told them. She could tell something was up. Paige was usually all smiles and laughter, but today she seemed irritated.

"Thanks," Camille said, rolling her eyes at Yaya. She led Paige through the salon and down the hall to Yaya's office.

Paige looked around, clearly impressed by the opulence and decor. "This is nice."

"Yeah," Camille said, taking a seat on the cream leather sofa, which was located across from Yaya's cluttered desk. "What's up?"

Paige sat beside her and said, "Is there something you need to tell me?"

Camille looked down and said, "I didn't know how to tell you."

"What do you mean, Cam? Come on, after all we've been through? You know there's nothing you can't tell me. I thought we were better than that. I don't understand."

"I'm sorry, Paige. And I know how hurtful this is. I thought about it all the way home from the shower. I can't believe how hurtful and disrespectful it is. It hurts me just as much as it hurts you," Camille replied. She hated the fact that she didn't tell Paige the name Kasey had chosen the moment she came home, but she was emotionally drained and didn't have the heart or the energy to tell her. She figured Marlon must have called and told her this morning.

"You not thinking you could tell me is what hurts the most,

Camille. Did you think I wasn't going to find out? Have you even told your brother yet?"

"Yeah, he knows, he was there when they brought the cake out," she told her. "Isn't that who told you about it?"

"No, what cake?" Paige frowned. "What are you talking about?"

"Huh? What are *you* talking about?"

"I'm talking about the fact that the school called regarding some boxes you had in the storage space of the dorm that you need to pick up by the weekend since you're not returning," Paige said in one breath.

Camille looked at Paige, unable to say anything. It felt as if time had suddenly stopped. *Shit, I forgot about that stuff*, she thought as she remembered the three boxes she left in the dorm basement before she left for summer vacation.

"Why the hell aren't you going back to school? What are you thinking?" Paige questioned.

"I . . . I don't want to go back to school. I changed my mind about what I wanna do. I was going to tell you, I swear." Camille's voice was barely above a whisper. *I should've just told her this weeks ago. I knew this was coming.*

"Let me guess, you wanna work in the salon and do nails for a living now, right?" Paige said sarcastically. "No, wait, you wanna be a personal assistant."

"No, Paige, I wanna be a makeup artist. I like working here and I'm good at it."

"Makeup? Camille, are you crazy? You had a full engineering scholarship. You mean to tell me you wanna throw your entire future away because you wanna make people up and live the glamorous life like Yaya? That's stupid and I'm not gonna let you do that. You are young and I don't think you realize the consequences of what you're doing, Cam!"

"I don't care about the glamorous life, and you know that. And I do realize the consequences. I know that the only thing

I liked about school was the fact that I was miles away from my mama! I wasn't all that happy. But working here, Paige, I learn so much and I love what I'm doing. I love living with you and being there for Myla; you are my family and I wanna be near you. Most of all, Paige, I found what I love to do and I'm good at it." Camille felt a tear falling down her cheek.

"Camille, baby, but you've gotta be smart about this. Makeup will still be there when you finish school if that's what you really feel that you wanna do. Don't throw this opportunity away. Do you know how many young ladies would die for an opportunity like the one you had?"

"I know how many women come in here every day and complain about their corporate jobs and wish they could go back in time and follow their true dreams. I know how many people I run into that complain about how miserable they are because they wasted all those years in school and aren't even working in the field their degree is in. I know that working here with Yaya, Taryn, and Monya is an experience and an education in itself and this is where I wanna be right now." She looked at Paige who was now crying as well. "Paige, if makeup doesn't work out, I can always go back to school and become an engineer. Please, give me a chance to see if I can do this."

The room remained quiet for what seemed like hours. Finally, Paige inhaled, and slowly spoke, "Camille Davis, I love you and I hope you know what you're doing. If you're sure this is what you wanna do, then fine. Promise me this, though."

Camille said, "Anything."

"Don't ever be afraid to come to me about anything. I'm here to support you, even if I don't always agree with you."

"I will," Camille said.

"I gotta get outta here. I'll see you when you get home." Paige stood up. Just as she stepped out of the office, she paused and turned back around. "Camille, what did you think I was talking about at first?"

"Huh?"

"You were saying something about Marlon and a cake? Did you all go to a birthday party or something?" Paige asked.

Camille shook her head. "I went with him to Kasey's baby shower yesterday. We—"

"Enough said," Paige interrupted her. "I don't wanna know what happened and I don't care. You know that. Love you, bye!"

Camille was relieved when she said that, grateful for the fact that Paige had resorted to not even talking about Kasey and pretending she didn't even exist most of the time.

"Bye-bye, ladies. Yaya, thanks for the use of your office. Taryn, don't forget you got me Friday afternoon," Paige said as she exited.

"I got ya, Paige," Taryn said, waving.

Yaya looked at her brother's girlfriend. She was a pretty girl and even though she resisted at first, she had really grown to like her. Yaya felt bad about the way she plotted and schemed with Celeste and Kasey to break them up and she was glad Quincy had wised up, thanks to Camille, and gotten back with Paige. The more she learned about Paige, the more she admired and respected her. She still wanted to make amends with Paige and considering the fact that Paige probably felt that Yaya had considerable influence in Camille's choice to leave college, she decided to take advantage of the moment.

"Let me walk you out," Yaya said and followed Paige out the door into the parking lot. As they stood beside Paige's champagne-colored Mercedes, she teased, "This car is ugly."

"I think you're still bitter that I bought it from Titus before you did." Paige laughed. "Hater."

She was right, Yaya was hating because she planned to purchase the car from Quincy's best friend but before she could even tell him, Paige bought it. At the time, it just gave Yaya another reason to dislike her. "Yeah, you're right. I do want to say something, though."

"Say it."

"Well, I know we didn't start off on the right foot when you and I first met but I'm glad you're with my brother. He's happy and I know you and Myla have a lot to do with that."

Paige smiled at her. "Yaya, that's all water under the bridge. We're cool. And your brother's happiness is because he is a good person."

"Well, that's true. But you're a good person too, Paige, and so is Camille. I know you're probably disappointed that she's not going back to school, but if she's serious about becoming an esthetician, then I'm willing to help her."

"An esthetician? Camille says she wants to be a makeup artist," Paige replied.

"An esthetician is a licensed makeup artist. She knows that in order to remain employed and further her career, she has to get her license. She enrolled in school last week." Yaya put her hands on her hips.

Paige nodded her head. "She didn't tell me any of that."

"She probably wanted you to absorb the fact that she left school first."

As if she knew they were talking about her, Camille walked out of the salon and over to Paige's car.

"Camille, why didn't you tell me you enrolled in school here?" Paige asked her.

"I was going to tell you once you got over the fact that I dropped out without telling you. I was going to come to you later and tell you my plan," Camille said, shrugging.

"Told ya," Yaya said.

"Lord have mercy," Paige said, sighing.

"Don't worry, Paige." Yaya put her arm on Paige's shoulder. "We're in this together."

Camille walked over and eased between both of them and put her arm on each of their shoulders. "Yes, we're all in this together."

Chapter 7

"So, you finally got a backbone and told your sis-in-law about dropping out. Don't you feel relieved?" Terrance asked after Camille told him she talked to Paige about her decision. They had been playing phone tag all week and she was glad to finally talk to him. It was almost six-thirty and she was sweeping the hallway, preparing to leave for the day. Yaya had already left and Monya and Taryn were about to do the same.

Camille was glad he couldn't see her rolling her eyes through her cell phone. "I always had a backbone. I was just waiting for the opportune time to tell her, that's all."

"You decided over a month ago that you wanted to pursue a career as an esteti—what's it called?"

"An esthetician," she answered. "Yes, and the opportunity just presented itself today."

"How did you tell her?"

"The school called and left a message about my stuff being in storage—"

"So, you didn't tell her, she found you out, scaredy-cat!" he teased.

"Be quiet. I'm at work, I will call you later," she told him.

"Wait, wait, wait. Don't try it. You called me, girl," he said, laughing.

"I called because I saw I missed your call, so technically, you called me."

"Okay, you're right, I did call you earlier. What are you doing tonight?"

"Why?" She couldn't help smiling.

"I have to go to a fund-raiser tonight and I was wondering if you would be my escort?"

She stopped and caught her reflection in the mirror. Her hair was pulled into a ponytail on top of her head and although she looked cute in the jeans, After Effex baby-doll tee and ballet-type shoes she wore, there was no way she could get herself together enough to escort Terrance to a fund-raiser.

"You've gotta be kidding," she told him. "I don't even get off for another thirty minutes and I'm definitely not prepared to go to a fund-raiser. Not tonight? I don't even have anything to wear," she said. "Why would you wait until today to call and ask me? Your date cancel at the last minute?"

"Damn, that's cold. You know I wouldn't even do you like that, Camille. Truth is, I wasn't gonna go, but the more I thought about it, the more I think if you went with me, I would have a nice time."

"Thanks for the compliment, but I can't go. I won't even have time to get dressed."

"Are you wearing your work clothes?" he asked.

"Yeah."

"Then what you have on is perfect," he told her. "I'll pick you up in about thirty minutes."

Before she could say anything else, he had hung up.

"What's wrong with you?" Monya asked as she walked by.

"Nothing. Terrance just asked me out."

"That's nice. I like him, he's cool." Monya nodded. They walked back into the main area of the salon and Monya announced, "Camille has a date."

Camille nearly died from embarrassment. "You didn't have to tell the world. God, Monya!"

"What? It's no big deal," Monya told her.

"A date with who? Terrance?" Taryn asked.

"Yep." Monya nodded.

Camille could not believe Monya and her big mouth. She shook her head and exhaled loudly as she emptied the trash cans.

"That's good, Camille. I know you've been feeling him for a minute," Taryn told her.

"We're just cool," Camille said.

"Where is he taking you?" Taryn asked.

"To some fund-raiser that I don't have to dress up for." Camille shrugged. "He says I don't have to change and he'll be here in thirty minutes to pick me up."

"Well, that gives a little time to make you fabulous." Monya grinned and clapped her hands.

"Let's get started," Taryn responded. "May as well start with your hair."

"I'll get my bag." Monya wasted no time heading to the small area where she stored her things. She didn't have an office like Taryn and Yaya had, but she had her own personal space and was satisfied with that.

"What are you all about to do?" Camille looked at her coworkers. "It's not that serious."

"Shut up and sit down, girl," Taryn said, pointing to the swivel chair that they used when they did waxing. Camille did as she was told; still thinking they were making a big deal for nothing. Monya came back in carrying a bag that she opened and removed the curling iron, combs, brushes, spritz, oil sheen, bobby pins, and even a mirror.

"Are you in beauty school at night and we don't know it?" Camille asked.

"I keep all this in case of an emergency such as this. Lean back," she said and took Camille's hair down. She began styling Camille's hair while Taryn worked on Camille's face. Twenty minutes later, they were finished.

"Not bad, Monya. We are the bomb." Taryn smiled and they gave each other five.

"That we are," Monya said. She spun the chair around so Camille could see herself in the mirror. "Voilà!"

Camille was stunned. She was gorgeous. Her makeup was flawless and her hair was now flowing in curls, not a strand out of place. "Wow. I look like a new person."

"Before and after are never the same, girl. It's the after effect!"

"It also didn't hurt that you're already a beautiful girl." Taryn winked at her.

Camille gave them both a hug. Glancing down at her watch, she saw that it was almost time for Terrance to pick her up. Butterflies filled her stomach and she wondered why she was getting nervous. She and Terrance had lunch a few times and they talked on the phone constantly, so there was really no need for her to feel this way.

"I know like hell you ain't biting your bottom lip after all the time I just spent perfecting them," Taryn snapped at her.

Camille hadn't even realized she was doing so, and immediately stopped. "My bad."

"Your lover boy just pulled up," Monya said, looking out the window.

"See you all in the morning." Camille grabbed her black Coach bag and put it on her shoulder.

"Hold on there, chick. Let him get out and come in for you," Taryn hissed.

"What?"

"Granted, I know this ain't your house and I ain't your

mama. But you still need to make him be a gentleman. And make sure he opens the door for you."

"Taryn, I keep telling you we're not like that," Camille said, laughing. She could see Terrance sitting in his car talking on the cell phone and she looked back at Taryn. She put her purse on the counter, took a seat and crossed her legs.

"Daaaaammmmmmnnnnn!"

Camille turned her head as Jarrod waltzed over and stood beside her.

"What do you want, Jarrod?" She rolled her eyes, jokingly.

"You look as good as one of those *Flavor of Love* girls! Where you going?" He grinned.

"Out," she answered.

"Yo, you could really be a model! I see what the cats in my shop be saying 'bout you now."

"Leave her alone, Jarrod." Monya pulled him away from Camille.

"Don't worry, I already let them know that you're my little sister and you're off-limits." He nodded assuredly.

"Like she wanna holla at any of them fools," Monya said, smirking.

The door opened and Terrance walked in. He looked nice in a pair of jeans, a plaid Rocawear shirt, and a pair of Timberlands.

"What's up, Tuff love?" Jarrod greeted him.

"Hey there, Jarrod. What's up, ladies? How y'all doing?"

"Hey Taryn, you got change for a hundred?" Jarrod asked.

"Yeah, I think I got sixty in my purse." Taryn nodded and began digging in her purse.

"Sixty? What the hell?" Jarrod's voice cracked.

"Uh, you owe me forty from last week, negro," she said.

"Oh." Jarrod said and then quickly turned to Terrance. "Hey Tuff Love, you got change for a hundred?"

"Naw, son, I can't help you." He turned to Camille and said, "You look nice. You ready to roll?"

Camille stood up and replied, "Yep."

"Wait a sec, you rolling out with this cat? No wonder you all sparkly and shit," Jarrod said, laughing.

"Shut up, Jarrod. Don't you have customers waiting on their change?" Camille snapped at him.

"We'll check y'all later," Terrance said as he held the door open and Camille walked out. She stood with her arms folded as she waited for him to open the car door for her. From the first time he had taken her to lunch, Terrance had been a true gentleman and always opened doors for her.

"Where are we going?" she asked when he got in the car.

"Girl, just sit back and ride," he told her. John Legend poured from the speakers and she did just that. They talked about her enrolling in esthetics school and Paige supporting her decision.

"Oh, goodness, Paige," she said as reached for her cell phone and dialed their home number. She didn't know how late it was going to be when she got home, and she didn't want Paige to worry. She called just in case, to let her know. There was no answer so she called Paige's cell phone.

"Hello," Myla, her eight-year-old niece, answered the phone.

"Hey there Ms. Myla, where is your mom?"

"Right here, Aunt Cam, hold on. Where are you? Mommy said we can go out to eat when you get home," Myla said in one breath.

"Hey, do you have on socks?" Terrance turned down the radio and asked.

"Who is that?" Myla asked.

"I'm out with a friend right now. I can't go," she told her.

"Is it a boy? Are you on a date?"

"Give me that phone, Myla," Paige said in the background. "Hey, what's up?"

"Nothing. I just wanted to let you know I'm going out tonight, that's all," Camille replied.

"Okay, thanks for letting me know. Have a good time," Paige said, and then added, "Are you with a boy?"

"Bye, Paige." Camille laughed and closed the phone. She looked down at her feet then turned and said, "No, I don't have on any socks. Why?"

"Don't worry, I brought an extra pair just in case," Terrance said.

"Why do I need socks?" she asked as she tried to think of places she would need socks. "Are we going bowling?"

"Nope," he said, laughing. "Guess again."

Just as she was about to say something else, he turned into the parking lot of Hot Wheels. She had heard all about the newest roller-skating rink from the teenage customers who came into the salon. The lot was full, and she could hear the music blasting from the building as she got out the car. Terrance popped his trunk, reached into a duffel bag and tossed her a pair of socks. She held them up and pretended to sniff them.

"Oh, you got jokes, huh?" He laughed and grabbed her by the hand.

"Skating, Terrance? I haven't been skating since I was like fourteen," she told him.

"I haven't either, and I'm older than you so get over it."

They entered the rink and he reached into his pocket and handed the young girl at the door two red tickets. Kanye West's "Gold Digger" blasted and neon lights blinked to the beat. Camille looked on the floor where teenagers were whizzing and dancing on skates.

"Thank you," the girl said, smiling.

"So, this is the fund-raiser you were telling me about?"

"Yeah, this is one of the senior class fund-raisers my high school alma mater has. I promised my cousin I would come support 'em," Terrance said. "You know I love the kids."

"Hey, Tuff Love!"

They looked and a handsome young man wearing a throw-back jersey and cornrows rolled over to them.

"What's up, Vashon!" Terrance gave him a hug.

"Thanks for coming out, man. Aunt Ida told me she was gonna see that you made it." Vashon nodded. "I didn't believe her."

"I told you myself I was coming," Terrance replied.

"But you lie all the time." Vashon punched Terrance play-fully in the stomach. He looked over at Camille and gave her a flirtatious look. "How are you?"

"Camille, this is my cousin, Vashon. Vashon, this is my friend, Camille," Terrance introduced them.

"Nice to meet you." Vashon extended his hand and Camille shook it. "You skate?"

"Not in a long time," she said, looking down at the skates that he wore.

"Come on Vashon, that's my jam," a young girl called out.

"A'ight, I'm coming," Vashon yelled over to the cute girl who was swaying to the music. "I'ma holla at y'all in a sec."

"A'ight," Terrance said and gave him some dap. They walked over to the counter and got their skates.

"So, you came because you love the kids, huh?" Camille asked as she laced her skates up and placed her shoes and purse into a locker.

"What? I do love the kids," he said, wobbling as he stood up.

"And your mother had nothing to do with your being here?" she asked.

"A little," he said and reached for her hand.

She stood up and tried to remember exactly how to keep her balance while on eight wheels. She was grateful for the thick carpet as she made her way to the wall beside the floor. She glanced over at Terrance, who didn't seem worried at all about busting his behind, unlike her.

As if he was waiting for the perfect moment, DJ began

playing Musiq's "B.U.D.D.Y" and Terrance stepped onto the shiny wooden floor. He moved his legs back and forth, making sure he was okay and then told her, "Let's roll."

Camille took a deep breath, stepped down beside him, and held onto the wall. People whizzed by, making her even more nervous. Terrance gave her a look as if he was tired of waiting and she said, "Okay. I told you it's been a while."

"I'm 'bout to leave you, girl," he threatened and rolled a few feet away.

Telling herself it was now or never, she pushed away from the wall and rolled beside him. She moved her legs and after a few wobbles, she was gliding across the floor, laughing and enjoying herself. She especially liked being beside Terrance, the feel of his arms around her waist as they went around the rink. Never in a million years would she think she would have this much fun while skating. Terrance was showing off while skating backwards when she felt someone behind her. She turned to see who it was and her body hit the floor, carrying Vashon down with her.

"Ahhhhhh," she screamed.

Terrance's eyes widened and he cracked up. He tried to stop but lost his balance and fell forward.

"Awwwww damn!" he cried out.

"That's what you get," she told him. Vashon got up and helped her to her feet.

"A'ight Norcrest High, it's time for a couples-only skate," the DJ announced.

"That's what's up," Vashon said and smiled. "Can I be your partner?"

"Uh, 'scuse me, Vashon." The girl from earlier rolled beside them with her arms folded.

"I think you already have a partner," she said, laughing. Terrance was getting up and she grinned. "And so do I."

They all coupled off and headed around the rink again, arm in arm to Robin Thicke's "Lost Without You". After the song ended, they took a break and sat down. Terrance introduced her to a couple of his old teachers who came over and spoke. It was apparent that people recognized him from the news and he entertained their questions and comments as well.

"You ready to hit the floor again?" he asked and she did. An hour later, Camille was disappointed when the last song was played and it was over.

"Did you have fun?" Terrance asked as they put their shoes back on.

"Yes, I did," she told him. "I'm probably gonna be sore as hell in the morning."

"You're not the only one," he told her. As they returned their skates, Vashon walked over.

"Thanks for coming out, cuz," he told him.

"I told you I was coming," Terrance said.

"It was a pleasure meeting you as well, Camille." Vashon gave her a hug that lingered a bit longer than necessary. She looked up and once again, his girlfriend was staring at them.

"Your girlfriend is waiting," she told him.

Vashon released her and then said, "She's not my girl. I've been trying to get with her all summer and now that she sees me giving attention to you, she's jealous."

"Oh, so you're just using me," she teased.

"Oh, no, you're hot, believe that, and if you weren't with my cousin, I would be spittin' mad game," Vashon said, winking.

"Boy, please, you're young enough to be—"

"Be what?" She gave him a warning look.

"His older sister." Terrance shrugged.

"A woman as fine as her, a brother would be down for incest," Vashon said, his voice full of confidence.

"We're outta here." Terrance hit Vashon upside his head.

❀   ❀   ❀

"So, did you have fun?" she asked him as they drove home.

"Damn right. I'm glad I asked you to come with me."

Camille was exhausted. She laid her head against the seat and closed her eyes. "Wanna hear something crazy?"

"What's that?" he asked.

"That was the third time in my life I've been skating."

"You're kidding," he said.

"No, I'm serious. I went once with my class in the third grade and again when I was fourteen when my friend had a birthday party." She thought about all the times she wanted to go when she was younger but couldn't because her mother was either too drunk to take her or too mean and hateful to let her go.

"Well, for someone only having been twice, you skated your ass off. Had all the little high school boys sweating you, even my cousin," he teased. "But I have to admit, you look good and I was glad to have you with me. I knew I would have a good time with you."

Camille's heart began pounding. Her eyes opened and she looked over at Terrance. He reached over and put his hand on her leg.

"I'm glad you invited me," she told him and put her hand over his. Terrance was the first guy she had ever really gotten close to, and it was scary for her. She prayed that her life was finally turning around and this was just the beginning of the good time she had yet to experience.

She could feel her phone vibrating in her purse and she took it out. There was a text message from her brother. She opened it and read, "It's a boy! Nine pounds, four ounces. Chauncy Montell Davis."

Chapter 8

"It's not that big, Yaya," Taryn said, looking around the small store. Located right next to the Q-Master's in Galleria Commons, it was a prime spot. Although the location was good, Taryn knew there were several other problems they would have to deal with. Renovating a former craft store into a nail salon was gonna take a lot of work and a lot of capital, which they really didn't have and the space was considerably small and would probably only hold one, maybe two, of the Princess massage chairs they used for pedicures and three manicure tables. The storage space would be limited and there would be practically no waiting area.

"Yeah, I see," Yaya said. "But I think we could make it work."

Taryn knew her friend was grasping at optimism and she had to be the voice of reason. "You wouldn't be able to have a Zen room or do massages. We would have to limit the services we offered."

"Not really."

"Yes, really. You know how you hate to be cramped." Taryn gave her a knowing look.

"How much is the space again?" Yaya asked the leasing agent who was waiting outside the store while they looked around.

"Nineteen-fifty a month." The short white man smiled.

Taryn looked over at Yaya who told him, "Okay, we'll get back with you."

"No problem. I hope we can work something out. Your brother is one of our best clients and he'll tell you we do what we can to make sure you're happy," he said as he handed a business card to each of them.

"Does that include coming down off the rent?" Taryn said when he was out of hearing distance.

"You're crazy," Yaya said. The walked into Q-Masters and talked to the guys for a few minutes before leaving. Taryn could see that her friend was disappointed about the shop.

"Well, we may as well make the most of this trip and get our shop on while we're here," she suggested.

"What time do you have to be back at the salon?" Yaya seemed to perk up a bit.

"I have a one o'clock brow appointment." Taryn looked at her watch and saw that it was ten-fifteen. "That gives us a couple hours."

"Let's hit it." Yaya smiled. It had been a while since the best friends had hung out while shopping, something they had often done before their schedules became bombarded. They went in and out of stores laughing, trying on and spending money.

"You know we gotta stop here," Taryn said, pointing to Frederick's of Hollywood. "You can get a surprise for Fitz."

"You mean you wanna get a surprise for Lincoln," Yaya replied, admiring the red leather bustier and garter hanging in the window. She was still waiting on the right moment for her and Fitz to make love.

"Guilty," Taryn said and pulled her friend into the store with her. She and Lincoln had a romantic weekend planned and she was excited. If things went as planned, this would be the first time they made love.

"Are you nervous about being with him?" Yaya asked. She knew this was a big step for Taryn, who always took her time before sleeping with men.

"Not really. I wouldn't call it nervous, maybe anxious," Taryn said, flipping through the racks of black leather items. "Did you decide when you're giving up the goods yet?"

"No, not yet."

"I'm surprised. I can't believe you're holding out."

"You're acting like I give it up on the first date, T!" Yaya shrieked, causing nearby shoppers to look over at them.

"Stop being so loud, girl. You know that's not what I meant. What about this?" She held up a black cat suit.

"Too much work to get in and out of, T." Yaya shook her head. "Easy access is the key, remember that."

"You are ridiculous," Taryn said, putting it back on the rack.

"So, what did you mean?"

"Jeez, Yaya, the only thing I meant was you enjoying getting your freak on and I know how much you like Fitz. So, I'm surprised you're holding out."

"In that case, I guess you're right. I'm surprised myself. But I just wanna take things slow. Maybe this time things will turn out different."

"Yaya," Taryn looked at her best friend. "Things will turn out different for you this time because for once you're not with a man for what he has and he can give you on the outside, but because of how he makes you feel and gives you on the inside."

Yaya thought about what Taryn told her and agreed. All the other men she had been with in her life were well-paid, established men who had it going on but rarely made her feel the way she felt when she was with Fitzgerald.

"Damn, T, now you're making me sound like a gold digger," Yaya said, laughing.

Things were going smoothly at the salon when they returned. Camille was just finishing up Taryn's client when they walked in.

"Everything okay?" Taryn asked, assessing Camille's work.

"Everything is good," Camille answered as she put Sea Breeze on a cotton ball and gently rubbed it on the woman's brows.

"Hey, Taryn girl," the woman said. "Camille hooked me up."

"Nice job, Camille," Taryn said, noticeably pleased.

"Thanks, I learned from the best," Camille said, winking.

"Aww, thanks Camille, that means so much to me." Taryn smiled. "I try to be a good teacher."

"Shut up, Yaya," Taryn said.

Camille walked with the woman over to the counter, took her money and pulled out the appointment book. "Two weeks, right?"

"Yes, ma'am," she answered, still admiring her brows in the window. "Preferably that Friday because my sister's bridal shower is that weekend."

"Hmmm, Taryn is out of town doing a fashion show that Friday, but she can do you Thursday."

"No, I have to work a double on Thursday. Can you take me?"

Camille looked at the woman with surprise. "Huh?"

"Can I make an appointment with you?"

She looked over at Taryn, not knowing what to say. She had done clients before, but this was the first time one had actually requested her.

"Take the appointment, girl. Give her a card!" Taryn laughed.

Camille gave the woman an appointment card and thanked

her. She was so excited. She had her first client. "Thanks so much, Taryn."

"I'm glad she doesn't do nails." Monya laughed. "I would have to watch my back."

"Yeah, I guess we need to make sure we're on time from now on, Yaya," Taryn responded.

"And to think we were gonna start taking her on the road with us," Yaya said, smirking.

"Are you serious?" Camille gushed. "Please don't play like this. I won't take another client, I swear."

"You keep doing your thing, Camille, and I promise you'll be on the road more than we are."

"I'd like to propose a toast," Fitzgerald said, raising his glass toward Yaya who was sitting across the table where they were having dinner.

"A toast to what?" Yaya picked up her glass of wine and held it up.

"To us," he said. "May the happiness I feel at this moment with you never end."

"Here, here," she said, smiling. Their glasses clinked as they hit against one another. She was also happier at that moment than she had ever been. The salon was doing well, she had finally figured out how to balance her personal clients, her salon clients, and make time for Fitz. Everything seemed to be going well. She looked into Fitz's eyes and saw the love he had for her. "I'm happy too, baby."

"I hope I have a little something to do with that," he said.

"You have a lot to do with that," she answered.

"So, have you figured out what weekend we can get away?" he asked as the waitress put their plates of food in front of them.

Yaya didn't know how to tell him that she didn't see the weekend getaway he wanted to take was going to happen any time soon. Although she had found the balance she needed, it definitely didn't include a vacation. Especially with the Geneva Johnson project coming up.

"I'm still trying to shift some stuff around," she told him. "I'm working on it."

He glanced up from his plate and said, "Qianna, we need this," calling her by her proper name.

"I know we need it, Fitz."

"And you're leaving again tomorrow?"

"Only for one day, two at the most. I'm doing some work for Geneva Johnson that came up at the last minute." She shrugged. She hoped hearing Geneva Johnson's name would make him see how important this job was.

"It's hard enough not being able to spend time with you and Carver together on the weekends," he said, sighing. He had also been stressing how much he wanted her to get to know his son. Getting to know Carver wasn't a problem to Yaya, it just wasn't on the top of her priority list. "I thought that since you hired the new nail techs and Camille was doing so well, it would free up some of your time."

"I thought so too," she said. Their conversation was interrupted by the sound of applause; she looked across the room and saw a man on bended knee, smiling at a woman who was holding her hand up and showing off a sparkling ring. Yaya smiled and said, "Awww, they got engaged. What's wrong, Fitz?" She frowned.

"That's Carver's mom," he answered. "She told me it wasn't that serious with her and that cat."

"Maybe she thought it wouldn't be a big deal to you," Yaya said before she took a bite of her baked chicken.

"Her thinking about marrying a man that's gonna be around my son is a big deal to me," Fitz snapped. Yaya was taken aback by his attitude and didn't respond. In her effort to make her new relationship different, she had made a conscientious effort to tone down her divatude in a sense. Any other time she would have let her man know that the only

woman he should be concerned about was her, but she never
had to deal with a baby mama before and somehow she knew
that wouldn't work.

"Have you ever been engaged?"

"No, not yet." She sighed. "Have you?"

"Once," he answered.

His answer surprised her. He had never mentioned it before, then again, she had never asked.

"Really?"

"Yeah, to my son's mother," he said, nodding. This fact didn't
surprise her. Fitz was the marrying type, especially if they
were having his child.

"What happened?" she asked.

He paused and then told her, "I realized that I wanted to
marry her for the wrong reasons, I guess. I was more or less
trying to do the right thing so she thought I wasn't in love
with her."

"Were you?"

Instead of answering, he remained silent. Yaya looked to
see what caused him to stop. He was staring at the newly engaged couple as they walked toward the door.

The remainder of the meal was filled with forced small
talk. Fitz was noticeably preoccupied. Her stomach began
tightening and Yaya couldn't eat anymore. She had hardly
eaten her food, but she was full. It was something that was
happening more and more frequently.

"You okay?" Fitz asked her. "You didn't eat that much."

"Yeah, I'll be back in a few minutes," she said excusing herself and going to the restroom. "I don't feel good."

Her stomach was bloated and it felt as if she could feel the
food floating inside of her. She stood inside the stall, unable
to take the discomfort. Not knowing what else to do, she
gagged and vomited. Relief came over her. After washing her
face and rinsing out her mouth with water, she went back to
the table.

"You ready to go?" Fitz asked. He had already had her food boxed up and the bag sat where her plate once had.

Confused by the sudden end of what she thought was going to be a long evening, she nodded. "Yeah, I guess."

The drive home was just as exciting as the second half of their dinner. Yaya knew that seeing his son's mother become engaged to another man had to be kind of devastating for him, but he was being downright rude. She was glad when they finally arrived at her home.

"I'll talk to you later," she told him.

"You don't want me to come in?"

"I'm really not feeling well," she said. Instead of waiting for him to open the door for her as she usually did, she opened it herself and got out of the car.

"Yaya, wait," he called after her.

She stopped and turned to him. "What?"

He walked over and kissed her gently. "I love you. I'll call you later to see if you're feeling better."

"Okay," she said, deciding to forgive him for his rude behavior considering the circumstances. *He loves you. There's no reason to even be worried about him tripping over her. She's engaged to someone else and he's with you.*

Chapter 9

"Well, Ya, maybe he was just surprised, that's all," Taryn said as Yaya told her about what happened at dinner. She wondered if her girlfriend was being melodramatic as usual, especially when Yaya said she had to throw up. *That girl will do anything for attention.*

"I know he was surprised, T," Yaya said, sighing. "But he was clearly bothered by the engagement. When I got back from the bathroom, he was ready to go. Food packed up and halfway out the door."

"Come on, Yaya, if you told him you didn't feel well, then he probably figured you weren't gonna eat anything else anyway. He was being considerate."

"Which is why even though I wanted to go off, I didn't," Yaya responded.

"I'm glad because you really didn't have a reason to go off." Taryn laughed. "What time does your flight leave tomorrow?"

"Seven-thirty," she said. "I'll only be gone overnight."

"Yaya, you know I'm not gonna be in the salon Friday and Saturday. I'm working with you on this Geneva Johnson thing, but you gotta have my back too." Taryn knew Yaya had been traveling more than they agreed upon, but she also knew how important working with a world-renowned celebrity was for the salon.

"I got you, T. I know you spending the weekend with your man!"

"You better try to take heed and spend some time with your man," Taryn teased. There was a beep and she looked at her phone. "This is my man now, I'll call you back."

"Bye, T," Yaya said and hung up.

"Hey, baby," Taryn greeted Lincoln.

"What's up, beautiful?" Lincoln's voice was so loud that she held the phone away from her ear. Loud music and laughing were in the background.

"What in the world," she giggled. "Where are you?"

"Hanging out with some of my boys," he answered. There was something weird in the way he was talking. His attitude was noticeably cocky.

"Okay, that's good."

"I just wanted to call and say hi to my beautiful girlfriend and tell you how much I love you."

"Uh, okay." She was shocked. He had never been so verbal with her. The Lincoln she was used to talking to was cool and suave. This Lincoln was loud and boisterous.

"And I wanted to tell you that I am coming to see you in a little while," he added.

"Really?"

"Yep, is that cool?" he asked.

Taryn smiled. "Of course that's cool."

"That's what I'm talking 'bout. I'm going see my baby!" Lincoln yelled out, "I'll see you in a little while."

Lincoln calling and saying he was coming over was totally unexpected. She straightened up her place, took a quick shower, chilled a bottle of Verdi and lit some candles. She considered putting on the sexy black ensemble she bought from Frederick's. *No, not tonight. Save that for the weekend.*

Flipping through her CDs, she settled on John Legend and waited on the chaise lounge.

Two hours later, the wine was chilled, the candles were melted, the CD had ended and Taryn didn't even realize she had fallen asleep until her eyes opened and she saw the clock read 1:16. *His ass ain't even show up! Wait! Before you get mad, maybe something happened. Call first.* She dialed his cell and his voice mail picked up. *Now, you can be pissed!*

"T, the credit card machine is printing with that red line across the top. I think it's about to run out of paper," Monya announced.

"Look under the register and see if there's a roll under there," Taryn told her. *Common sense should tell you that.*

"I already looked. There's none there," Monya replied.

"Dammit," she whispered, unable to hide her frustration. *Do I have to do everything myself?* She looked under the register and didn't find any. *This is not my day.* The last thing she needed was to tell her clients they couldn't take credit cards.

"Hey everybody." Camille walked in with Terrance right behind her.

"Camille, if you knew you were gonna be late you should've called." Taryn looked up from the client she was working on. "You know we're short staffed today because Yaya is gone again."

"I'm sorry, Taryn. We're running low on receipt tape and ink for the computer so I stopped at OfficeMax and picked some up." She reached into the plastic bag she was carrying and held up a package of receipt tape. "I didn't wanna take the chance of running out."

"Well, I guess that means your timing is perfect," Monya said, taking the paper from her, then whispered, "I'm warning you to tread lightly, though. She's been tripping all morning."

"What's wrong with her?" Camille leaned over and asked.

"She hasn't said yet, so it must be big." Monya shrugged.

Taryn pretended not to hear them. She knew she was being a bitch, but she couldn't help it. Holding it together after last night was a challenge. Not wanting to cancel clients and lose money, she decided to juggle Yaya's customers in with her own and try to fit in the walk-ins. Camille had morning classes and until she came in, they had to tag-team answering the phones. Her patience was worn thin. She had yet to talk to Lincoln and was glad he hadn't called yet. It gave her time to think of how she would cuss him out when she finally did talk to him.

"Afternoon, ladies," the mailman said when he walked in. "I have a certified letter."

"I'll sign for it," Camille quickly spoke up, happy for the distraction. She signed the green card and passed Taryn the white envelope. "T, I think you should open this. It looks important."

Taryn took the letter out of her hand and opened it. She blinked to make sure she was reading correctly.

"Oh, hell naw!" she said, her anger growing by the second.

"What's wrong, T?" Monya walked over to see what was wrong.

"This girl has lost her mind!" Taryn continued reading.

Unable to wait for Taryn to tell her, Monya took the paper from her hands and read for herself. "Oh, this is some bull!"

"Can someone tell me what's going on?" Camille put her hands on her hips.

"Celeste has filed a workman's compensation claim against us!" Monya replied.

"What? How?" Camille couldn't believe the nerve of her. "She hasn't worked here in months."

"I don't know how, but it looks like this trick is trying!" Monya snapped.

"Who's Celeste?" Terrance asked.

"A chick that called herself working here a couple of

months ago, if you call standing around doing nothing *work*."
Monya folded the papers and put them back in the envelope.
"T, don't even let this stress you."

Taryn looked at Monya. "I'm not stressed, but she's about
to be. Believe that!"

"T, don't call her," Camille said as Taryn stormed down the
hall toward her office. She knew that Celeste was in for it,
and she was glad.

"What the hell is your problem?" Taryn yelled into the
phone when she heard Celeste's voice on the other end.

"I beg your pardon?" Celeste asked. "I don't have a problem. But you're acting like you do."

"Girl, I will . . . what is this fake-ass workman's comp claim,
Celeste? You're too lazy to find a job so you think *we're* supposed to take care of your ass?"

"That claim is as real as I am. Working at that salon was a
health hazard to me and my baby."

"Oh, yeah, your *supposed* pregnancy," Taryn snapped.

"That's right, my pregnancy . . . by your *supposed* man!"
Celeste was assertive in defense of herself. "Look, Taryn, I
don't care if you don't like me. I don't care that you and Lincoln are all in love. What I do care about is me and my baby,
and taking care of us. As far as my workman's comp claim, it's
as legitimate as Lincoln being the wonderful father I know he
will be; whether he or you like it or not. I suggest you don't
call me regarding this anymore or I'll sue you for harassment
in addition to workman's compensation. You wanna talk to
me, you call my lawyer!"

Taryn was beyond furious when she heard the dial tone in
her ear. Not knowing who else to call, Taryn scrolled through
the phone book in her phone until she came to Jimmy's number.

"Don't worry about it. I'll come to the salon as soon as I
leave the office," he assured her.

"You'd better make it quick or you're gonna have to be my defense attorney when I go kill this bitch," she told him.

"I got you on that too if you need me," he said, laughing. "I could use the exposure of a good murder trial."

"I'll see you later," she said, sighing. Her day had gone from bad to worse and as much as she wanted to leave for the day, there was no way she could.

"Hey, beautiful."

"Oh, no, this is not a good time." Taryn looked up and saw Lincoln in her doorway. "I can't deal with you. Not right now."

"Baby, what's wrong?" he asked, walking toward her, looking fine as ever in a long-sleeved black tee, jeans, and Timberlands; the diamond earrings he wore were large enough to make even her jealous.

Taryn rolled her eyes at him. "Please don't try to act like everything's all good, Lincoln."

"Girl, you know this ain't no act! Everything is all good now that I'm here with my baby." He walked over and tried to put his arms around her.

Pushing him away, Taryn's frustration increased. "I'm telling you, I'm not in the mood, Lincoln. I got too much going on right now."

"You mean to tell me you're too busy to deal with your man?" Lincoln sulked.

"You were too busy to deal with me last night, so what's the damn difference?"

"Last night? What are you talking about?"

"Nothing," she said, walking past him. She could feel his grip as he pulled her toward him. Looking down at his hand on her, she scowled at him and his fingers quickly released their hold.

"Taryn, why are you tripping? What the hell happened last night?"

"Your showing up at my house like you called and said you were, didn't happen. That's why I'm tripping!" she yelled.

Lincoln looked confused. "I ain't talk to you last night, did I?"

"Look, I know you're used to dealing with chicken-head hoes like Celeste, but I ain't one of them, okay? Get the hell outta my way. Unlike your baby mama, I got a job to do, and my customers are waiting."

"Wait, Taryn. If I called you and said I was coming over, I'm sorry. I was hanging at my boy's house last night, and we got drunk. I couldn't even drive home. I spent the night there," he said, his voice apologetic.

Taryn took a deep breath and looked into his eyes. She thought about the crazy way he sounded on the phone when he called and figured he was telling the truth. "You don't even remember talking to me?"

He shook his head. "No, we were seriously ripped. I'm sorry, T, I really am. I promise it'll never happen again." He pulled her to him again and this time, she allowed him. He leaned down and kissed her, tenderly.

"You know I'm still pissed, right? "she said when their kiss ended.

"And you know I'ma make it up to you, right?" He kissed her again; this time, his hands roamed along her back and landed on her behind, where he squeezed.

"Stop it," she squealed, unable to contain her laughter.

"What else did I say last night?" he asked.

"I'll never tell," she said, winking, "I gotta get back to work."

"Can a brother come over and see you tonight?"

"If he can remember to call first," she teased and walked out.

All eyes were on Jamison Grossman when he walked into After Effex just as they were closing. Taryn could see almost see the drool in the corners of their last clients' mouths when the door opened and he stepped in clean as ever in a dark green suit.

"Well, well, well, my true love has come to find me," one lady said.

"Girl, please, the only reason his fine ass would be looking for you is because you stole his wallet," the woman sitting beside her said, laughing. Jimmy cleared his throat and smiled politely.

"Monya, control your customers," Taryn said, snickering. "What's up, Jimmy?"

"Hey, Mr. Grossman," Camille said, grabbing her purse.

"Didn't I tell you to call me Jimmy." He winked at her. "I sent that paperwork to the credit bureaus for you, so hopefully we'll get this mess cleared up soon."

"Thanks, Mr.—I mean . . . Jimmy," Camille replied. "I'll see you all tomorrow."

"I'm outta here too." Monya sighed. "It's been a long day."

"Bye, girls," Taryn told them.

"Where's Qianna?" he asked, looking around.

"Out of town working," Monya answered as she walked out the door behind Camille.

"It figures." He laughed, then turned to Taryn. "Where's the paper you were telling me about?"

"On my desk, I'll get it." Taryn went into her office and got the letter. She waited as Jimmy flipped through the pages.

"Well," he said, flipping through the pages. "According to this, the fumes that Celeste Peterson was exposed to and constantly inhaled while she was employed here, has caused her to suffer from debilitating migraines and constant pain."

"That's crazy. She sat right where Camille sits here in the receptionist area, which, as you can see, is a fair distance away from the nail station. Lincoln put in a huge ventilation system throughout this damn place, which constantly runs, so there are no fumes for her to inhale."

Jimmy removed his jacket. "Can I sit down? It's been a long day and my feet are tired as hell."

Taryn smiled at him. "I can do something even better for you."

"Oh, really? What's that?" He licked his lips, seductively.

"Boy, please, don't even try it." She lightly smacked his shoulder. "Come over here and take off your shoes and socks."

She turned the water on in one of the large cushioned massage chairs with foot basins attached that they used for pedicures. Checking the temperature of the water to make sure it was perfect, she poured sea salts and oils in.

"You're kidding me, right?" He laughed.

"No, come on, hurry up and sit down." She took the jacket from him and hung it on the coat rack.

"I don't do pedicures, girl, you'd better stop trippin'. That's some foo-foo gay-type stuff and I don't get down like that," he said in an overly masculine tone.

"Jimmy, please, save the machismo for your homeboys, boo." She gently shoved him toward the chair. He stared wide-eyed as the chair hummed and the water swished.

"I don't know."

"Boy, sit down and take your shoes and socks off."

"This will remain under attorney-client privilege," he warned as he sat in the large leather seat. While he removed his shoes and socks, she gathered all the supplies she would need. Music and Jarrod's loud voice could be heard through the walls, so she put the iPod on the surround sound speakers and played Maxwell.

"You are ridiculous." Taryn laughed at Jimmy's awkwardness. "Put your feet in the water and sit back."

Hesitant at first, Jimmy complied. His body relaxed, his eyes closed, and a goofy grin was on his face. "This feels wonderful."

"I know, all my gay clients think so," she said, sighing. His eyes flew open and he looked horrified. She quickly added,

"I'm just kidding. So, did you do something special with Bianca like I suggested?"

"I tried to take her out the other night as a matter of fact, but she declined," he replied.

Taryn gave him a knowing look. "Tried how? And where did you try to take her?"

"A new client of mine has opened a winery. They had a invite-only tasting."

"That sounds so nice," she told him.

"I thought so too. But she had committed herself to go to a Pampered Chef party with her sister, so she didn't go." He shrugged.

"A Pampered Chef party? What?" Taryn tried not to laugh.

"Her sister, Darla, can be kinda persuasive," he told her. "She's five-seven and about three hundred pounds, built like an NFL linebacker. I think she can take me if I pissed her off. That's why I try to stay on her good side."

Taryn was so busy talking and laughing with Jimmy as she massaged his feet that she jumped when her cell phone rang.

"Are you home yet, sweetie?" Lincoln asked after she answered.

"Um, not yet," she said. "I'm working on my last client now."

"Damn, it's almost nine o'clock," Lincoln said, sighing.

"I know, Lincoln, it's not gonna be that much longer." She glanced at Jimmy who seemed to be in a place of total bliss. "I'll call you when I get home."

"I guess Lincoln figured out I wasn't your date, huh?" Jimmy smirked when she hung up her phone.

"Yes, he did," she said, sighing.

"That's good," he replied. "See, things worked out for you guys."

"It's still a little early to tell." Taryn poured lotion into her hands and worked it into his calves. "I'm still trying to feel him out."

"He's the one who did the work on the salon for you, right?

That means you've known him for a while. Weren't you all friends before? Damn, that feels good."

"Yeah, we've been friends for a minute," she said, nodding. "But, you know how men are, and I'm not trying to get hurt."

"Come on Taryn, you know anyone you let in your life will eventually hurt you in one way or another. The trick is finding out who's worth the pain."

Taryn stared at him, letting what he said sink in. She almost told Jimmy about Celeste and her saying Lincoln was the father, but she felt that was too much information. For some reason, having him know that was embarrassing for her.

"That's true, Jimmy. But the ones that you think are worth the pain are the ones who hurt you the most."

Chapter 10

"I thought you were getting here at three."

"I overslept this morning so I had to catch a later flight." Yaya paid for her smoothie and put her change in the Louis Vuitton purse, which matched her carry-on luggage perfectly. Her layover was only forty-five minutes, but that gave her plenty of time to grab a quick snack and make it to the other side of the airport where her departure gate was. "I land at eight-fifteen."

Fitz's voice was strained. "I guess that means we're not going out tonight then, huh?"

"Baby, I'm exhausted now. By the time I get home, the only thing I'm gonna wanna do is go to sleep. We can go out tomorrow night." Her call-waiting beeped in her ear and she saw that it was the salon. "Hold on. Hello."

"Hey Yaya, where you at?" Taryn asked.

"In Charlotte, about to board the plane. How are things going?" She could feel stares of male travelers while she walked past them, as she listened as Taryn told her all about Celeste's workman's compensation claim and Lincoln's failure to show up at her house due to his drunken stupor. *Damn, a lot can happen in two days*, she thought. "Well, did he come over last night?"

"It was late when I got home, so I didn't even call him," Taryn said. "You know I'm not trying to sweat him."

"I know that's right," Yaya said, laughing. Her phone beeped and she realized she had forgotten Fitz was on the other line. "Damn, T, that's Fitz."

"You need me to pick you up?" Taryn asked.

"No, my car is parked at the lot. I'll swing by your place later on tonight."

"Cool."

"Baby, I'm sorry. That was Taryn and she was telling me about—"

Fitz interrupted her, "I'm beginning to feel like I'm not one of your top priorities, Yaya."

"You are one of my top priorities, Fitz. It's just that there's so much going on right now that it seems that way," she told him. She knew that she was wearing herself thin and she didn't want her relationship to suffer, especially since it was still in the beginning stages. Fitz was a good man, and she wanted to make it work. "I promise, I am going to make time for you."

"Not me, Yaya, us. I gotta go. I'll talk to you later."

"Fitz, wait a minute," she said but he was gone. Not wanting their conversation to end the way that it did, she dialed his number. His voice mail picked up and she hung up. Finally arriving at the gate, she sat down and tried to relax for a minute. The stress and strain of everything she had going on was taking its toll on her. She had barely touched her smoothie and she felt so full that it made her stomach ache. They began calling for first-class passengers to board. *There is no way I can fly with my stomach feeling like this.* She threw the cup in the trash, grabbed her bag and walked over to the flight attendant.

"Excuse me, I need to run to the restroom," she said.

"We have one on the plane. You can go ahead and board and use it before we prepare for takeoff," the blond woman said, smiling.

"I'm not feeling well and I'd rather use the one here in the airport. Do I have time?"

The woman looked at Yaya's first-class boarding pass then nodded. "If you hurry and go now, you should be okay."

"Thanks," Yaya said and rushed to the restroom. Grateful that there wasn't a line, she walked into the first stall and threw up. Satisfied that she felt well enough to get on the plane, she washed her hands, brushed her teeth and headed for her flight.

"Are you gonna be okay?" the flight attendant asked when Yaya returned.

"Yes, I should be fine now," she answered. She got on the plane and settled into the plush leather first-class seat. Before turning her phone off, she dialed Fitz again, but still didn't get an answer. *I hope he doesn't call himself ignoring me*, she thought, taking out her iPod and putting her earphones in. She had too much other stuff going on to chase down a man who didn't understand her need to succeed.

"Surpise!" Fitz smiled at Yaya. She had just made it home and found him waiting on her doorstep holding a bouquet of flowers.

"Do you have stock in a florist?" she said as she walked over and kissed him. All of the tension they had earlier vanished as she wrapped her arms around his neck as they tasted one another.

"Damn, I missed you," he whispered into her ear and she felt herself melt.

"Now, that's what I call a homecoming," she said, taking the flowers from him. Fitz grabbed her suitcase and followed her into the house.

"How was your trip?" he asked.

Laying the flowers on the bar, she walked over and hugged him again. "Not as good as my homecoming."

"You should stay home more often. There's no telling what you'll get." He kissed her again. She could feel his hands running along her back, causing her desire to increase. She knew that for her, there would be no more waiting. She wanted him.

"Can you give it to me now?" She gave him a seductive look and pulled him toward her bedroom. She cut the lamp on her nightstand on, slightly illuminating the pitch-black room.

For a moment, Fitz looked shocked. Yaya kicked her shoes off, and then began unbuttoning her blouse, staring at him as she did so. Fitz's eyes widened and stared at her full breasts covered by the black lace bra she wore, her hardened nipples protruding through the fabric. He took a step forward, but Yaya held her hand up and stopped him. Yaya loved undressing for her men. It was a turn-on for her and them. Taryn and Monya often teased her saying she really wanted to be a stripper but was scared. She reached and unfastened her jeans and slid her hands inside.

"Damn," Fitz groaned and she turned her back to him as she slid them off and stepped out of them. She then unhooked her bra and it fell to the floor. Wearing only her black lace panties, she looked over her shoulder and gestured for him to come to her. He walked and stood behind her; the feel of his hardness aroused her even more and she reached around for his hands. She took his forefinger and sucked it, then rubbed it on each of her nipples. "Oh, damn."

"Feel good?" she asked, taking his other hand and placing it on her inner thigh.

"Damn, right," he answered, and began sucking on her neck. His finger traveled along her thigh until it rested between her legs. Yaya turned and faced him, kissing him again.

He began taking his clothes off and she got into bed. It had been too long since she had been with a man and she was ready. She looked at Fitz's nude body for the first time. She couldn't stop her eyes from traveling down his sexy chest, along his firm stomach and resting on his manhood. It's not as big as I thought it was gonna be, but it's not bad.

"Do you have a condom?" she asked as he climbed in bed beside her.

"Uh," he paused.

"Don't worry," she said, smiling, reaching into the night-stand, pulling out the small plastic wrapped rubber. She almost threw them away after she broke up with Jason, but figured she would need them eventually.

"You have condoms ready at hand?" He gave her a strange look.

"Just in case of emergencies like this one," she said, laughing as she opened it. "Get on your back."

Fitz rolled onto his back and she put the condom on him. She nibbled on his abdomen, working her way up his body, her lips lingering on his chest and sucking his nipples. She could hear his breath quickening and her tongue left a trail from his shoulder blade to his neck, as she found her way to his lips. He covered her mouth with his and she straddled his body. She could feel her wetness and the heat from within her center as she mounted herself on his hardness.

"Oh, shit Yaya," he murmured. "You're so damn wet."

She tightened her muscles as she began riding, slow and intense. "You like this?"

"Yes," he answered and pulled her mouth to his again. She increased her speed, maintaining a steady rhythm. She could feel the heat coming from his body and his chest began glistening with sweat. She braced herself and arched her back, anticipating the satisfaction she was working toward. Yaya stared as Fitz gripped the headboard and bit his bottom lip. "Yaya . . . I . . ."

Yaya could feel Fitz holding her body on top of him and then let out a long moan.

Oh, hell naw . . . this did not just happen . . . there's no damn way . . . it ain't even get good yet! She told herself his dick was still hard and there was no way he came yet and she went to ride some more, but reality showed her otherwise when she felt his limpness and heard him say, "Damn, that was the bomb!"

Yaya rolled from on top of him, too shocked to say anything. She climbed out of bed and went into her bathroom. *What the hell just happened? Did I miss something? Not only is he barely average in size, but he can't last, either? What the hell am I gonna do?*

A knock on the bathroom door caused her to jump. "Hey, you almost done? A brother needs to clean up."

"Oh, I'm sorry," she yelled. She wanted to add, *and so are you*, but she held her tongue. She quickly washed up, slipped into her bathrobe and psyched herself up to be nice when she walked out. "I laid a towel and washcloth on the sink for you."

"Thanks, baby." He leaned over and kissed her tenderly. "That was intense. You truly know how to satisfy your man."

She forced a smile and replied, "Thanks, you know how I do."

"Damn right." He winked and went into the bathroom.

Yaya didn't know what to do. Her first instinct was to call Taryn and share the details of their passion-filled, seven-minute lovemaking session to her best friend, but she couldn't, at least not while he was within earshot. She quickly threw on a pair of shorts and a tank top and went into her living room.

"Are you on your way?" Taryn asked when she answered her phone.

"No, I'm at home." Yaya's voice was barely above a whisper. "Fitz was here when I pulled up."

"That was nice," Taryn remarked.

"Yeah, but what just happened wasn't nice at all, T. I don't know how to deal with this crap." Yaya walked in the kitchen and opened the refrigerator, which was nearly bare. *I need a drink, a strong one.* There was a bottle of Smirnoff in the cabinet and she found a can of pineapple juice. *This will have to work.*

"What happened, Yaya?"

"Okay, I was kinda psyched to see him when I got here and I showed him *my appreciation* for his thoughtfulness," Yaya admitted.

"What? You gave him some? What happened to waiting this time?" Taryn giggled. "So, how was it? What went wrong."

"It was over as soon as it got started, that's what went wrong."

Taryn laughed so hard. that Yaya knew she had to be crying.

"It's not funny, T. Stop laughing!"

"Okay. I'm sorry," Taryn said, trying to catch her breath.

"T, help me. Tell me how to fix it!" Yaya hissed.

"Come on, Yaya, you're being dramatic now. All first times are awkward, you know that."

"I can handle awkward, this was FAST!" Putting ice in two glasses, Yaya peeked out the doorway to make sure Fitz was still nowhere near. Taryn was still laughing in her ear. "Stop laughing, Taryn."

"I'm trying to, but you're still being funny. Look, maybe it's been awhile since he got some, you know how guys are."

"T, I think he thinks that it was *good*, which it *wasn't*."

"Give him another chance, Yaya. Everyone deserves a second chance. Where is he now while you're calling me? Shouldn't you be cuddling?" Taryn teased.

Yaya poured a fair amount of vodka in her glass and just enough juice to turn the clear liquid yellow. She took a long swig and said, "That ain't even funny. He's in the room. I came out here to fix a drink."

"At least you worked up a thirst, that's a good sign," Taryn

told her. "Go lay in bed with your man, Yaya. Talk to him,
laugh with him, snuggle up next to him, fall asleep in his arms
and then, when you both wake up, make love to him. It will
be better next time, believe me."

Yaya repositioned herself so she could see the clock on her
nightstand and saw that it was six-fifteen in the morning. Fitz
nuzzled the back of her neck as he spooned his body with
hers. The warmth of his body felt good but it didn't satisfy her
any more than his failed attempt to do so fifteen minutes earlier.

"Are you okay, baby?" he asked.

"Yeah, I'm good," she replied.

"I love being with you," he said, kissing her ear. "This
morning was even better than last night."

"Yeah, it was," she lied. *I'm going to kill Taryn*, she thought
to herself and tried to evaluate her situation. She loved
Fitzgerald, that fact was clear, but could she really be with a
man who couldn't satisfy her sexually?

Chapter 11

Camille was used to being swamped on Fridays, but today seemed as if everyone in town came in to get their nails, brows, and makeup done or purchase products from the salon. There was no wait between clients and between answering the phones, taking payments, making appointments, and serving as backup for walk-in clients, Camille wasn't sure if people were coming or going. By the time the door was locked and the neon pink OPEN sign was shut off, she was beat.

"Aight, are y'all rolling to State Street's tonight, or what?" Monya said out of the blue. "I heard it's gonna be off the chain tonight."

"I told you, I'm down," Taryn replied. "I haven't been there in a minute. DJ Terror with his fine ass. Tobias Sims. Too bad he's married."

"I already told Fitz I was going. It'll give me something *fun* to do for a change." Yaya smirked, giving Taryn a knowing look.

"You need to stop." Taryn threw a wad of paper at Yaya.

"What? He's meeting me there later. And so is Lincoln."

"You hanging out with us, Cam?" Taryn asked.

Camille shook her head. "I can't get into State Street's. You have to be twenty-five. I'm not even twenty-one."

"Girl, please. You can get in. You work for After Effex! Besides, you've never hung out with us," Monya told her.

"She's too busy hanging with Tuff Love," Taryn teased.

"Whatever, you know we're just friends." Camille smiled.

"Friends with benefits, probably," Yaya giggled.

"We are not." Camille sucked her teeth. She tried to change the subject. "Besides, I'm too tired to go anywhere."

"It's been a long week for all of us, Cam, that's why we need to go party." Monya snapped her fingers and moved from side to side as if she was on the dance floor.

"We're all tired. And don't try to change the subject. Terrance is your man," Yaya added.

"He is not. I keep telling you, we're just friends. He doesn't even want a relationship right now," Camille replied.

"Oh, really, is that what he said?" Taryn asked.

Camille nodded. She and Terrance were laying on his couch watching *Flavor of Love* a week ago when they began talking about finding someone special. She thought it would be the defining moment when their relationship would transition from friendship to something more. Instead, he told her that his interest in a serious commitment was nonexistent and he had no desires to have a steady girlfriend. She was disappointed, but acted like it was no big deal. The kiss he gave her was what was a big deal to her. It was much more than a friendly peck. Their mouths explored and tasted one another for longer than a minute. It was clear by his actions, he wanted to be more than just friends, but what he said was totally different.

"Yes, that's what he said," Camille answered.

"And you're fine with that?" Yaya asked.

"I enjoy being Terrance's friend. We're cool, that's it."

Camille was becoming frustrated. *Hell no, I'm not cool with it, but what can I do?* She and Terrance constantly talked on the phone, went to lunch, dinner, movies, all the things couples do. She had fallen for him and thought he felt the same way. There was no way she wanted to stop being with him because all of a sudden he said that he didn't want a committed relationship. His saying that didn't make her stop feeling the same way about him.

"Then you need to come to the club with us tonight. You might meet a few new friends." Taryn walked over and put her arms on her shoulder. "I'll pick you up at ten."

The line outside State Street's was wrapped around the building. Camille looked down at the black stiletto shoes she bravely wore and knew there was no way she would be able to stand in them long enough to get in.

"Look at that line," she whined as she walked beside her coworkers.

"I know, I told y'all the club was gonna be banging tonight," Monya said.

"By the time we make it to the door, it's gonna be time to leave," Camille replied.

"I hope you don't think we're standing in line," Yaya said, laughing. "Cam, you got a lot to learn about the life of a celebrity makeup artist."

"We don't do lines," Taryn told her as they walked past the crowd and stepped to the front door of the club.

"Well, well, well, look who decided to grace us with their presence tonight. The fly women of After Effex!" The bouncer wore a grin so wide, he looked like a kid on Christmas morning. "What's up, beautifuls?"

Butterflies fluttered in Camille's stomach at the thought of being turned away at the door. She would be an embarrassment to them all.

"Hey, Mack!" Yaya kissed him on his cheek. He held the door open for them without even checking their IDs and she walked right in along with everyone else.

Camille usually hated being the center of attention, but being with Yaya, Taryn, and Monya gave her a newfound sense of power. They were the baddest chicks to step foot in the club and she knew it. Her black-and-silver halter top fit perfect, along with her black Baby Phat jeans. She wasn't even as self-conscious about her entire back being out, like she had been when she first got dressed. *This is gonna be the bomb*, she thought, observing everything and everyone as she moved to the sound of Timbaland and Nelly Furtado singing "Give it To Me."

"Come on, Cam," Monya said, motioning toward a set of spiraling steps.

"What's up there?" Camille asked, trying to look past her.

"VIP, girl!" Monya answered. "You have so much to learn!"

Camille walked up the steps and the bouncer waiting at the top held the red velvet rope for her to pass through.

"What's up, cutie?" A guy smiled at her.

"Hi." Camille smiled back. *He is fine.* He wasn't as tall as Terrance, but he had to be at least six foot three and he was cut like an NFL player. He had the deepest dimples and prettiest smile she had seen, which she could see even in the dimness of the club. She almost hated having to leave him.

"Hey, Yaya, T, and Monya!"

"Hey, Terrell! What are you doing here? Nicole must've took you off house arrest for the night." Yaya walked over to a big guy dressed in a sports coat, jeans, and shades. The diamonds he wore in his ear had to be at least two karats.

"Still trying to be a damn comedian, huh, Yaya? I keep telling you to stick to your day job," he said, walking over and hugging her along with Monya and Taryn. "What's up, fam? And who is this fresh—"

"Back the hell off, Terrell," Taryn warned. "This is our new assistant, Camille. Camille, this is Terrell, he's married and a flirt, but he's good people."

"Nice to meet you, Camille. I see you fit right in with the beauty crew, as we know them as. I take it you're a triple threat like they are?" He hugged Camille.

"Triple threat?" she raised her eyebrows and asked.

"Fine, fabulous, and fly as hell. That's why they can't keep a man, they're dangerous forces to be reckoned with," he said, laughing.

"Shut the hell up, Terrell." Taryn rolled her eyes as they all sat on the leather sofas. "Yaya and I have men, thank you."

"Unfortunately, Mr. Right hasn't found me yet." Monya stuck her tongue at him.

"That's because your ass is probably still hiding," Terrell said, laughing, then turned to Camille. "And where is your man?"

"I don't have one either," she said, smiling.

"Really?" He winked.

"I have a friend," she replied.

"Ohhhhhh, a friend," he said, laughing. The waitress came over to take their drink orders. He leaned over and asked Camille, "What are you drinking, *friend?*"

Shaking her head, Camille told him, "I don't drink."

"Come on, don't be a punk," he egged her on.

"Leave the girl alone. There's nothing wrong with her not wanting to be an alcoholic like the rest of us," Yaya said. "Besides, she's the designated driver. But I'll take a redheaded slut."

Camille gave Yaya a grateful look. After dealing with her alcoholic mother for most of her life, drinking was something she never had a desire to indulge in. She had surprised herself by coming out to the club, period.

"Oh, that's cool." Terrell nodded. He ordered himself a whiskey sour and then asked Camille, "Since you're the designated driver that means I can get a drink, right?"

"Sure, I'll make sure you get home to your wife in one piece." This time she winked at him.

"You've been around them too long, I see." Terrell shook his head.

Camille listened as they all talked and drank, enjoying her surroundings. Terrell was hilarious and she learned that his brother was none other than the club's DJ who Taryn was talking about earlier.

"Excuse me, Yaya," one of the bouncers came over and said. "There are a couple of guys who are asking for you. One of them claims to be your boyfriend. I told them I couldn't let them up here without you escorting them."

"Oh, hell, that's probably Fitz. I forgot he was meeting me here. I'll be back," Yaya excused herself. "Taryn, you need to be coming with me because you know your man is downstairs too!"

"Yes, he is." Taryn stood up and the two women left, followed by the bouncer.

A waitress came over and put a glass containing what looked like a pineapple slurpee in front of Camille.

"Uh, I didn't order this," Camille quickly told her.

"Compliments of the gentleman over there."

Camille turned to see who she was talking about and saw the fine guy who spoke to her earlier.

"Could you please tell him thanks, but I don't drink," Camille said, looking at the appealing beverage.

"I already told him. Don't worry, it's just a virgin piña colada," the waitress replied. "It doesn't have any alcohol."

"Aw, that's so sweet. He sent you a fake drink!" Terrell laughed.

"You're just jealous because you didn't think to do it first." Yaya stuck her tongue at him.

Camille lifted the tall drink and held it in his direction, mouthing the words, "Thank you."

Looking over the balcony, she watched as more and more

people entered. The dance floor was packed and the line at the bar stretched across the club and the DJ was hyping the crowd. *Taryn is right, he is FOINE!*

"Enjoying your drink?" a voice said over the sound of Jay-Z. Camille turned to see the guy who bought her the drink standing beside her.

"Yes, I am. Thanks again," she told him.

"I'm Lex." He held his hand out and she shook it.

"I'm Camille," she replied.

"Nice to meet you, Camille. Would you like to dance?"

She almost declined, but her adrenaline was pumping and she wanted to dance. "Sure," she told him as she stood up.

The guy took her by the hand and they walked down the steps. They passed Taryn, Yaya, Lincoln, and Fitz as they approached the dance floor.

"All right now, Cam!"

"Don't hurt him girl." Yaya winked.

Dancing with a man wasn't something Camille was used to. She could count on two fingers the number of times she had been to a club and she didn't dance either time. Tonight, she was determined to have fun. *You can do this. Just move to the beat. You know how to dance.* Camille began moving to the beat; awkwardly at first, praying that she didn't fall in her high heeled shoes. Lex smiled as his moves met hers. She looked and Yaya and Taryn were on the floor as well. Her confidence level increased and she felt comfortable enough to move a little more. Before long, she was handling her business on the floor, backing that thang up and having a ball. DJ Terror must've sensed her love for Jay-Z because he played an entire medley and she didn't want to come off the floor.

"That was fun," she said when they finally stopped dancing.

"Yeah, it was. You can move." Lex led her through the crowd. The rest of her friends were sitting at a large table near the dance floor.

"Camille, I ain't know you had moves like that." Monya looked impressed.

"I can do a little something," Camille said, laughing.

"I'm gonna get us something to drink," Lex said. "Another piña colada?"

"I'd like that," she said, smiling.

"Having fun?" Taryn asked.

"I'm having a ball." Camille nodded. "What's up, Fitz? Lincoln?"

"What it do, Camille?" Lincoln said, his voice a little too loud. He was leaning on Taryn and Camille could tell that he was tipsy.

"You are so loud, you know that?" Taryn asked him.

"And you are so beautiful, you know that?" Lincoln said and then kissed her.

"Get a room," Fitz teased.

"Stop hating." Lincoln smirked.

Lex returned with their drinks and Camille introduced him.

"Hey, Sonya!" Lincoln yelled. They all looked to see who he was talking to. A woman who Camille had never seen before waved and walked over to the table. Her light skin, thick curly hair, and green eyes let Camille know that she had to be biracial.

"Hey there," she said.

"I didn't expect to see you up in here tonight." Fitz smiled after he introduced everyone.

"My new boyfriend is about to start doing business here, so I came with him," she answered.

"You got a man already. You've only been here a few weeks. You go girl," Taryn commented.

"Yeah, he's right over there." Sonya waved her hands and called out, "Sweetie, over here!"

"What's up?" The man, who Camille assumed was Sonya's

boyfriend, began walking toward them. He was built and for some reason, he reminded Camille of a bounty hunter, but he was dressed to kill in all gray.

"Oh my God! Diesel!" Yaya jumped up.

"Yaya!" The man grinned. The two of them seemed oblivious to everyone else as they ran to greet one another. The guy picked Yaya up off the floor as he hugged her and she squealed in delight. Sonya didn't look too pleased.

"I take it they know each other," Fitz said to Taryn.

"Yeah, they go back a while," Taryn said, laughing. "Diesel and Yaya used to be really close. They used to be known as wild and crazy. When they worked together, everyone was sure to have a good time."

"Sonya, this is Qianna. My friend I was telling you about," Diesel said to his girlfriend.

"So, Yaya is your nickname?" Sonya looked from Yaya to Diesel.

"Yep," Fitz answered, walking over and taking Yaya's hand.

"Fitz, this is my friend, Diesel," Yaya said.

"Yes, this is my boyfriend, Diesel." Sonya put her arms around Diesel. "And baby, this is Yaya's boyfriend, Fitz."

"What's up?" Fitz stared at him.

"You told her about Qianna and ain't say nothing 'bout me? I'm jealous," Taryn said, jokingly, breaking the tension.

"You know I talked about you, T." He gave Taryn a hug. "Where the hell is Monya?"

"Up in VIP, probably drunk as hell," Taryn replied. "So, what brings you to town?"

"Well, they got me here to do some promotional stuff for the club," Diesel answered. "So, I'm back in town for a while."

"That's what's up." Taryn took her seat.

"Well, I say we order another round to celebrate the damn reunion!" Lincoln smiled.

"I actually have some people I have to go meet with. I'll buy the round the next time." Diesel turned to Yaya. "I'll talk to you later."

"Cool." Yaya smiled and then said to Sonya, "It was nice meeting you."

"Same here," Sonya said, flatly.

"Wild and crazy, huh?" Fitz asked when Sonya and Diesel were gone.

"That was back in the day." Yaya shook her head. "Come on, let's go dance."

Fitz allowed her to pull him and Camille watched them on the floor. They made such a nice couple.

"I'm going get me another drink," Lincoln announced, standing up.

"I hope you know you're not driving," Taryn warned him. He leaned over and kissed her, then headed to the bar.

Monya walked over to the table. "Hey, I just saw a dude that looked just like Diesel."

"No, you just saw Diesel," Taryn told her.

"Shut the hell up! Are you for real?" Monya's eyes widened.

"Yep, he's here."

"Did Yaya see him?"

"Yeah, she saw him." Taryn nodded. "And they were happy to see each other."

"Damn, I hate I missed that. Did Fitz say anything?" Monya seemed fascinated.

"Not really."

"Well, he'd better hope he lasts longer than seven strokes tonight, or he's in serious trouble," Monya said, sighing.

Lex choked on his drink and Camille's mouth hung open.

"You'd better believe it," Taryn agreed. "I just hope that it doesn't run in the family."

Chapter 12

"How was it?" Yaya asked, walking into Taryn's office and taking a seat. "I waited for you to call all weekend."

Taryn pretended to be confused. "What are you talking about?"

"Don't even try it, Taryn." Yaya reached into the candy jar sitting in the desk, grabbed a handful of M&M's and popped them into her mouth.

Taryn picked up the jar and put it on the shelf behind her. "It's too early for candy. And you already keep whining about your stomach hurts. I wonder why."

"I told you the doctor said it's reflux and to stay away from spicy foods and avoid stress. Chocolate isn't spicy and it's good for stress," she said while chewing. "And you know I'm stressed."

"Why are you stressed?" Taryn waited for what she knew was going to be a dramatic response.

"You know why I'm stressed, T. I'm out working and promoting the salon. I got Geneva Johnson blowing my phone up, they sold my Prada boots back that they were supposed to be holding at Nordstom, we have to pick out the design for our long-sleeved shirts because the weather is about to change, there aren't enough hours in a day to get everything done and to top it all off, I'm dating Fast Fitz!" Yaya snapped. "And my best friend is holding out on me."

"I'm not holding out on you, Yaya," Taryn told her. "We had a nice weekend."

Taryn and Lincoln did have a nice weekend, once he sobered up from Friday night. He rode home with her from the club and fell asleep before they even made it home. Once they arrived, she tried waking him up, but it was a struggle. She yelled his name, pulled on his shirt, even slapped him a few times, but she could not get him to move. An hour later, she was tired, cranky, and pissed and decided to just leave him asleep in her Armada. She changed clothes and climbed into bed. It was almost four o'clock when she heard him knocking. She dragged herself out of bed and opened the door for him. Neither one said a word as he followed her to her bedroom, then, fully dressed, he lay across her bed. Again, she tried to get him up, but he wouldn't budge. Frustrated, she grabbed a blanket out of the top of her closet and went into the guest bedroom and fell asleep.

The sun was peeking through the curtains when she heard him in the bathroom. She closed her eyes and pretending to be asleep when he walked into the room and called her name.

"Taryn, baby, why are you sleeping in here?"

She didn't answer. She nearly jumped when she felt him climb into bed beside her and pulled her close.

"Baby, you sleep?"

She still didn't answer. She was pissed and trying to think of how to cuss him out when she felt his fingers gently massaging her breasts and his soft lips on her neck. Her nipples hardened at his touch and heat began growing between her legs. His hardness pressed against her behind and his hands reached under her top, pulling it over her head. Lincoln rolled her over onto her back and stared at her.

"Good morning," he said and kissed her. She could taste the mint of toothpaste and the coldness of his tongue was a surprising treat. He positioned himself over her, removing her pants.

"What are you doing?" she whispered.

"Waking you up." He smiled as he bent her knees and touched her wetness. The thickness of his fingers made her even wetter. "Damn, I can't wait to eat breakfast."

"Wait, Lincoln . . ." She forgot what she was going to say as his tongue plunged into her and he gently sucked. Her eyes closed and she grasped onto the bed as he teased her clitoris and licked her inner walls, taking her to heights of pleasure that she had never reached. He seemed to be enjoying himself as he satisfied her. Suddenly, she couldn't take it anymore. "Lincoln . . . please."

"Please what?" he asked, still tasting her.

"Please . . . stop," she begged, clenching the sheets.

"I can't," he replied. "Not until you come."

"O . . . kay," she tried not to scream as her heart pounded from excitment. "You . . . can . . . stop . . . I'm about to."

"Mmmm, hmmmm," he responded by moving his tongue even faster and deeper.

Unable to hold on any longer, Taryn screamed as she climaxed. Her chest rose and fell so hard with each breath, that she could see it. "That . . . was . . . the . . . bomb! I need a minute . . . to catch . . . my . . . breath."

"Nope, no rest for the weary. We're not done yet." Lincoln laughed and kissed her, softly at first. Her hand caressed his chest, down his stomach until it found what she was searching for. He moaned as her fingers wrapped around him and rubbed back and forth. The sound of his moaning as he did so and the feel of his erection caused her desire to rise. His mouth covered her hard nipples and he teased them, nearly driving her mad. She was already wet again, and he made sure by touching her again. Still throbbing from his oral pleasure, her center nearly erupted. Taryn spread her legs wider and soon, his manhood replaced his finger. He carried her on an erotic journey she never wanted to end. Never in her life had Taryn had such a powerful sexual experience. *Thank God it doesn't run in the family,* she smiled to herself.

It wasn't until after he had collapsed on top of her and she was running her fingers along his smooth, mocha shoulders that the reality of what they had done hit her. *CONDOM, we didn't use a CONDOM!*

"Taryn, I'm not trying to be funny, but I could care less about how nice your weekend was. You know what I wanna know. You can spare me the intimate details, believe me." Yaya folded her arms. "I just wanna know if it's me that has the problem."

Taryn looked at her best friend, trying not to laugh. "And what exactly does that mean?"

"Well, if both brothers have a lack of stamina, then that's different. But, if not, it has to be me."

"You?"

"Yes." Yaya nodded. "My stuff, my power, my juicy fruit, it's mega. It's mega and he can't handle it."

Taryn could no longer hold her laughter. She nearly doubled over. "Yaya, you are truly a diva in every sense of the word—"

"Shhhh, listen."

Shouts were coming from the salon area. The two of them made a mad dash to see what was going on. They both stopped dead in their tracks when they saw the source of the commotion. Celeste and Camille were standing face-to-face, screaming at one another. Monya was trying to pull Camille away and the few customers were standing around them, gawking. At first glance, it looked like it was going to be an unfair fight. Celeste, average height, over two hundred pounds, looking homely as ever in baggy jeans, sweatshirt, and thick glasses; and Camille, her hundred-twenty-pound frame perfectly proportioned to her five-three height, looking like a glamour girl in black leggings and matching After Effex T-shirt tied stylishly in the back.

"Look, I asked you to leave. Why are you being so damn difficult?" Camille yelled.

"I'm not leaving until I see Taryn. This ain't got shit to do with you, so sit the fuck down somewhere and mind your damn business!" Celeste responded.

"You want me to sit down? You sit me down then, trick." Camille snatched away from Monya and leaped toward Celeste, who took a step back. "What you jumping for, huh, heifer? Because you know I'll kill your ass if you don't get out my face. I mean that!"

Yaya looked at Taryn and told her, "See why I ain't wanna open a shop in the damn hood?"

"What the hell is going on?" Taryn walked to the center of the crowd. Yaya followed. Even Jarrod and some of the guys from next door came in to see what was happening.

"All I said was I needed to talk to you and Camille seems to have a problem with that." Celeste turned to Taryn.

"Girl, don't nobody wanna talk to you," Yaya replied.

"Well, considering the fact that we don't have anything to talk about, it may be a problem. As I recall, you only wanna talk through your lawyer." Taryn tried to remain calm.

"Well, something came up and I felt I needed to tell you this face-to-face; woman to woman."

"And what woman would Taryn be talking to, because if you're referring to yourself, it would be more like woman to whore," Camille snapped.

"Ain't that the truth." Yaya said, smirking.

"This ain't got nothing to do with either of you, shut the hell up!" Celeste took a step closer to Taryn. "We need to talk in private."

"No, we don't." Taryn shook her head.

"Fine, let me just give this to you then." Celeste reached into her pocket and handed Taryn a crumpled piece of paper.

Taryn looked at it without touching it. "I don't want that crap."

"Look, I came over here because I had a doctor's appointment earlier," Celeste told her, still holding the paper out.

"That's your business." Taryn still didn't move.

"I had my prenatal testing done last week and I got the results," Celeste continued.

"Monya, call the police. Maybe they can get her the hell outta here," Yaya said.

"I know that you're seeing Lincoln and he *is* my baby's father. I came over here to warn you, I tested positive for chlamydia, gonorrhea, *and* herpes. I got it from him." Celeste forced the paper into Taryn's hand, turned and walked out the door.

Chapter 13

"Okay, show's over." Yaya's voice broke the silence. "The drama whore is gone and we can all can go back to what we were doing."

The crowd slowly departed, and she looked over at her best friend who was still standing in the same spot, staring at the floor. The crumpled piece of paper was still in her hand.

"Taryn, you a'ight?" Jarrod asked, putting his hand gently on her shoulder.

"I'm good, Jarrod, thanks," she said, still looking down.

"I got her, Jarrod." Yaya nodded at him.

"That shit wasn't even cool," he commented. "That girl's a straight scallywag, believe that."

"Come on, T, let's roll for the rest of the day," Yaya suggested.

"Naw, I'm good. Besides, I got two appointments." Taryn's voice was barely above a whisper.

"Camille can handle it." Yaya could see the hurt on Taryn's face. *I'ma kill Celeste! She better watch her back, because she has fucked with the wrong person.*

"Naw, I have a—" The door opened and Taryn stopped

mid-sentence. Silence filled the room as the door opened and Fitz walked in followed by Lincoln.

"What's up, everyone," Fitz spoke.

"What's going on?" Lincoln smiled.

No one made a sound. They all stared at the two good-looking brothers who obviously had no clue about what just happened.

"What the hell is wrong with y'all?" Lincoln asked as he walked up to Taryn. He leaned to kiss her but she turned her head.

Fitz turned to Yaya who just shook her head. "T, I'ma grab your purse and meet you outside. I'll drive."

Taryn looked over at her, nodded and walked past Lincoln and out the door.

"Taryn, wait!" Lincoln called out as he went after her.

"Yaya, can you tell me what the hell is going on?' Fitzgerald said as he followed Yaya into her office. She unlocked her desk drawer and removed her leather bag and keys.

"Your brother's baby mama just left here, that's what just happened," Yaya said, slamming the drawer shut. "And her ghetto ass caused a scene in our place of business!"

"What? Who are you talking about? My brother doesn't have any kids!" Fitz frowned.

"Well, according to Celeste, she's carrying his kid!"

"Celeste? Who the hell is Celeste?"

"The girl that used to work here? She used to answer the phones when we first opened," Yaya replied.

Fitz looked deep in thought, then he started smiling. "The big girl with the glasses? The one who used to always complain about T not liking her and she ain't know why? That's funny."

"What's funny?" Yaya put her hands on her hips.

"You think my brother would get with that? She's not even his type. She's so . . . what's the word I'm looking for? Homely!" He snapped hs fingers.

"Look, all I know is she claims he's the father. This has been going on for a few weeks now. He hasn't said anything about it?" she asked. He and Lincoln were so close; she was surprised he didn't know about the Celeste situation.

"I know you mentioned that old girl was suing the salon for workman's comp, but not about this. Lincoln ain't said nothing at all." Fitz seemed hurt by hearing this from her.

"I don't believe a bit of it. But today she comes in and announces that she has chlamydia, gonorrhea, and herpes. The nasty whore told everyone she got it from him."

"What? She's lying!" Fitz's voice was anger-filled.

"She has been known to do that," Yaya said, putting her bag on her shoulder. "I gotta get T's things, I'll be right back."

When she returned from Taryn's office, he was mumbling into his cell phone. "It was too late for me to call. You know how early your ass goes to bed. I'm swing by later, is that cool? Yeah, that does sound good."

"I'm ready," she said, standing in the doorway.

"A'ight, Micha, call me when he gets off the bus. Talk to you later," he said, standing up nervously and closing his phone. "Uh, that was—"

"Your son's mother, let's go, Taryn is waiting for me," she said, walking back into the salon. "T and I are gone for the day."

"We got everything under control. We're good." Monya nodded. "Right, Camille?"

"Yaya, I'm sorry about—" Camille told her.

"It's okay, Camille." Yaya smiled. "At least we know you got our back. Thanks."

Taryn was leaning on Yaya's car talking to Lincoln when they walked out to the parking lot. She was still holding the crumpled sheet of paper. Yaya could see that she was crying.

"You ready?" she asked Yaya.

"Taryn, you gotta believe me," Lincoln said, reaching for her hand.

Taryn snatched away from him. "Unlock the door, Yaya."

Yaya hit the lock and Taryn opened the passenger door and got in.

"Just give her a little while to calm down, Lincoln," Yaya told him.

"She won't even listen to me. I keep trying to tell her that chick is lying, and it's like she doesn't care," Lincoln yelled.

"She will listen once you give her the chance to calm down," Yaya retorted. Lincoln walked away, looking defeated.

"Taryn! TARYN! Come on now, don't be like this!" Fitz was standing in front of Yaya's car, trying to get Taryn's attention. Taryn turned her head away.

"She's mad. Let her calm down," Yaya snapped.

"She can't get mad at Linc because old girl came in here lying, that's crazy!" Fitz said.

Yaya glared at him. "Leave it alone, Fitz."

"This is some bullshit," he said, frowning at Yaya.

"What?" She looked at him like he was crazy. She knew they needed to leave before things got worse than what they already were.

"I'm just saying, she's being unreasonable." His voice calmed down a bit.

"And I'm just saying she needs some time to sort all this out." Yaya moved past him and got in the car. She shut her door, started the engine and drove off.

"Where are we going?" Taryn asked after a few minutes of riding.

"Where you wanna go?" Yaya inquired.

"I don't know. I don't know. I don't know." Taryn leaned her head against the seat and closed her eyes.

"We can always go find Celeste and kick her ass." Yaya glanced over. Taryn was rolling her eyes at her while biting her lip. Yaya knew she was trying not to smile. "Sound like a plan?"

"First of all, you know the only things you fight over are shoes and your brother," Taryn told her.

"No, those are the only two things I fought about in the past. This just happens to be the first time I've had to fight for my best friend. And it wouldn't be me fighting by myself, it would be us fighting together," Yaya said, laughing. "She may be a big bitch. But she can't take either one of us. We can take turns."

Taryn finally laughed. "You are so silly."

"We can always go get drunk," Yaya suggested.

"It's too early to get drunk." Taryn reached into her bag and pulled out her dark Dolce & Gabbana shades.

"Those are cute. Where did you get those?"

"Lincoln and I went to the outlet mall and I picked them up."

"And you didn't get me a pair?" Yaya whined. She and Taryn always shopped for each other and Taryn knew she loved Dolce & Gabbana almost as much as Prada.

"Quit whining!" Taryn reached into the bag again and handed Yaya her matching pair.

"Aw, T. You are so wonderful," Yaya squealed, putting the shades on and checking her reflection in the rearview mirror. "I'm so glad you're my best friend."

"Watch the road!" Taryn yelled as the Lexus swerved.

"These are really cute."

"Why don't we go meet with Chester about the new shirts. The least we can do is be productive."

"Taryn Green, do you always have to be the responsible one?" Yaya asked. Suddenly, Taryn began to cry. Yaya slowed the car down and looked for somewhere they could stop and talk. She spotted the Krispy Kreme and quickly turned in. "T, it's okay. Taking care of the shirts is a good idea."

"That's not what it is," Taryn said, sniffling. "I'm so pissed!"

"I'm pissed too, T! But, don't worry about it." Yaya turned

to face her best friend. "This was just another one of Celeste's ploys to get at you and break you and Lincoln up. She's a snake. If you let her get to you, then she wins."

"I'm pissed at myself, Yaya."

"Why? For what?"

"When I slept with Lincoln, I didn't use a condom." Taryn looked down. "How responsible is that?"

Yaya was too stunned to respond. Taryn had always been adamant about them being careful and protecting themselves. It was her that made sure they had yearly checkups, reminded them about monthly breast exams, and even bought them condoms. Yaya couldn't understand or even fathom. Just as she was about to ask Taryn how she could allow such a thing to happen, she caught herself. Over the years, no one had made more stupid mistakes than Yaya, and Taryn had always been there to pick her up each time she had fallen short. She had finally been given the opportunity to do the same. *Now is not the time for a lecture, it's time for support.*

"It's all right, T." She took her sunglasses off. "It happens to all of us. It's happened to me a couple of times, you know that."

"But you didn't find out the person it happened with may be full of STDs." Taryn pulled a tissue out of her purse and dabbed at her eyes.

"She's lying, Taryn. You know that."

"What if she's not? What am I supposed to do?"

"You do what you told me to do, T. You get tested and move on from there. I'll go with you."

"Thanks, Yaya," she said.

"Okay, my stomach is growling and the hot sign is on," Yaya said, opening the door and getting out.

A few moments later, as they sat inside eating fresh glazed doughnuts and cold milk, Taryn asked, "Does the fact that Fitz is fast, change the way you feel about him?"

Yaya took a few moments to think before she answered.

"No, I think that's what frustrates me the most. I'm still in love with him. I love being with him, talking to him, spending time with him. I just don't like sleeping with him."

"Does he know he doesn't satisfy you?"

"Hell no. I care too much about him to tell him. I wouldn't dare blow his ego like that." She looked over at Taryn and said, "It was the bomb, wasn't it?"

Taryn looked up. "What?"

"It had to be the bomb. That's why your ass ain't wrap up, because you were caught up," she said, sighing. "It's me. I got the ill-nana. It's mega!"

"You are crazy, Yaya." Taryn cracked up. Yaya was happy to see her cheering up. "I'm so glad you're my best friend."

Yaya's stomach began bloating and she could feel herself getting sick. *Not now, not again.* She hadn't eaten anything other than the handful of candy from Taryn's desk since lunch yesterday because she figured there was no point. The only reason she was eating the doughnuts was because she was starving and thought since the candy didn't make her gag, she was okay.

"I gotta go to the bathroom," she said, jumping up and running into the restroom. When it was all over, she stood over the commode, panting and sweating. *Maybe I need to see the doctor when I go with Taryn.*

Yaya was surprised to see Fitz's Honda station wagon in the parking lot when they returned to the salon a few hours later. She was even more surprised to see him in the parking lot leaning into a car talking to another woman. As soon as she pulled into her reserved spot in front of the building, the woman pulled off and drove away.

"Ain't this a—"

"Yaya, don't start tripping. You know Fitz ain't stupid enough to do anything disrespectful out here where everyone knows you and him," Taryn interrupted her.

"Okay, I'm not even gonna trip. I don't even wanna know

who the hell it was," Yaya said, grabbing her purse out the backseat and getting out the car.

"Hey, y'all are back." Fitz walked over, smiling.

"Yep," she half-smiled back at him.

"I'll see you inside," Taryn told Yaya as she walked by and opened the door to the salon.

"I'll be there in a minute," Yaya said, nodding.

"Has she calmed down?" Fitz asked, putting his arms around Yaya.

"She's working through it," Yaya replied.

"Look, baby, I don't want what's going on between Lincoln and Taryn to affect you and me. Okay?" He stared into her eyes with such intensity, that Yaya could see the love he had for her.

"Okay," she said, shrugging, and then told him, "Your little friend didn't have to leave because of me."

"What little friend?"

"The girl you were just talking to, in the Saturn. I wasn't gonna clown."

Fitz gave her a strange look and then smiled. "Who? Micha?"

"Micha?" she repeated, feeling like a fool.

"Carver needed a haircut," he answered. "She dropped him off. I'm trying to spend as much time with him as I can. I don't want her *fiancé* to think I can't still handle my son."

"Carver?" she asked.

As if he could hear them talking about him, Carver came running out of the barber shop. "Daddy, can I have two dollars?"

"Stop running," Fitz told him.

"Hi, Ms. Yaya." the cute little boy stood next to his father. They looked just alike, only he didn't wear locks in his hair like his father.

"Hi Carver. How was school?"

"It was good," he said then turned back to Fitz. "Can I have two dollars?"

"For what?"

"I want some cookies and a juice," Carver answered. "Mommy picked me up from after school before I got a snack. I'm hungry."

"You're always hungry," Fitz told him.

Yaya reached into her purse and pulled out a five-dollar bill, passing it to Carver. "Here you go, sweetie."

"Thanks, Ms. Yaya." He grinned at her.

"No problem," she answered, then told him, "and make sure Mr. Jarrod gives you your change!"

"I will!" Carver turned and ran back into the shop.

"He is so adorable," she told Fitz.

"And what about his father?" Fitz walked over and kissed her.

"His father ain't bad either," she said, laughing. The affectionate moment was interrupted by the sound of motorcycles pulling into the lot. Yaya recognized her brother's bike instantly. "Oh goodness. Here comes trouble."

"Hey there, sis," Quincy said, taking his helmet off. "What's up, Fitz?"

"Hey Q." She walked over and gave him a hug.

"I'ma go check on Carver," Fitz said and went inside.

"What are you doing on this side of town?" Yaya asked, sneaking a peek at the other rider, parked next to Quincy. Whoever it was had yet to remove their helmet.

"I heard there was a bit of drama earlier from one of the barbers, so I came through," Quincy replied.

"So now you're checking up on me?" She folded her arms. "I can take care of myself, Q. Everything is under control."

"I didn't think it wasn't, Yaya. I just came to make sure you and everyone was all right," he retorted.

"Everyone is fine. I told you I handled it," she said.

"I don't know how this is gonna work out. When are you finding time to work here when you're still doing your celebrity work, Yaya? You swore you were cutting back on being on the road and now you're Geneva Johnson's personal stylist."

"What?" Yaya couldn't believe Quincy was saying all this to her. It was as if someone had fed him misconstrued information and he was using it to say "I told you so."

"Running a business is no joke, Yaya," Quincy continued.

"See, this is why I didn't even want to open my salon down here. Because I knew you were gonna have people reporting my every move to you," she said, her anger rising. "Someone is giving you a bunch of WRONG information, and now here you come!"

"Yaya, don't even start with the melodramatics. I came because it's my responsibility—"

Yaya didn't let him finish. She turned to get into her car but stopped when she heard her name being called.

"QIANNA!" The other rider took his helmet off and climbed off the bike. Qianna didn't move and stared as Diesel walked toward her. She rolled her eyes at Quincy who was shaking his head at her. *Lord, he looks good.*

"What?" she asked Diesel, reminding herself she was pissed.

"We need to take a walk, now!" Diesel pulled her by the arm and she didn't resist. They walked around the building to the back lot. He led her to a set of empty crates that were stacked against the building and sat down. "What was that all about?"

"Nothing. I can't believe he came over here to check up on me. After all the hard work I've put into this salon, he still doesn't think I can handle it and he's still looking over my shoulder," she told him. "Diesel, of all people, you know how bad I wanted this."

"And you got it, Yaya. It's yours!" Diesel told her.

"If that were the case, my brother wouldn't have his little barbershop spies sneaking, peeking, and reporting my every move!"

"I don't think he has spies, Yaya. You know Q doesn't even

roll like that. What I do think is that your salon is no different than anyone else's, and people are gossiping." Diesel shrugged. "Come on, Yaya. You know how black people are."

Yaya shook her head. "Gossip? Q is listening to gossip?"

"Have you called and talked to him about how you're handling your schedule? When was the last time you and your brother sat down and talked, period?" Diesel asked her.

It had been a while since she and Quincy had really talked. With everything she had going on with the salon, traveling, and Fitz, her relationship with her brother had been placed on the back burner. Especially because she still felt bad about almost coming between him and Paige. "It's been a minute. But that's because we've both been busy. He had a new girl and I—"

"You need to talk to your brother," he said, softly, and took her hand. His touch made the hairs on her neck stand up.

"I need to talk to my brother." She smiled. They walked back around to the front of the building, arm in arm. Fitz and Carver were waiting out front when they returned.

"Fitz, you remember my friend, Diesel?" she said.

"Yeah, how you doing?" Fitz nodded.

"I'm good," Diesel told him. He turned to Yaya and said, "Handle your business."

Yaya didn't say anything, she just nodded.

"Your little friend ain't have to leave because of me," Fitz commented. "Let's roll, son."

Chapter 14

"Oh now she is just foul," Paige said when Camille told her about Celeste's actions in the salon. "Celeste is a wench, in every way possible."

"I know that's your cousin, Paige, but I hate that girl."

"Don't say *hate*. She's not worth the energy to hate. Just say you can't stand her," Paige replied.

"Well, I can't stand her then. You know what I was thinking the entire time she was standing there in the middle of the salon?"

"That she is crazy?" Paige asked.

"Well, other than that. I was wondering how desperate a person has to be if your sole purpose in life is to make other peoples' lives miserable," Camille said, sighing. "Then, when she said she had all those nasty STDs, I realized she wasn't desperate, she was pathetic."

"She's been like that her entire life. Celeste is a master at playing the victim. She creates all this madness for attention and then when all eyes are on her, she acts like it's everyone else's fault. I've had to deal with it forever." Paige sat on the sofa beside her. Camille looked at her and wondered what the hell made Marlon ruin what they had together. Paige was smart, beautiful, intelligent, funny, loving, and a good mother. She didn't see any of those qualities in Kasey. *I don't even know how the hell she even became a nurse. She must've gotten her nursing license from a damn mail order catalogue.*

"I'm telling you, it took all I could not to beat her tail, Paige."

"Ohhhh, Aunt Cam! That's not nice." Her niece Myla came and sat between them, carrying a plastic bucket that held her barrettes.

"I'm sorry, you're right." Camille leaned over and pinched Myla's chubby, dimpled cheeks. "Did you see the pictures of Ms. Kasey's baby? Daddy sent me an e-mail."

"Yeah, I got the e-mail." Camille nodded. She glanced at the photos her brother sent her of the scrawny little runt who he claimed was her nephew. The baby wasn't cute at all, which made her desire to see him in person nonexistent.

"Are you going to see him?"

"Not any time soon," Camille answered.

"Did you finish your homework?" Paige asked Myla.

"Yep."

"Laid your uniform out?"

"Yep."

"Wonderful. You are getting so responsible. I'm so proud of you," Paige told her. "Now go run your water and jump in the tub."

"But, Mom, Aunt Cam is gonna put my hair in a bun," Myla protested. "We haven't even had dinner."

"The chicken's still in the oven. By the time you get out, it'll be time to eat," Paige replied.

"I'll do it after you get out the tub. Go ahead." Camille swatted Myla's bottom as she ran past.

The little girl paused and looked back at them. "Are you trying to get rid of me so you can talk some more? That's all you had to say."

"GO!" Paige and Camille said simultaneously.

"That girl is a trip," Camille said, laughing.

"She's grown as hell, that's what she is," Paige told her. "Why haven't you gone to see the baby?"

"Because for one, he's ugly and two, I'm not feeling my mother, my brother, or his wife," Camille said, sighing. "The fact that I didn't go back to school isn't sitting well with any of them right now."

Since confessing to him that she had dropped out of school to pursue her esthetics career, the conversations between Camille and her brother were mostly arguments and ended in one of them hanging up on one another. She had yet to talk to Lucille or Kasey because she refused to answer her phone when they called, but based on the disgusting messages they left her, they weren't pleased with her decision either.

"You're wrong for that, you know that, right?" Paige stood up and walked into the kitchen.

Myla called from upstairs, "Aunt Cam, your phone is ringing!"

"Answer it," Camille responded, flipping through the channels until she found Lifetime.

"Here, it's Terrance." Myla gave her a knowing look.

"Thanks, Ms. Myla." Camille stuck her tongue at her. "Hey."

"You got a new secretary, I see," Terrance said, laughing. "Business must be pretty good these days."

"Funny," she told him.

"Well, something must be going on. I didn't talk to you all weekend. I called you twice today and left messages and I still haven't heard from you. So, are you igging me or is it that you want me to sweat you?"

"Neither," she answered. "I've just been working hard. Yaya and Taryn were out the shop this weekend and today, I had too much drama. I was gonna call you later, I promise."

"Well, I was gonna head over to the Red Dragon for margarita Mondays and I wanted you to join me. That is if you're not too busy."

"I'm sorry, Terrance. I promised my niece I would do her hair tonight," Camille replied. She wanted to see him, but didn't wanna seem like it was a big deal. *After all, according to him, we are just friends.*

"We can go when you finish. They don't close until late. Wait, you're not braiding her hair, are you?"

Camille laughed. "No, I'm not braiding it. I should be done in an hour."

"I will pick you up then," he told her.

"Another date with Terrance?" Paige asked, walking into the room.

"Yeah, we're going to the Red Dragon." Camille shrugged.

"The Chinese restaurant?"

"Yeah, they have margarita Mondays or something." Camille stood up.

"I thought you didn't drink," Paige said, smirking.

"I don't. I can get a virgin one."

"Speaking of virgin . . ."

"Oh God, Paige." Camille rolled her eyes at the ceiling. "Yes, that's still my classification. My virginity is still intact."

"Well, I was just asking because I know you've been hanging out with Terrance a lot."

"Terrance and I are just friends, Paige. We're not romantically involved. I'm gone to do Myla's hair and change clothes," Camille told her.

"Cam, I'm not trying to get in your business or seem overbearing. You are still holding on to the most precious gift you can give to a man."

"We had this conversation six years ago, Paige. As a matter of fact, we've had it several times since then."

"And we're gonna keep having it until your wedding day."

"I can't see that happening anytime soon. My luck with men sucks!"

"You don't need luck when you have God. Paige gave her a

big hug. "I love you, Cam. I just want what's best for you and for you to be happy."

"Yeah, Ma, I have them. They're in my trunk," Terrance said as they walked to the car. "I'm about to go somewhere right now. I'll bring them by tomorrow."

He opened the car door and Camille got in. She looked up and saw Myla waving out of her upstairs window. She waved back and blew her a kiss.

"Ma, I'm on the way . . . okay, I'll be there in a few minutes." He closed the phone and exhaled loudly.

"Change of plans?" she asked innocently.

"More like a detour. I promised my mother she could use my luggage. I need to run by her house and drop it off," he said, starting the car. "She's gonna have a conniption if I don't bring them tonight."

"When is the trip?" Camille asked.

"Week after next," he said.

The ride to his mother's house was fairly quick and there were several cars parked out front when they arrived at the nice-looking brick home with the well-manicured lawn.

"Is she having a party?" Camille counted a total of six vehicles as he helped her out the car.

"Ha, no, two belong to my mom. That's my stepfather's truck and van. And it looks like my aunts are over here. The other two belong to them," he said, opening the trunk and taking out two large suitcases and a shoulder bag.

"I'll take that one," she said, reaching for the shoulder bag.

"Why, thank you." He smiled and kissed her. "By the way, you look very nice tonight, as usual."

"Thank you," she replied.

"We shouldn't be here that long." He opened the front door without knocking or ringing the bell. "Hey Ma!"

"Boy, do you have to yell every time you walk in this house?" his mother fussed as she came into the living room.

She was dressed in a mint-green sweatsuit and a pair of white Nikes. "Oh, hey there Camille. Why didn't you tell me you were bringing company?"

"Hi, Ms. Irene, how are you doing?"

"I'm fine. Y'all come on into the den." His mother hugged her. They followed her down the hallway and into the sunken den where two other women were sitting, watching TV.

"Camille, these are my sisters, Naomi and Virgie. This is Terrance's girlfriend, Camille, the one who works down at After Effex," Ms. Irene introduced her. Camille looked over at Terrance, who wore a look of embarrassment. "The one he told us about the other week."

"Nice to meet you," Camille said, smiling, not wanting to make the situation awkward.

"We've heard so much about you," Naomi said.

"Yes, Vashon told me Terrance brought a pretty girl to the skating party. I thought he was lying," Virgie added and they all laughed.

"Let me take those bags," Ms. Irene said, reaching toward Camille. "It's about time you dropped them off. I asked you about these bags a week ago."

"Ma, your trip isn't even until next month," he told her.

"That's not the point. You shoulda brought 'em when she asked." Naomi playfully hit his arm.

"Nobody's trying to wait until the last minute to pack. Some people prepare for their trips." Virgie pointed her fingers at him then turned to Camille. "You want something to eat, baby? Irene made some really good pork chops."

"No thanks. We're about to leave," Terrance answered quickly.

"She can answer for herself," Ms. Irene told him. "Camille, you're more than welcome to some food. You want something to drink?"

"No, ma'am, I'm fine," Camille told her.

"Okay, Ma, you got the bags and now we're about to go," Terrance nodded toward the door.

"It was nice meeting you," Camille said to Naomi and Virgie. "Nice seeing you again, Ms. Irene. I hope you get the chance to come by the salon so we can hook you up for your trip."

"You know I will baby," she said, hugging Camille. "You both enjoy the rest of your evening."

"Thanks, Ma. Bye Aunt Naomi, Aunt Virgie." Terrance hugged all three women and nearly dashed out the door.

"They are nice," Camille commented as they devoured a pupu platter and sipped margaritas at the restaurant.

"Go ahead," he told her.

"What?" She tried to control herself but couldn't. She began laughing so hard, tears began streaming.

"I'm glad you find them so hilarious," he told her.

"They are. And they're cute," she said when she could finally talk.

"I'm sorry about the whole girlfriend thing. I keep telling my mother we're just friends and she keeps thinking otherwise," Terrance explained. "She always asks about you. I'm beginning to think she has a crush on you."

"I get the feeling she's like that to all the women you bring around," Camille said, shrugging.

"I rarely bring women around my family. And I guess you can see why. My mother and her sister can be like vultures. I have to be very selective."

Camille didn't know whether to be flattered or not. "Good thing you had to bring the bags or I wouldn't've had the pleasure of meeting them, huh?"

"No, that's not true. As a matter of fact, I was gonna invite you to have dinner at my aunt's on Sunday."

"I thought you were selective." She sipped her drink.

"You can handle my family. You proved that tonight. Besides, they already think you're my girlfriend," he said laughing.

"So, you just wanna use me?" She frowned.

"Not like that, Camille," he said, motioning for the waitress. He ordered another drink. "I mean, I want you to come to be with me."

"Terrance, what's going on between us?" She was tired of trying to read how he felt about her.

"What do you mean?"

"What am I to you? Am I your friend? Are we dating? I mean, what?"

He reached across the table and took her hand into his. "Camille, you are my friend. This is the closest relationship I've been in since my breakup a year ago. I like you, you know that."

The waitress brought his drink back and he damn near drank it in one gulp.

"I like you too Terrance. But I'm beginning to more than like you," Camille replied.

"Camille, you know I'm not ready for a relationship right now." He shook his head. "I have feelings for you too."

"You do?" She was surprised to hear him say that.

"Of course I do. Cam, you think I call you everyday and spend time with you because I don't have anyone else to hang with? No. You're beautiful, and smart and funny. You make me laugh and you have so much going on in your life that it's damn near entertaining," he teased.

"Don't be a hater. You're jealous because your life is boring," she told him.

"Okay, that may be true," he said, shrugging, finishing his drink. "I don't ever want you to feel like I don't like you or I don't feel the same way about you that you feel about me. It's just that when I am in a committed relationship, it's not something that I take lightly, so I don't jump into them that often."

Camille slowly nodded. She knew that he was being honest with her. "I can respect that."

She still didn't know where that left him and her. Truth of the matter was that the more time she spent with him and the more she was with him, the more in love she fell.

Chapter 15

"Well, everything came back negative," Dr. Whitman said through the phone.

"Everything?" Taryn repeated, making she heard correctly.

"Yes, ma'am, everything. You are disease free, child free, and HIV free."

"Thank so much, Dr. Whitman." Taryn smiled. She had taken the tests three days ago and waiting for the results had been hell. She had been praying so hard, that she knew God was tired of her calling his name every fifteen minutes.

"It's not a problem. Just make sure you're taking the necessary precautions. You know better because I taught you better," Dr. Whitman scolded. She had been Taryn's gynecologist since she was sixteen years old and was easy to talk to.

"I will, Dr. Whitman," she said, putting the phone on her desk and yelling, "THANK YOU, GOD!"

The tears began to fall and she began praying once more, this time thanking God for his mercy and seeing her through this and vowing to never let it happen again. She was in the middle of her praising when she heard someone knocking.

Everyone in the salon had gone for the day, and she was doing some last-minute paperwork when Dr. Whitman called.

"Who the heck can that be?" she asked out loud as she went to see. Jimmy was peeking through the door, waving when he saw her coming. She smiled as she let him in. "We're closed."

"I can always leave," he retorted.

She locked the door behind him. "Come on back into my office. Let me cut this light off right quick since the *closed* sign doesn't seem to be working."

"Okay, closed. You called me, remember." He followed her into the office and sat on the sofa. "Nice office."

"Thanks," she said, picking up the used tissues on her desk and tossing them into her wastebasket.

"You all right, T? You look like you're kinda upset."

Nodding her head, she told him, "I'm fine."

"Does this have anything to do with the restraining order you wanna take out on Celeste? What's going on?"

"Well, I may not have to do that, come to find out." She sat in her seat and smiled. She had called Jimmy and told him she needed the restraining order as soon as possible, but now that her tests were negative, there didn't seem to be a point.

"What's changed between yesterday and today?" He took the tailor-made navy-blue suit jacket off and laid it on the sofa beside him.

"I got a little bit of good news, that's all," she said. "You want me to hang that up for you?"

"No, it's fine," he said.

"You want something to drink? We got juice and stuff in the fridge." She was still trying to get her nerves together.

"Taryn, sit your ass down and tell me what's going on. What did Celeste do now?" he commanded. She stared at him, shocked by the tone of his voice, and slowly took her seat. She told him about Celeste coming into the salon causing the scene and embarrassing her with the announcement about

her medical status. Taryn also confessed about her unpro-
tected encounter with Lincoln and the news Dr. Whitman
had just given her. His only response was, "Wow."

Once again, the tears began to fall and Jimmy walked over
and hugged her tight. She inhaled the scent of his cologne,
enjoying the feel of his strong arms. *HELLO, what are you
doing? He's married and you've got a man!* She quickly
pushed away from him, reaching on her desk for another tissue and wiping her eyes. "I'm sorry."

"There's no need to apologize. I can imagine how emotionally draining this is for you. I'm just glad your tests came back
negative."

"Me too."

"Taryn, this girl seems to be mentally unstable and the restraining order may still be a good idea. Just because you
don't have an STD doesn't mean she's done harassing you."
He brushed the hair from her eyes. She stared at his handsome face, his skin the color of dark chocolate. His mustache
and goatee were trimmed perfectly and he put her in the
mind of Big Boi from OutKast. *An intelligent thug who can
wear the hell out of a suit.*

"Yeah, that's true. I just want her to stay the hell away from
me for her sake." Taryn plopped back down in her chair. "I
swear if she comes around here again, it's not gonna be pretty.
We had to keep Camille from kicking her behind when she
was in here the other day clowning."

"What was Camille's little-bitty self gonna do?" Jimmy
laughed.

"She may be small, but from the way she was about to swing
on Celeste, she looked like she could handle her own. And
she wasn't backing down either," Taryn said matter-of-factly.

"Is Lincoln worth all this?" Jimmy asked.

"Huh?" Taryn was taken aback by the question.

"Is he worth everything you're dealing with?"

Taryn thought about the Celeste situation, Lincoln's drinking, and the fact that he may very well have a baby on the way. When she became involved with him, she didn't expect to take on all of this.

"I don't know," she replied, her voice barely above a whisper.

"Taryn, you know your self-worth and what you want out of life. I don't have to tell you all that. But sometimes, we become so caught up in the thought of being in love that we don't see situations for what they really are. Take it from someone who knows for a fact." The way he said it, Taryn knew he was speaking of his own situation. He was still trying to make it work with his wife, but he was still unhappy in his marriage. "I can only go on what you tell me, and what I see. And I can tell that you really care about Lincoln at this point. But before you become even more involved and find yourself to the point of no return with him, know that he's worth it."

They continued talking for a little while longer until he noticed the time. "Damn, I didn't even realize it was that late."

Taryn looked at her own watch and to her own surprise saw that it was after nine. They had been talking for almost two hours. "I'll walk you out," she told him.

Jimmy grabbed his jacket. "You're not leaving?"

"No, I still have some last-minute stuff to catch up on," she told him.

"I have to go to the courthouse in the morning to take care of some stuff for Camille. I'll take care of the restraining order and have Celeste served by the end of the week." He embraced her once again; this time his hands lingered along her arms when they released.

"Before this is all over, my bill for your service is gonna be outrageous," she said, shivering, wondering why she was cold all of a sudden.

"I'm sure we can work something out," he said, grinning. "My feet are looking kinda rough these days and I could use a good pedicure."

"Oh, really? I thought you weren't into that foo-foo gay stuff?"

"I'm not," he replied. "But you gotta do something to work off these billable hours. They ain't cheap, you know. I'll call you tomorrow."

"Bye, Jimmy," she said, locking the door behind him. She had just sat back down in her office when she heard knocking at the front door again. She rushed to open it. "What did you forget this time?"

Instead of Jimmy, it was Lincoln who stood peeking in the glass door. She stopped and stared back at him. She had ignored his calls to her cell, home, and salon, having no desire to talk to him.

"Can I talk to you?" he asked, his voice sounding as pitiful as he looked.

She hesitated, and then slowly unlocked the door. Lincoln walked in and stood in front of her. She folded her arms and stared at him. "So, talk."

He reached into the pocket of the jeans he was wearing and pulled out a slip of paper. "I went and got tested, Taryn. I'm clean. I don't have any diseases. Here's the proof." He handed the paper to her.

She looked at the paper verifying that he was indeed negative for chlamydia, gonorrhea, syphilis, herpes, and HIV. She stared at the name and date, making sure it was his and current.

"Baby, I'm sorry. I told you I hadn't been with that girl and if I have, I swear I don't remember. She's lying." He took a step toward her. "Contrary to popular belief, I don't go around sleeping with each and every female I come into contact with, and if I do sleep with someone, I always wrap up."

"You didn't wrap up with me, Lincoln," she retorted.

"I know I didn't. And I'm sorry about that. It was just that I . . . I was so caught up in the moment. It was the first time in a long time, longer than I could ever remember, that I was actually making love to someone. And that was the greatest feeling I have ever had," he explained. "Taryn, I love you. I need you in my life."

"Lincoln, this is just so much for me to handle," Taryn said.

"Baby," she could hear the shaking in Lincoln's voice. He got down on his knees and wrapped his arms around her waist, staring up at her. "I can't lose you, Taryn. Baby, I'm begging."

Taryn looked down at him and saw the tears in his eyes. She felt her own tears welling up. "Lincoln."

Lincoln buried his face into her abdomen and held her tightly. She reached down and rubbed the thick waves in his hair. Taryn had never had a man become this emotional over her before and she knew it had to be love. *Is he worth it? Is he worth all the drama and chaos? Is he worthy of all that you are and all you have to give?* The love she saw in Lincoln's eyes when he looked back up at her gave her the answers to the questions she had been pondering.

"Taryn, tell me you still love me," he pleaded. "Tell me we can move past all this bullshit and move on."

"I love you, Lincoln," she said softly.

Lincoln's face lit up and a big grin spread across his face. "What? What was that?"

"I said I love you, Lincoln," she said, smiling. He stood up and kissed her so hard, he nearly knocked her over. She wrapped her arms around his neck and then, without warning, he picked her up into his arms. "Boy, put me down!"

"Thank you," he said when he finally put her down.

"Thank you for what?" she asked.

"For believing in me, and trusting me. I swear, nothing like this will ever happen again," he said, smiling.

"It better not," she told him.

"And I'm going to take care of this whole Celeste situation. She won't be bothering us anymore, believe that." He became serious. "There's no way she is carrying my kid."

"Don't worry, I'm already working on it," she said, hoping that the restraining order would handle Celeste once and for all.

Chapter 16

Yaya pulled into the parking lot of Jasper's where she was meeting Fitz for dinner. She looked around the lot for the burgundy Honda Accord station wagon he drove, but didn't see it. Lincoln and Taryn had smoothed their mess over and now it was time for her and Fitz to do the same. She hadn't talked to him in a couple of days; he hadn't called her, so she decided if she wanted to make up, she was going to make the first move. She was surprised he agreed to meet her without arguing. She checked herself in the mirror before getting out the car, and walked inside.

"Good evening, welcome to Jasper's," the hostess greeted her. "Are you dining alone or meeting someone?"

"I'm meeting someone," Yaya answered. "I didn't see his car in the parking lot, so he probably isn't here yet."

"Would you like to go ahead and be seated or wait?"

"I think I'll wait at the bar, if that's okay." Yaya told her. She walked over to the bar and ordered: "Amaretto sour with a splash of grenadine and pineapple juice."

"Coming right up," the bartender told her. She sat on the

tall leather stool, enjoying the band. The bartender placed her drink in front of her. "Eight bucks."

She reached into her bag and passed him a ten-dollar bill. She checked the time to make sure she wasn't too early. Fitz agreed to meet her at seven-thirty and it was going on quarter to eight. *He's fifteen minutes late!* Dialing his number on her cell phone, she told herself to remain calm. He didn't answer the first or second time she called him. She ordered another drink and waited ten more minutes. *I can't believe I got stood the hell up*, she thought as she paid for her last drink. Her cell began ringing and she answered it.

"Hello."

"Yaya, hey, I'm sorry I missed your call. I couldn't get to the phone." Fitz's voice was so low she could barely hear him.

"I guess you also couldn't get to the restaurant on time either, huh?" she snapped.

"I'm sorry. Man, it's just that, you're not gonna—"

"Look, are you coming or what? If not, I can leave now and make it home in time to watch *Top Model*," she interrupted him.

"Yaya, I'm not gonna be able to make it to dinner."

"What?" Her anger was growing. "Fine, thanks for letting me know."

"Yaya, wait a second, let me explain. Micha called and—"

"Save it, Fitz. Go be with your son and your baby mama, okay?" She closed the phone and hopped off the stool, heading for the door. She was in such a rush that she didn't see her brother until she bumped smack into him.

"Damn, Yaya. Where the hell is the fire?" He grinned.

"My bad, Quincy. I didn't even see you," she replied. "What are you doing here? Meeting Paige?"

"Naw, I'm meeting Diesel to talk business," Quincy told her.

She frowned at him. "Since when did you and Diesel start hanging so close?"

"You know he and I have always been cool. Now that he's back in town, we've been riding before the weather gets too bad. We've tossed a few ideas around and we're trying to make some things happen," Quincy said, shrugging.

"That's good. If anyone can make things happen it's you and Diesel," she said, smiling.

"What are you doing here? I know you ain't eating alone."

"No, I was supposed to meet Fitz, but once again, his baby mama called and he canceled on me," she replied. "So, I'm leaving."

"Don't leave, eat with us."

Yaya turned to see Diesel standing behind her, looking gorgeous as ever even in the jeans and plaid Mecca shirt he wore.

"What's up, D? Naw, you two are here on business, I'm outta here," she said, grinning.

"Aren't you a businesswoman? And we can always use a woman of your caliber on our squad, right Q?" Diesel turned toward Quincy.

"She is woman of many talents. And her business is the talk of the town right now," Quincy agreed. "I think you should join us, Yaya."

Yaya looked at both men and then put her arm through each of theirs. "Gentlemen, lead the way."

"So, how do Monya and Taryn feel about you traveling so much with Geneva?" Quincy asked, taking the last bite of his smothered chicken.

"They really don't mind. They know the publicity is great for the salon and we all do what we have to do for the good of the business," she answered.

"Everyone is pulling their fair weight, then?" Quincy continued.

She looked up and gave Diesel an irritated look. He nodded for her to answer and she replied to her brother, "Everyone is doing more than their fair share of the work in the salon, Q. That's why we stay busy. We can't stand to turn clients away."

"The only reason I ask is because Monya is there like six days a week," he told her.

"That's because Monya is all about the money. Those women pay her top dollar because she is the best at what she does. Monya has a waiting list of over thirty people," Yaya said. "Her role in the salon is to be the head nail technician. But, she's more than that. Monya holds the salon down when T and I aren't there. Which, by the way, we try to be. Taryn and I are the owners and estheticians, and we handle our business, but Monya and Camille are what hold that shop together. Our Carol's Daughter retail sales are through the roof."

"What is Carol's Daughter?" Quincy frowned.

"That's the line of beauty products we sell in the store, Q. Shower gels, facial cleansers, hair products, the whole nine," she told him.

"Kind of like Bath and Body Works, but for us," Diesel added. "They have a great men's line. I use this ylang and patchouli facial scrub that is really good because I have dry skin."

"Really, I was looking at this new AMBI stuff in the store the other night," Quincy replied.

"Naw, man, try the Carol's Daughter line. I have the Big Kahuna set too. Yaya turned me on to it about a year and a half ago and it's all I use. Now before—"

"AHEM!" Yaya cleared her throat loudly, trying to get their attention. "You two are worse than women. Let me find out."

"Don't even play like that," Quincy warned. "That ain't even funny."

"You can't get mad at a brother for taking an interest in his personal hygiene." Diesel stroked his chin playfully.

"Vain. That's what you are, vain." She shook her head.

"Is something wrong with your food? You hardly touched it." Diesel looked at her plate. "You know that ain't like you."

"No, it was fine." Yaya looked at the plate of baked fish and vegetables that she hardly touched. She was afraid that taking more than two bites would have her running to the bathroom and she didn't wanna have to explain that to Diesel and Q.

"Maybe she's trying to be cute since you're here, Diesel," Quincy teased.

"Please, I know better than that," Diesel said, laughing. "Yaya may wear a size ten, but I don't see how because she can eat like she wears a twenty."

"Shut up." Yaya hit his arm.

"He knows you better than I thought," Quincy said, snickering. "Well, I gotta get outta here. It's been real. I will talk to both of you tomorrow."

Yaya stood up and hugged her brother. "Okay, thanks. This was a lot of fun."

"I love you, girl." Quincy kissed the top of her head.

"I love you too Q," she said. He tapped his fist against Diesel's and was about to walk off when Yaya stopped him. "Q, wait!"

"What?"

"You forgot the check so you can pay it on the way out," she said, laughing, snatching the receipt off the table and handing it to him. He shook his head in disbelief as he took it from her.

"That was so foul," Diesel told her.

"What? It was a business dinner. He can write it off on his taxes," she said innocently. "What are you complaining about? You got a free meal!"

"Ohhhh, check it out. You hear that?" Diesel began moving to the music that was flowing through the speakers.

"Oh no." She shook her head. The band was playing Stevie Wonder's "All I Do", one of Diesel's favorite songs.

"That's us, come on." He stood up.

"No," she said, shaking her head.

"Old habits die hard, let's go, you know you want to."

She rolled her eyes.

"Don't even try it," he said and held his hand out to her. She stared at it, not moving. "Yaya, don't play with me."

"There's no one dancing," she said, frowning.

"So? Since when did that matter to us? Let's go," he said, still holding his hand out. She stood up, fixed her shirt and took his hand.

The fact that they were the only couple on the floor wasn't what made them the center of attention; it was the way they moved together. Her uncle taught her how to swing dance from the time she could walk, and she loved it. She discovered Diesel also knew how to swing out a few years ago at a party they were both at. They had become each other's select dance partners from that moment on. Dancing with Diesel was one of her life's pleasures. He twirled her around the dance floor, back and forth to the rhythm, and they swayed in each other's arms.

They became lost in their own world and she closed her eyes as he sang along with the music, *"Well let me tell you girl think of how exciting it would be, if you should discover you feel like me."*

By the time the song ended, they received a standing ovation. He bowed and she curtsied, laughing at each other. The band began playing "Cruisin'" by Smokey Robinson.

"Shall we?" She gestured with her hands.

"One more won't hurt," he said, pulling her to him and gliding to the music.

"Where is your girlfriend?" The question had been burning in her mind all night, but she waited until the right time to ask.

"At home," he told her. "This was supposed to be a business meeting with me and your brother, remember? No need for her to be here. Where's your man?"

"He's with his baby mama, I suppose. No need for him to be here." She smiled.

Diesel didn't answer, just tightened his hold on her body. She enjoyed the hardness of his body and the strength of his arms as her head lay on his shoulder. Her mind traveled to the first time they slept together. He had hosted a Super Bowl after party in Atlanta and she did the makeup for the ten go-go dancers he hired and stayed to enjoy the festivities. Diesel was the most creative party promoter she had ever met, and seeing his visions come to life excited her. The party, attended by any and everyone who was hot was in attendance. Rappers, sports stars, singers, choreographers, photographers, you name it. The party was a huge success. The next morning, Diesel showed up at her hotel room door with a dozen white lilies and breakfast on a cart. They ate, went shopping and then he took her to dinner, to thank her for all of her help. They returned to her room, one thing led to another and they stopped denying the chemistry they had from day one. Yaya knew it had to be love. They left no parts of one another's bodies untouched, un-tasted, and unsatisfied. He set the bar for any other man she would ever sleep with and no one else had come close. They only slept together that one time. They were both at a point in their lives where they knew neither one was ready for a relationship. The attraction was there, the chemistry was apparent, but their careers and lifestyles would not allow it to happen. They settled for being great friends.

The song ended too soon for Yaya. She knew it was late, but the thought of going home alone saddened her.

"You ready to go?" Diesel asked as they returned to the table. "I promised Sonya I would stop through for a minute."

"May as well," she said, shrugging. She didn't know why she was tripping.

"What's wrong, Ya? You a'ight?" He touched her shoulder.

"Yeah, I'm just trying to remember where I put my keys," she lied, reaching for her purse.

"Probably in the bottom of that big-ass purse of yours." He laughed. "How much was that bag anyway? 'Bout a grand?"

"No." She frowned at him, glancing at the black Juicy Couture bag she had just purchased.

"I bet," he said, laughing. "You were always the fly girl. I gotta give it to you."

He walked her out to her car. She unlocked the doors and got in. "I'll talk to you later, Diesel."

"Yeah, this was fun, Yaya," he said. "I enjoyed hanging out with you. We haven't done that in a long time. We gotta do it again really soon."

"I don't think your girlfriend would be too pleased," she said, sighing.

"I don't think your man was feeling me too much either. I don't know why. We're just friends, right?"

"Right," she said.

Once she got home, showered and got into bed, she checked her voice mail messages. There were three urgent ones from Fitz telling her to call him as soon as possible; Micha had an emergency that he was dealing with. *What? Did Micha break a nail? No, maybe she needed him to kill a spider in her bedroom.* Whatever it was, Yaya didn't care. She wasn't used to being second choice and she wasn't about to start now. She had tried to make it work with Fitz, but they were just too different.

The next morning, Yaya was wakened by her cell phone playing Rihanna's "S.O.S.," letting her know it was Taryn. What the hell did she want this early in the morning? Yaya rolled over and grabbed the phone off the nightstand.

"Whaaaat?" she said, seeing that it was only seven-thirty.

"How come you ain't call me last night?" Taryn hissed though the phone.

"What?"

"Why didn't you call and tell me about what happened? You know I'm pissed at you, right?"

"Ain't nothing happen. We had dinner with Q, danced to two songs, he walked me to the car and then I left. That was it."

"What? Yaya, wake up. Are you dreaming or something?"

"If I was dreaming, I would at least be bragging about a kiss good night, retarded," she mumbled. "Diesel and I are just buddies."

"Diesel? When the hell were you with Diesel?" Taryn sounded totally confused.

"Last night at Jasper's. Isn't that what you're talking about?"

"No, Qianna. I'm talking about Micha, Fitz's ex. She was in a car accident yesterday evening. It was terrible. Her fiancé didn't make it. You didn't know?"

Yaya sat up, rubbing her eyes. "Huh? No, I didn't know."

"Yeah, he's dead."

The familiar feeling of nausea hit Yaya once again. Dropping her phone, she ran into the bathroom and put her head in the toilet, regurgitating what felt like her entire inner being.

Chapter 17

"That's terrible," Camille said when she heard the news about the car accident. "Terrance and I saw it on the news last night."

"I know. Yaya didn't even know until I called her this morning," Taryn said.

"What did she say?" Camille asked.

"She threw up," Taryn replied.

"Uhm, is it just me or has she been doing that a lot?" Camille had been noticing that Yaya threw up all the time. Sometimes, she didn't think anyone noticed, but being the child of an alcoholic enabled Camille to pick up on a lot of hidden behaviors.

"Well, she says she has reflux. Which is why she can't eat a lot," Monya told her. "Some of it's nerves too. She's been stressed lately."

"I just don't want her to be bingeing and purging. I saw a movie on Lifetime about that and the girl died," Camille told them.

"Girl, please, Yaya definitely ain't anorexic or bulimic. Does she look like she's losing weight?" Taryn asked.

"Well, I don't know, but . . ." Camille replied. "She might be pregnant."

Monya and Taryn looked at each other and cracked up laughing. Jarrod walked in and asked, "What's so funny?"

"Ca—Camille thinks—thinks—" Monya was laughing so hard she couldn't talk.

"Camille thinks Yaya might be pregnant," Taryn finally said.

It was Jarrod who laughed loudly this time.

"I don't get it. Why is that so funny?" Camille looked at them like they were crazy.

"The last thing Qianna Westbrooke wants in her life is a baby. She's too selfish for that," Monya explained. "She's been on birth control from the moment she turned fifteen and fell in love with a little tag with the name Gucci." Jarrod informed her. "She decided right then and there that nothing or no one would ever come between her and any item she wanted."

"She's been on birth control since forever," Taryn added.

"A baby is nowhere in her future plans," Monya agreed.

"If y'all weren't so damn funny, I would be offended," Yaya said, surprising all of them by coming in through the barbershop door rather than the front.

"It's sad, but true," Taryn said.

"I do want to have a baby someday. I just need to make sure I have everything in order before I do," Yaya told them.

"And what is everything?" Monya winked at Camille.

"First of all, a husband who can support me and his child."

"And?" Taryn asked.

"A nice home comfortable enough for my family."

"And?"

"Enough money in the bank to sustain my lifestyle for two years because I don't plan on working."

"Wow, two years?" Camille said, surprised.

"And?" Taryn, Jarrod, and Monya all said simultaneously.

"What is this? Why is this a big deal?" Yaya put her hands on her hip.

"There's more?" Camille asked.

"And?" they all repeated.

"A platinum, princess cut, five-karat ring and matching platinum Range Rover, which will be gifts from my husband for bearing his seed. And a new wardrobe for my pre- during, and post-pregnancy figures," she snapped.

"And if she doesn't have all of those things . . ." Monya said.

"Then it's not time for me to have a baby," Yaya replied, sitting down in the waiting area. "How did my having a baby become the topic of conversation anyway?"

"Uh, we were talking about Angelina Jolie," Taryn lied.

"Oh," Yaya said.

"Yo, I heard about the accident. You talked to my man yet?" Jarrod asked.

"Yeah, I talked to him. I called him as soon as I found out. Micha is being discharged this morning and Kareem's funeral is on Saturday," Yaya told them as she walked to the back. "He's supposed to call me later."

"Let me know if there's anything we can do," Jarrod said. "Yo, Camille, can I get twenty dollars til later?"

"Jarrod, you already owe me ten from yesterday." Camille shook her head.

He reached into his pocket and took out a wad of money, passing her a ten-dollar bill. "I forgot about that. Can I get twenty now?"

"Get outta here, Jarrod!" Taryn lurched at him and he ducked, rushing out the salon and back into the barbershop. "Didn't I tell you to stop giving him money? You ain't learned yet?"

"He said he didn't have change." Camille shrugged. "I wanted some chips out of the machine."

"And you believed him? Jarrod always has money," Taryn told her.

"Why do you think he conveniently never has change for the machine? He makes more money off that little trick than he does cutting hair," Monya said, snickering. "Don't feel bad. He owes me about two hundred dollars. We really need to see about getting a machine of our own."

"Okay, Geneva Johnson just called," Yaya came in and announced a couple of hours later.

"No, Yaya, I can't cover for you this weekend," Taryn quickly retorted.

"I don't need for you to cover for me, thank you." Yaya rolled her eyes at her. "*True Diva* magazine is doing a cover piece on her. They want to capture her getting the star treatment. She'll be here Friday at noon and they're bringing a crew. Get ready."

Yaya turned to walk away and Taryn yelled, "Wait, Yaya. Hold up?"

"What?"

"She's coming here to After Effex for the shoot? This Friday?"

"Yep."

Taryn looked at Monya who looked at Camille who looked at Yaya. The significance of what Yaya was saying sunk in.

A smile slowly spread across Yaya's face. "I'm tired of being in the spotlight by myself. It's everyone's time to shine. We need to get ready. Camille, call Chester and see if those shirts and jackets are ready."

"I'm on it," Camille said, rushing for her palm pilot to get the number.

"If anyone, I mean anyone ghetto, loud or embarrassing is on those books for Friday, call and change their appointment," Monya instructed.

Everyone was in busy mode. Calls had to be made, inventory checked, cleaning had to be done. And clients still had to be serviced. They had three days to prepare and it was organized chaos. Camille loved it. She called Terrance and canceled their plans for the evening, explaining what was happening.

"Are you serious? Geneva Johnson?" He seemed as excited as she was.

"Yes, Geneva Johnson. Do you know what this is gonna mean for the salon? We're already booked solid now. People are gonna have to call a year in advance. Taryn and Yaya are really gonna have to open a second location," she told him.

"I would love to get a quick interview. You think maybe Yaya will ask for me? It wouldn't be that long. Whenever she gets a break in her schedule, no matter what time." Terrance was talking so fast, Camille almost couldn't understand what he was saying.

"Are you crazy? You want me to ask Yaya? Are you trying to get me fired or cussed out? You know how Yaya is," Camille told him.

"Just ask, for me, please," Terrance begged.

"I'll try," Camille said, not wanting to disappoint him. "But I'm not making any promises."

"I'm not asking you to." She could hear the smile in his voice.

"I gotta get back to work," she told him.

"Okay, call me later when you get a chance."

"It'll probably be late when we get outta here," she warned him.

"I don't care how late it is," he said. "Call me."

Camille didn't get the nerve to ask Yaya about the interview until Thursday night. They were putting the finishing touches on the salon and Chester, the designer who Yaya and Taryn worked with, had just brought in their new long-sleeved shirts and denim jackets. Camille couldn't believe how fly they were. The jackets had *After Effex* embellished in hot pink and teal blue on the front pockets and on the back, set off with rhinestones and studs. He had created every type of shirt imaginable, long-sleeved tees, golf shirts, button-down, V-neck, scoop neck. Each one was custom-made for each of them.

"Wow, this is incredible," Camille said, looking through her personal pile.

"Well, I do aim to please." Chester snapped his fingers.

"I love this dress." Yaya came out wearing the short minidress, "But where's the belt?"

"Yaya, baby, that's a shirt," Chester told her.

"This big thing is a dress?" she asked. "Monya, let me see your belt."

Monya took off her belt and passed it to Yaya who wrapped it around her tiny waist. Sure enough, it looked like a dress.

"Okay, if that's the look you're going for, that'll work," Chester said, laughing.

"You know I'ma work this with some tights and my black Michael Kors boots. Hello!" Yaya did her imitation of a top model walk.

"Take off my shirt, Yaya. NOW!" Taryn growled.

"This is your shirt, T?" Yaya looked down at the pocket and saw Taryn's name. "My bad."

"You're so damn funny." Taryn cut her eyes as Yaya walked to the back.

Sensing Yaya's good mood, Camille figured there was no better time than the present to ask about the interview for Terrance. "Yaya?" She knocked softly.

"Yeah," Yaya answered. "Come in."

Camille walked into her office as she was pulling her jeans up. "Oh, my bad. I can come back."

"Girl please, I ain't got nothing to be ashamed of. What's up? Taryn still griping because I modeled her shirt as a dress?"

"Uh, no, I was wondering if maybe, tomorrow, I mean, I know we're gonna have a lot going on—"

"Camille, spit it out, damn, unless you're about to ask for the day off. Because that ain't happening," Yaya snapped.

"No, nothing like that," Camille said. "Well, you know Terrance does the weekend sports report and I mentioned that Geneva was coming to the salon and—"

"Let me guess, he wants to meet her," she finished.

"No, he wants to do an interview with her," Camille said.

"On camera?" Yaya frowned.

"Yes," Camille said, nodding.

"Cam, why did you wait until *now* to ask me this?" Yaya sat down and shook her head at Camille.

"I knew we had a lot to do and I didn't wanna be a bother and . . ."

"You were scared to ask. Be honest." Yaya waited for Camille's answer.

"Yeah, I was scared," Camille admitted.

"Camille, I may be a bitch, but I don't ever want you to feel like you can't come and ask me something. Or can't come and talk to me about anything. We're family. Outside of Quincy, this salon is the only family I have. Hell, if I can't depend on y'all, who can I depend on?" Yaya shrugged.

Camille nodded at what Yaya was saying. She understood exactly how Yaya felt. It was the same way she felt most of the time. She did have Paige and Myla. "I feel you."

"Let me call Geneva and see what her schedule is. I'll let you know what she says," Yaya told her.

"You don't have to check with her agent or manager?"

"Girl, I'm her makeup artist, I deal with her directly. I make her beautiful . . . well, in her case, presentable."

"Thanks, Yaya." Camille smiled. Yaya stood up and gave her a hug.

"You're doing your so-called *friend* a big favor by doing

this, you know. I hope he appreciates that," Yaya said. "I know you said you and Terrance are friends and you're cool with that. But I know you like him more than that. I just want to give you a bit of sisterly advice. Whatever rules you establish at the beginning of the relationship, even if it's just a friendship, are the same rules throughout unless you both agree to change them. You have to constantly remember the rules, Camille. Even when you feel like they've changed, unless you've both agreed, remember the rules."

Camille wondered why Yaya felt the need to tell her this, but she didn't question it. "Thanks, Yaya."

A little while later, Yaya came into the salon and told her, "Call your *friend*. Geneva says she can do a studio interview with him on Saturday. Taryn and I have a funeral to attend, but I told her you would be responsible for her makeup."

Chapter 18

Geneva Johnson was an unusual-looking woman. It wasn't that she was ugly, because Taryn didn't believe any of God's creatures were ugly. She was just had an unusual combination of facial characteristics. She had a keen nose, thin lips, and an extended forehead. Her hair was fairly thin and she always wore tracks. Taryn personally didn't have a problem with hair extensions; she wore them herself from time to time. But Geneva changed her extensions like she changed clothes. She would be curly and blond in the morning and long and straight in the evening, and no matter what style she wore, the only thing Taryn thought when she saw her on TV or in the magazines was, her tracks look terrible. One thing that couldn't be denied, dissed or dismissed was Geneva's banging, athletic body; tall and lean, but curvy with enough junk in the trunk to make J. Lo do a double take. Taryn could see the guys panting through the window as she walked into the salon.

"Hi, welcome to After Effex," Camille greeted her as she did all the clients that came in the door. "I'm Camille."

"Hello, Camille, I'm Geneva." Geneva smiled. "Nice to meet you."

"We've been expecting you, Geneva. I see you have a twelve o'clock appointment and you're right on time," Camille responded, and then turned to Taryn. "This is Taryn, the co-owner of the salon."

"It's a pleasure." Taryn shook Geneva's hand, trying not to stare at the red weave in her hair.

"I'll let Taryn and Yaya know you're here. Can I get you something to drink?"

"Fiji if you have it," Geneva answered.

"Coming right up." Camille already had the water chilling in the kitchenette, located in the back of the salon. Yaya had already informed them of Geneva's likes and dislikes and idiosyncrasies, so they were well-prepared for the day. Geneva introduced her to her entourage, which included her personal assistant, publicist, security guard, and her sister. There was also the photographer and reporter from *True Diva* magazine.

"What's up, Geneva? You find the salon all right?" Yaya walked up and gave her a hug.

"Yeah, it was fairly easy." Geneva looked around. "This place is so nice. I love the colors."

"Here you are, Geneva." Camille came in carrying a tray holding a glass of crushed ice and a chilled bottle of Fiji water.

Geneva's assistant opened the water, poured it into the glass and passed it to her. She took a tall swallow and said, "That's perfect."

"Have you met everyone? Camille's our receptionist and artist in training, Taryn's my partner, and Monya is the salon manager," Yaya said. "We also have two other part-time nail techs that come in as needed."

"Can I get anyone else anything to drink?" Camille offered.

They all declined, so Taryn asked, "You guys ready to get started?"

The schedule for Geneva had already been mapped out. It started with a Swedish body massage, body scrub, mud bath, manicure, pedicure, eyebrow threading, waxing, and full makeup. The photographer would be taking pictures of it all. Yaya whisked Geneva to the Zen room and Camille and Monya took care of the entourage. They wanted to make sure that not only Geneva was treated like a VIP, but everyone else as well. Taryn and Yaya knew firsthand that the assistants to the stars were very well connected. Good news traveled fast, but horror stories of bad service traveled faster.

"You wanna go ahead and get your manicure and pedicure out of the way first, before Geneva needs you for something?" Monya asked the remaining ladies.

"Well, we hadn't planned on getting anything done." Geneva's publicist frowned.

"Nonsense," Camille said, leading her to a Princess chair. "This is After Effex, where before and after are never the same. You can't walk out that door the same way you walked in."

Seeing that everything was under control, Taryn went into the Zen room to assist Yaya. Geneva was laid out on the table on her stomach, talking nonstop about a guy she had spent the weekend with.

"He was cute, but I need someone more rugged in bed, you know what I mean?" Geneva asked. "I'm an athlete."

"You are crazy, Geneva," Yaya told her as she rubbed the oil into her skin. Geneva was sharing bedroom stories of her ex-boyfriend, Deon Carroll, a shining star in the NFL.

"Taryn, you're a woman of above average size, don't you prefer a man who takes charge and handles his business?" Geneva looked up at Taryn. Yaya's eyes shot across the room at her best friend and Taryn could feel her praying that she wouldn't say the first thing that came to her mind

Oh no, this wench didn't. What the hell is that supposed to mean? You Raggedy Ann, bad-weave-wearing heifer. I will reach over there and push your ass off that table.

"Girl, yes, I don't need anyone I gotta tell what to do," Taryn said, squinting at Yaya. She could see her relief.

"Thank you! I'm tired because I'm telling you harder, softer, left and right." Geneva cracked up.

"I'm going to go make sure everyone is okay out here," Taryn said. "You good, Ya?"

"Yeah, T. Go ahead."

The photographer followed Taryn out the Zen room and stopped her in the hallway. "You handled that very well."

"Thanks," she told him. "It was hard."

"I'm really feeling this spot. I'm really feeling the fact that you didn't go all the way out in the burbs to open it, but opened it right here, you know, y'all kept it real."

Taryn didn't dare tell him that Yaya had a conniption when they opened it up here in the middle of the hood. "We try to be an example for the community. You know so many times people leave and do well and never return. We did well and brought our blessings here to bless others."

"That's real talk right there. I'ma hook ya'll up," he said, smiling.

She didn't know what he meant, but she took it for what it was and said, "Thanks, we'd appreciate that."

By the time Geneva Johnson and her crew walked out the door, Taryn was glad to see her leave. Her jokes were corny, her stories were boring, and she bad-mouthed anyone she thought they would be interested in hearing about.

"Baby, she couldn't have been that bad," Lincoln said, laughing.

"She was arrogant and ignorant, Lincoln. A deadly combination. And Monya was worried about our regular clients not being loud and ghetto." She ran her fingers along his chest. "I feel bad for Camille. She has to deal with *that* tomorrow."

"Yaya doesn't seem to have a problem with her." He reached for the remote and flipped through the channels.

"Well, come to find out, Yaya charges her double what she charges anyone else plus travel expenses. I knew there had to be some reason she was so gung-ho about having her as a client," Taryn explained.

"Yaya is coming to the funeral, right?"

"Yeah, she'll be there."

"That's good. Fitz was worried but I told him everything was cool."

Taryn stared up at Lincoln. "Worried about what? Yaya?"

"He didn't want her to trip in case he had to be there to support Micha."

"What does he mean, *support?*"

"Nothing, T. I guess like if she got upset and needed to be escorted out or something. People would expect him to do it," Lincoln replied.

"No they wouldn't. They would expect the ushers to do it. The only reason Yaya and I are going to pay respects to Kareem, who we didn't even know, by the way, is to support Fitz and Carver. Now, if Fitz is going to be the shoulder for Micha to cry on, then Yaya doesn't need to go," Taryn informed him.

"Good grief, T. He's not going to be the shoulder for Micha. We're all going to pay our respects and support Carver, period. Let's leave it at that," he suggested. "We'll all go to the funeral and have a great time."

"What? How are we going to have a great time, Lincoln? You are sick."

"Come on, you know the best cake in the world is the one somebody's aunt made for the repast after the funeral. Don't trip. And the macaroni and cheese, man, I can't wait!"

Taryn couldn't help but laugh. "You are really sick."

"Yeah, lovesick," he said and kissed her.

Taryn woke up in the middle of the night to find Lincoln gone. She got up and walked to the front of her house, peeking out the window. His car was gone out of the driveway.

Walking back into her bedroom, she noticed his bag was still in the corner and his suit and tie he brought to wear the following day was still hanging in the doorway of her closet. She called his cell but heard it vibrating on the dresser. *Don't go looking for anything you don't wanna find,* she warned herself, looking at the sleek RAZR phone. *Just go back to bed.* She climbed back into bed and closed her eyes, but was unable to go back to sleep. It was two hours later when she finally heard her front door creak open and felt him climb into bed beside her.

"Where did you go last night? Or rather this morning?" she asked as they got dressed.

"Huh?" he asked.

"If you can *huh*, you can hear. I asked where you went. I woke up in the middle of the night and you were gone." She waited for his answer.

"Oh, I forgot my tie. I thought about it while I was asleep and ran home to get it. The church is in the opposite direction and I wasn't sure if we were gonna have time to run get it so I went and picked it up." He answered as if it was a simple explanation. "I wasn't gone that long. Did you miss me, sweetie?"

Taryn contemplated telling him she knew he was lying but decided to let this little situation play itself out. She was a firm believer in what's done in the dark always came to light and when daylight broke, she was going to be ready.

The service was very nice and well-attended. Taryn, Lincoln, Yaya, and Fitz sat near the back of the church. The choir was amazing and from what people were saying, Taryn could tell that Kareem was a good man, well-respected and well-liked. All was going well until they opened the casket for the final viewing. *I hate when they do this,* she thought, *this just upsets the family all over again.* The organ began playing softly and a soloist began singing "Sweet, Sweet Spirit," one of Taryn's favorite hymns. The instant she heard it, she looked over at Yaya, and held her hand tightly. It was the song they sang at her uncle's funeral and she knew it would be hard for her. Yaya's uncle was the man who raised her and Quincy and they had been very close.

"There's a sweet, sweet spirit in this place." The woman's voice was beautiful. *"And I know it's the spirit of the Lord."*

The casket was opened and Taryn could make out the silhouette of Kareem's face. Soft sniffles turned to slow whimpers as the family slowly made their way to say their final good-byes.

"Sweet Holy Spirit, sweet heavenly dove, stay right here with us, filling us with your love."

Yaya's grip on Taryn's hand tightened. Taryn looked over and saw that she wasn't looking well at all. "Yaya, you all right?"

Yaya nodded and dabbed at her eyes with her handkerchief.

A loud wail filled the sanctuary as Micha, dressed in a simple black dress, leaned over the casket. "Why Kareem, why? Don't leave me!"

"Without a doubt you know that we have been revived when we shall leave this place."

Micha's weeping set off a whole other level of grieving in the church. The ushers and a few other men grabbed her and dragged her down the aisle. Fitz, unable to remain seated, got up and joined them. If Taryn hadn't been so worried about Yaya, she would've been pissed. Yaya began rocking back and forth as the crying became louder.

"Come on, let's get her outta here," she said to Lincoln. She gathered their purses. "Come on, Yaya. It's okay."

They slipped out just before utter pandemonium erupted. Taryn rubbed Yaya's back as they walked in the parking lot. Fitz was nowhere to be found. *It's a good thing he's ghost right now, because he has a good cussing out coming to him.*

"Is she going to be all right?" Lincoln said softly in Taryn's ear.

"She's going to be fine. She just needs some air," she said, nodding. "We can take her home seeing that your brother seems to have disappeared."

Lincoln looked up. "He's probably just inside. I can go get him."

"Leave and you better climb in that casket with Kareem." Taryn gave him a threatening look.

"You're right, she can just ride with us," Lincoln said, taking the keys out of his pocket. "It's not a problem."

Lincoln tried making small talk as they drove to Taryn's house. Once they arrived, he offered to go and get them something to eat. He was making a true effort and Taryn valued that. So much so that she temporarily overlooked his middle-of-the-night disappearing act.

"I'm not hungry," Yaya said.

"Yaya, you need to eat. I can go for some Ochie's," Taryn suggested. She knew that it was one of Yaya's favorite restaurants but she rarely ate their food unless someone went and got it for her because it was located in the grimiest part of town.

"Ochie's it is." Lincoln smiled.

Taryn went and walked him to the door. "Thank you."

"For what?" He frowned.

"For being a decent guy," she told him.

"You can thank me later." He kissed her, playfully sucking her bottom lip. "Because you know I was really feenin' for some funeral cake."

"I'ma give you some cake, all right," she said and closed the door. Yaya was sitting on the sofa and she went and sat beside her.

"Man, I don't know where all that came from. I didn't even know Kareem."

"It was a funeral, Yaya. All funerals are emotional. No one

expected you to be an ice queen," Taryn told her. "Now a drama queen, that's a different story."

"I need a drink," Yaya said, slipping out of her DKNY pumps.

"Coming right up." Taryn went into the kitchen to pour them a glass of wine.

"I didn't even wanna go, but Fitz made such a big deal about being there as a couple and showing our condolences to Micha. I could be taking Geneva Johnson's money right now," Yaya said. Taryn heard the doorbell chimes in the hallway as Yaya called out, "I got it. It's probably Fitz."

"No fighting in my house, Yaya," Taryn warned her, although she thought Fitz was deserving of a good slapping right about now. She waited a few moments.

"Uh, T, you got company," Yaya beckoned.

Taryn grabbed the two glasses of wine and went to see who Yaya was talking about. She was shocked to see Jimmy standing beside her best friend, who was giving her a goofy look.

"Hey Jimmy," Taryn said, ignoring Yaya's gaze.

"Hey Taryn, I couldn't get you on the phone and I went by the salon and you weren't there. So, I decided to try my luck here when Monya said you were in town," Jimmy said, standing with his hands in his pocket. It was one of the few times she had seen him looking casual. Even in the black Sean John sweatsuit and matching Jordans he wore, he was still debonair.

"What's going on?" she said, knowing something must be wrong for him to go through all the trouble.

"We got a problem, a big one," he said.

Chapter 19

"You nervous?" Terrance asked Camille as they walked up the sidewalk and into the television station.

"Yeah, are you?" she asked him.

"Not really. I've done interviews before. I keep telling myself that this one is no more important than the other ones I've done before," he said.

"You look really nice," she said, admiring the gray suit her wore with the yellow shirt underneath. "Your mom got that one?"

"Oh, you got jokes, huh?" he said, purposely bumping into her. She almost dropped the heavy makeup case she carried.

"I'm sorry," he apologized. "You want me to take that for you?"

"No," she snapped. "I can carry it myself."

They walked along the long corridor and entered a large office, arriving at what he proudly announced, "This is my space."

She looked at the cluttered desk and told him, "Indeed it is."

"Laugh now, but soon, you'll have to go through my secretary to see me," he said, nodding.

"Is that a fact?" a man's voice asked. Camille looked around to see a short, burly man with a full gray beard to match his hair smiling at them.

"Camille, this is the station manager and my boss, Mr. Hardy," Terrance introduced them.

"Nice to meet you," Camille said, shifting the bag into her left hand so she could extend her right one.

"The pleasure's mine, young lady," Mr. Hardy said. "Terrance, you let this beauty carry her own bag?"

"I offered to carry it for her, Mr. Hardy, but she declined my services," Terrance explained. "You know how these modern women are, sir."

"So, you allowed her to carry it, even though she declined. In my day, a woman didn't have a choice whether or not she was gonna be treated as a lady. I took it upon myself to always be a gentleman." He winked at Camille as he took the bag out of her hand and extended his arm. "If you come with me, I'll show you where you can set up for Ms. Johnson."

Camille smiled and hooked her arm into his. "Why thank you, Mr. Hardy."

Terrance opened his mouth to protest, but shook his head and followed them. The dressing room was set up for her to work. Camille looked around and her heart beat in anticipation. *This is it, my first celebrity client. My first big-time job. God, please don't let me mess up.*

"Everything look okay?" Mr. Hardy asked. "We got the Fiji water right over there for her."

Camille saw that there was a bowl of ice with bottles of Fiji water chilling, but there were no glasses. "Would you all happen to have any glasses to pour it in?"

"Glasses to pour it in?" Mr. Hardy asked. "What's the point of having bottled water if you're gonna pour it in a glass?"

"That's what she likes." Camille shrugged.

"Well, I don't think she's gonna like it today because we don't have any glasses," he answered.

"Don't worry." Camille picked the bag off the floor and placed it on the counter. She unzipped it, and pulled out a small bag holding two carefully wrapped glasses, which she brought just in case. She looked over at Mr. Hardy and asked, "Got any crushed ice?"

"Awwww come on." Mr. Hardy threw his hands in the air and turned to Terrance. "See, this is why I don't do celebrities! Come get me when the diva arrives."

"I like him," Camille said to Terrance when Mr. Hardy was gone.

"He is a character," he said, laughing. "I gotta go look over my notes and prepare. She should be here in about twenty minutes. You good?"

Camille looked around the room and nodded. "I'm good. And don't worry, you'll be great."

He walked over and hugged her. "Thanks. I'll check you in a little while."

Alone, Camille pulled her After Effex smock out the bag and put it on. She began arranging her brushes, sponges, and cosmetics so that they would be right where she needed them. She also set up her iPod and speakers so she would have music to work with. Sitting on the nearby sofa as she waited, Camille said a quick prayer. *Okay, God, I don't ask for much, but you've given me more than I even knew I wanted, so thanks. Help me out here. I know this is what you've called me to do and I need for you to help me do a great job.*

"Camille, Geneva's here," Mr. Hardy said, walking into the dressing room. Geneva was right behind him, wearing dark shades and a jet-black weave in her hair. Her entourage was still in tow. Although she was excited about doing her first celebrity face, after meeting Geneva at the salon and seeing her nice-nasty persona in action, she had mixed emotions. Yaya and Taryn told her to be polite, steer away from dangerous subjects and do the superb job they knew she could do.

"I thought Yaya was playing when she told me you were gonna be doing my makeup." Geneva half-smiled.

"It's nice to see you again too, Geneva. No, Yaya was serious, and here I am," Camille replied. "I know you're on a tight schedule, so I'm ready when you are."

Geneva took a seat and Camille put a cape over her. She hit the pause button on her iPod and Tamia's "Almost" began playing. Yaya told her to pick something that would be upbeat, yet soothing to work with, so Tamia seemed like the perfect choice.

"Would you like some water before we begin?" Camille asked.

Geneva looked over at the bottled water and glasses, which were laying out for her "There's no crushed ice?"

"No, unfortunately not," Camille answered.

"Then, I don't think so." Geneva removed her sunglasses and lay back. Camille took a deep breath and began to work. She tried to remember each and every thing Taryn and Yaya had taught her about technique, color, blending, textures, and creativity. More importantly, she remembered to have fun with it.

"How long have you been doing this?" Geneva asked.

"For a while," Camille answered.

"You look as if you're barely out of high school, you can't have been doing it that long," Geneva responded.

"I did faces while I was in school," Camille lied.

Luckily, Geneva's attention turned to her personal assistant and they began chatting up a storm. When Camille was done, she stood back and looked at Geneva's finished face. *Damn, I'm really good.* She couldn't help smiling. *I actually made this chick pretty!*

"You done?" Geneva looked up at her and asked.

"Yes." Camille swiveled the chair around so Geneva could see her reflection. She held her breath and waited for her reaction. *Please let her like it, and if she doesn't, just don't let her say anything that'll make me punch her in her face so hard I knock that makeup off her face.*

"Wow, I'm impressed." Geneva nodded and posed in the mirror.

"It looks nice," her personal assistant told her.

"Great job," her sister agreed.

Terrance walked in and spoke. "Hi, Ms. Johnson, I'm Terrance Oxford. I'll be doing your interview this afternoon. I just wanted to say hello before we begin."

A wide grin spread across Geneva's face and she stood up. "Well, that was nice of you, Mr. Oxford."

"Well, I'll see you in the studio. We'll be ready in five minutes," he said, smiling.

"I'm looking forward to it," Geneva responded.

"I can touch you up while their doing the mike checks." Camille remained professional.

"Who is that you're listening to?" Geneva pointed to the iPod.

"Tamia." Camille removed the cape from round her neck.

"Nice." Geneva looked in the mirror again and said, "Not bad. Not bad for a *rookie* at all. Let's go. Terrance Oxford is cute and I'm looking good."

"Wait," Camille said, reaching into the bag and grabbing her digital camera. She took several shots of Geneva and then said, "You're good."

"Baby, I'm great." Geneva winked and walked away.

Thank God that's over. Camille picked up the few items she would need to touch Geneva up.

"Pssst, how do I look?" Terrance whispered, standing in the doorway.

She shook her head at him. "You look fine. Wait." She

grabbed a MAC compact and sponge and began to lightly apply it on his face.

"Wait, what are you doing?" He frowned. "I don't need makeup."

"I'm just covering the blemishes and getting the shine off. What you need is a facial," she told him.

"I gotta go, Cam! Come on, I just need you to fix my tie." He rushed her.

She adjusted the silk material and fixed the handkerchief in his pocket. "There."

"Wish me luck," he said, grinning.

"You don't need luck when you have God," she said, smiling.

"Great job," Mr. Hardy said, walking into the dressing room. Camille was packing up.

"Yeah, Terrance was really good. He actually made Geneva likable and funny." Camille nodded.

"I was talking about the job you did."

Camille was stunned. "The job I did?"

"I've been in the TV business for years. I started as a gofer and worked my way up and I know a great makeup artist when I see one. You didn't have the cleanest sheet of paper to paint on, if you know what I mean and you damn near created a masterpiece," he said, matter-of-factly. "We could use someone like you on our staff, even if it's on an on-call basis. Do you have a card?"

Camille quickly handed him a business card. She couldn't believe this was happening. Never in a million years did she expect to be offered another job.

"I'll be calling you, Camille. You're young, vibrant, pretty, talented, and you're going places. I admire that," Mr. Hardy said.

"Thank you, Mr. Hardy," she told him. She couldn't wait to call Paige, Yaya, and Taryn and share her great news.

"You are the bomb!" Terrance came in, swooping her into his arms.

"Stop playing," she said when he put her down. "I'm so proud of you. You were terrific."

"No, you did an awesome job. You weren't lying when you said you had skills," he said. "Camille, I truly owe you big-time. Mr. Hardy thought the interview went so well that he wants to increase my airtime."

"Well, he offered me a job too, so I think we're even." She beamed with pride.

"What? That's incredible." He picked her up and swung her around again.

"Put me down, Terrance," she said.

"We're celebrating tonight. Go home and get even more beautiful than you already are; if that's possible." He placed her down and stared into her eyes. "I can't believe how incredible this day has been. You are truly a blessing."

"Terrance, I didn't do anything." She turned to look away but he pulled her chin up, leaning down and kissing her. She became lost in the experience of his taste once more. She loved his taste, his touch, and she wanted more.

Chapter 20

"What do you mean, Celeste is missing?" Taryn put her hand on her hip. Yaya knew the familiar pose meant her best friend was about to go postal.

"We went to serve her with the restraining order Friday morning. They said she wasn't home. We tried again Friday evening and same thing. I get a call a little while ago from a friend of mine at the police station saying her mother was trying to file a missing person's report. No one has seen or heard from her since Thursday," Jimmy informed them. "Have she tried to contact you at all?"

"No, I haven't seen or heard from her since that day at the salon," Taryn replied.

"What about you, Yaya?" he turned and asked.

"Hell no," Yaya snapped. "She knows better than to try and call me. I don't have anything to say to her."

"It's only been two days. She's probably laid up somewhere with somebody else's man," Taryn told him. "She's been known to do that."

"Well, do you know if Lincoln has had any type of contact with her?" Jimmy questioned.

"No, he hasn't," Taryn answered quickly. "I don't understand why her being missing is even a big deal."

"If she's as psychotic as you all say she is, the fact that she may be plotting to hurt you is the big deal," he responded. "We're talking about a woman who has already gone through great lengths to harm you already."

"The chick is crazy, Taryn," Yaya agreed. "We know that for a fact."

"So, now what are we supposed to do?" Taryn stared at Jimmy, waiting for his answer.

"Be careful, for now. That's all we can do. Be mindful of where you are and your surroundings. If she tries to call or shows up, call the police immediately. I got some buddies on the force and I already talked to them about keeping watch out on you for me," Jimmy said gently. There was something curious about the way he and Taryn were interacting, Yaya noticed.

"I don't need security, Jimmy." Taryn sat down on her sofa and gulped down her wine. "I'm a big girl. I can take care of myself."

"It's just a precaution, just in case Celeste tries anything." He took a seat beside her. Yaya could see Taryn's stress level rising.

"Jimmy, can I get you something to drink?" Yaya offered, going to refill her and Taryn's glass.

"No, I'm good," he told her. "Hey, why don't you camp out at Yaya's until we figure out what's going on with this girl."

"That's not a bad idea," Yaya called from the kitchen as she filled their cups.

"I'm not letting that crazy-ass girl run me away from my own house. Are y'all crazy?" Taryn yelled.

"Calm down, T," Yaya told her, passing her the now full glass. "Take a sip."

"I'm not going anywhere."

Jimmy put his arm around Taryn. "You don't have to leave if you don't want to. Just promise me you'll be careful."

"I promise." Taryn forced a smile. Yaya blinked to make sure she wasn't imagining things. If she didn't know any better, she would've sworn there was something going on between the two.

The door opened, and they all jumped. Lincoln walked in with the food bags. Taryn hopped up to help him. "Hey, baby, that was fast."

"They weren't that crowded, plus I called the order in while I was on the way so they could have it ready when I got there," Lincoln said, his eyes glued to Jimmy.

"You remember, Jimmy, our attorney," Taryn quickly told him.

"Yeah, what's going on, man?" Lincoln placed the bags on the breakfast bar.

"Hey, Lincoln." Jimmy stood up. "I gotta get outta here. Keep your phone on at all times. I'll be calling periodically to check on both of you to make sure you're okay."

"Yes, sir," Yaya said, saluting him.

"Is anyone gonna tell me what's going on?" Lincoln folded his arms and waited for someone to answer.

"Celeste has conveniently disappeared. No one has seen or heard from her since Thursday," Taryn said, sighing.

"She hasn't tried to contact you, has she?" Jimmy asked Lincoln. "Have you talked to her?"

"What the hell is that supposed to mean?" Lincoln snapped. "Why the hell would I talk to her?"

Yaya interrupted before the two men squared off. "Because she's been harassing all of us, that's the only reason he's asking, Lincoln."

"Then there's the fact that she's supposedly carrying your baby. Call me if you hear anything," Jimmy said, closing the door behind him.

"That fool was about to get punched dead in his lip," Lincoln said after he was gone. "How he gonna try and carry me like that? Have I talked to her?"

"He's just doing his job, Lincoln. He's trying to protect Taryn." Yaya tried to ease the tension.

"I guess that's why his ass was at the salon with her ass till almost ten o'clock the other night, huh? Protecting her." Lincoln stormed down the hallway.

Yaya thought she could see steam coming from the top of Taryn's head. She started to say something, but Taryn held her hand up and told her, "Don't!"

Without saying another word, Yaya went into Taryn's guest bedroom, grabbed a pair of shorts and a T-shirt out of the drawer and changed into them. The best friends kept a set of clothes at each other's houses just in case. She still hadn't heard from Fitz, and she was pissed. She decided to just make herself a plate, try to eat without throwing up, watch a little TV, and maybe take a nap on Taryn's chaise lounge. She dabbled a bit of macaroni and cheese, cabbage and peas and rice on a saucer, picked up her glass of wine and settled on the large comfy chair. She picked up the remote to the forty-two-inch flat screen TV and turned to Lifetime.

"It's not how it looks," Taryn finally said.

"I didn't say anything, T." Yaya picked at her food. She knew Taryn better than anyone; and she knew that one thing Taryn did not do was mess around with married men, no matter how fine, successful, and attractive they were. Taryn believed marriage was a sacred covenant with God and one thing she was not going to do was disrespect the man upstairs.

"Jimmy came by the salon because I called and told him I wanted to take a restraining order out on Celeste. We talked for a little while and he left. That's it," Taryn advised her.

"T, you don't need to be telling me this. You need to be going back there with your man and explaining it all to him."

"I will," Taryn replied. "I just need for you to know that there's—"

"Taryn, we've been best friends for over ten years. I know there's nothing going on between you and Jimmy. You don't have to tell me." Yaya smiled at her. "There's no way you would be creeping with him and not tell me if it was good or not."

"You are really a sick individual, Qianna Westbrooke," Taryn said, laughing.

"You better go talk to your man," Yaya teased. "He's the one that's looking sick right about now."

Yaya had just fallen asleep when she thought she heard Fitz's voice. She opened her eyes and glanced up and saw that he was standing in the living room talking to Lincoln. *Damn, how long have I been asleep? It's almost dark.*

"Hey, you." Fitz walked over and kissed her gently on the forehead.

She rolled her eyes at him, as she snuggled under the comfy blanket she kept specifically at Taryn's house. *I hope he is not about to try and act like he didn't just abandon me at the church and everything is all good.*

"I thought you were out for the night," Taryn said.

"What time is it?" Yaya asked, still groggy.

"Almost eight. You must be tired, Ya. You were sleeping hard," Taryn told her. "Why didn't you go get in the bed?"

"I can take you home." Fitz sat on the end of the chair beside her. He looked nice in his black suit. His dreads were pulled back into a ponytail and hung down his back. There was something different about him. Something small, but different and she tried to figure out what it was. He seemed sort of reserved in some type of way.

"Here." Taryn passed her a glass of ice water and she sipped it. Her throat was dry and the water was soothing as she swallowed.

"Thanks, T." She passed her the now empty glass.

"You don't look good. Yaya." Taryn put her palm against Yaya's forehead.

Yaya felt terrible. *I knew I shouldn't have tried to eat that food*, she thought as she sat up. Her head was pounding and she felt dizzy. There was no doubt; the moment she stood up, she would be vomiting her insides out.

"Put your shoes on, baby. Let me get you home so you can go to bed." Fitz reached to help her up.

"I'm fine." She pushed his hand away. *Get it together and make it to the bathroom*, she tried to will herself into feeling better. Closing her eyes and inhaling deeply, she eased her body off the chair. Fitz grabbed her blanket off the floor. "T, can you grab my purse for me so I can get my medicine?"

"Sure," Taryn told her, passing the bag.

"Thanks," Yaya said, taking it with her into the bathroom. Once inside, she locked the door and turned the faucet on, hoping it would drown out the sound of her throwing up. Pain radiated through her stomach as she heaved into the commode. She flushed the toilet and rambled through her purse for the Aciphex antacid prescription she had just re-filled. She popped three tablets into her mouth, rather than the two she was supposed to take, praying that it would bring her some relief. She rinsed her mouth out with the small bot-tle of mouthwash she now carried with her, washed her face and walked out.

"You a'ight?" Lincoln put his hand on her shoulder.

"Yeah," Yaya told him.

"I guess Moscato and Ochie's don't mix, huh?" He laughed.

"Anything goes with Moscato," Taryn corrected him.

"What's Moscato?" Fitz asked.

"Some bourgeois wine Taryn buys all the time. They killed a whole bottle this afternoon when we got here, but she got like a case in her pantry." Lincoln shook his head.

"What are you doing snooping in my pantry?" Taryn in-quired.

"Looking for cereal, which you don't have," he said, laughing. "No cereal, no beer, but she got plenty of Moscato."

"That shows where her priorities are," Fitz added.

"And where her money goes," Lincoln joked.

"No, I use your money to buy my wine," Taryn told him.

"Well, it's getting late." Fitz turned to Yaya. "You ready to go?"

"Yeah, let me get my clothes," she told him

Lincoln asked, "How's Micha?"

"She's holding up as well as can be expected. That's why I gotta hurry up and get outta here. I promised her I would stay there tonight because Carver's been having nightmares," Fitz explained. "He's taking Kareem's death kinda hard."

Yaya shook her head in disbelief. "You know what. Now that I think about it. I'm just gonna stay here tonight. You can go ahead."

"Come on, Yaya, don't be like that," Fitz told her.

"Don't be like what, Fitz? You want me to act like I don't feel like an afterthought in your life right now?" Yaya snapped.

"You shouldn't feel that way at all. How you gonna get mad at me because I'm trying to be there for my son when he needs me?"

"Your son or your son's mother? Because that's who you were running after at the church." Yaya was breathing so hard, she could see her chest rising and falling as she breathed.

"That's so selfish of you." Fitz frowned. "Now, all of a sudden because I can't spend time with you when *you* want me to, I'm treating you like an *afterthought*. It's always about YOU, huh, Yaya? The funny thing is, you're the one who's been treating me like an *afterthought* for months now. You'll find time for me *after* you're done working at the salon, *after* you've been on a world tour with Geneva Johnson, *after* you're done hanging with your girls."

"Whoa, I think y'all need to chill out before someone says something they'll regret." Lincoln walked over to his brother.

"Why don't you hang out here with Yaya for a while before you leave."

"I don't need for him to hang out with me." Yaya rolled her eyes then turned and told Taryn, "I'm gone to bed."

I can't stand him, she thought as she sat on the side of the bed. *I can't believe he called me selfish. This was the first relationship that I ever had where I didn't go into it expecting anything in return except to be loved. That's what I get for lowering my damn standards. And he has the nerve to call me selfish. If I was selfish, I wouldn't have dated his broke, baby mama drama having, UPS truck driving, raggedy Honda Accord station wagon, nappy dread, lazy in bed, seven-minute ass.* She was so hot that she could feel beads of sweat forming on her forehead.

"You okay?" Taryn walked in and asked.

"Is he gone?"

"Yeah, he left." Taryn nodded. "I don't know what to say. But, you can't be mad at him for being there for his son, Yaya."

"I don't have a problem with him being there for his son, T. I swear I don't. But if it's all about Carver, and that's it, why can't Carver spend the night at his dad's house? He has his own room there too," she pointed out. She looked down at the bed and recalling Taryn's detailed account about her and Lincoln, asked her, "You did wash these sheets, right?"

Chapter 21

To Camille's surprise, there were several cars parked outside of the town house when she got home after leaving the television studio. She felt like she was floating on air. The afternoon had gone perfect and she was excited with anticipation of what Terrance had in store for the rest of the evening. She recognized the Mercedes-Benz that belonged to Meeko, Paige's cousin and there was also Paige's mother, Darling's car. *I wonder what's going on?*

"Aunt Cam's home!" she heard Myla yell when she walked in.

"Hey Camille, we're in here," Paige called from the den. Camille strolled in to see Paige, Meeko, Darling, and Nina, Paige's best friend, sitting.

"Hey everyone," she spoke and gave everyone a hug.

"How did it go?" Paige asked. "I told them you had your first celebrity client today."

"It was perfect!" Camille gushed about everything that happened. "The station manager asked for my card and says he wants to hire me."

"That's wonderful, Camille," Darling said, grinning.

"So, what's going on?" Camille sat down. "Or is this a surprise party to celebrate my first gig?"

"I wish," Paige told her. "We can always order food and turn it into that."

"I'm just kidding," Camille said, laughing.

"Cam, has Celeste called or been to the salon lately?" Paige's voice turned serious.

Camille looked at her, shaking her head. "Not since that day she came in clowning about her STDs."

"You haven't heard anything from her since that day?" Darling asked.

"No, not at all." Camille shrugged. "I know Taryn was talking about taking a restraining order out on her. So maybe that's why she's been keeping her distance."

"She never got the restraining order," Meeko told her. "She's been missing since Thursday night."

"Missing?" Camille laughed. "Who misses her?"

Paige tried not to laugh, but a giggle escaped. "That's not funny, Cam. Her mother misses her, I guess. That's who's filing the missing person's report. She swears someone at the salon has killed Celeste or something because Celeste is suing them."

"That's ridiculous. I know plenty of people who have better reasons than that to kill her, including you," Camille slipped and said before she could stop herself. "I mean, my bad."

It was Nina and Meeko who couldn't stop laughing this time.

"That's not funny," Darling scolded them.

"That was a good one, Darling," Nina said. "And it's true."

"This is probably just Celeste's way of getting everyone's attention, again," Paige said, sighing.

"Well, let me go call Terrance and cancel our plans. Celeste is always messing something up." Camille stood up.

"Don't cancel your plans, Camille. You deserve to cele-

brate your accomplishments. You go and have a good time."
Darling stood and gave her a hug. "We're proud of you."

"Thanks, Darling." Camille felt the tears swelling in her
eyes and tried to blink them away. It was a shame that Darling had more love and respect for her than her own mother
did.

"But if you hear anything from Celeste or anyone says anything about her, you let us know, okay?" Darling wiped her
own tears away. "I know she's a troublemaker and has made a
lot of enemies in her life, but she's still my sister's child and I
have an obligation of sorts. And they say Celeste is claiming
to be pregnant too."

"I understand." Camille nodded and went to get ready. She
really could care less if Celeste was missing, kidnapped or
otherwise indisposed. It was the last thing she would be
thinking about tonight.

"Can I ask you a question?" Camille said as they walked up
the steps to Terrance's apartment. He had taken her to the
Melting Pot, a fondue restaurant that she had wanted to go to
for months. The dimly lit, secluded table provided the perfect romantic setting and the food was awesome. They decided to take their dessert back to his place and eat it while
watching movies.

"Anything," he said, smiling.

"How many relationships have you had?"

He seemed caught off-guard by her question, but told her,
"Two. One in high school and one after college."

"After college? That was kinda recent." She waited as he
unlocked the door.

"It's been a minute ago," he said, holding the door open for
her.

"Do you all still talk?"

"Huh?"

She placed her purse on the coffee table and took off her shoes. "Is talking about this making you uncomfortable? I thought journalists were supposed to be the most open people in the world."

"I don't have a problem talking about it. I'm just wondering why you wanna talk about it tonight, that's all. This is a celebration."

"Why not talk about it tonight. And this is a celebration. But I still wanna know. So, do you still talk to your ex?"

He paused and then said, "No, I don't talk to her. It wasn't a pleasant breakup. I'm the last person in the world she wants to talk to."

"You broke her heart? What did you do? Cheat?" Camille asked, opening the Styrofoam boxes that held thick slices of strawberry shortcake topped with whipped cream. She reached into the cabinet and got two saucers to put them on.

"What makes you think I did something?" He frowned, picking a strawberry off the top of the cake and popping it into his mouth.

"You said she doesn't wanna talk to you. What happened?"

Terrance slowly chewed and swallowed, then said, "Fine, you asked. I dated a girl for about two years, things were going great, she moved in, we even talked about marriage, kids, the whole nine."

"Sounds like a love story to me," Camille said, shrugging. He picked another strawberry and placed it into her mouth. They went into his living room and sat across from each other on the sofa.

"I'm not done. One night, we get a little inebriated and hmmm, how should I put this? Let's just say I was pleasuring her orally when in a fit of passion, she yells out *'You gotta stop! If Tuff finds out, he'll kill me!'* You can imagine how quickly I sobered up."

"Come on, she was drunk. I can see if she called out someone else's name, but it was *yours*." Camille tried not to laugh.

"A drunken man always speaks a sober mind, don't ever forget that. If I'm the one that's going down on her, why would I be the one who'd kill her if I found out? Either way it goes; that shit wasn't right."

"So, let me get this straight, you broke up with her because she called *your* name out during sex." A giggle slipped from Camille.

"Oral sex," he corrected her. "Anyway, I knew something was up and she was cheating. I became suspicious and tried to find out who she was tipping with. But that I-spy crap was making me crazy. There was no way I was gonna become one of those dudes who hide in the bushes at the mall, waiting for his girl to walk by and jump out. Instead, I just confronted her. I asked her to be honest and 'fess up about the guy she was seeing."

"And she did?"

"No, she told me I was wrong and she wasn't seeing a guy," he said, shrugging.

"You accused her of cheating and she wasn't?"

"No, she wasn't seeing a guy, it was a girl. She was still trying to explore her sexual identity. I wasn't willing to deal with that. She was pissed, but it was over."

"Damn." Camille sat back and stared.

"So, how many relationships have you been in?" he asked. "I've divulged all the embarrassing secrets of my past, it's time for you to do the same."

"Other than my alcoholic mother and horse of a sister-in-law, which you already know about, I don't have anything else embarrassing to share," she said, chuckling.

"No crazy ex-boyfriends?"

"Nope."

"No wild sexual escapades?" he teased.

"No sexual escapades. Those are kinda hard to have without a boyfriend. Yours truly is still pure," she confessed.

"How? Why?" He seemed confused by her confession.

"Paige taught me a long time ago that my virginity is price-less and something I should save until I met the right per-son," she told him.

"And that's never happened?"

"Not until now." Her eyes met his. He didn't say anything, but she could see the desire in his eyes. She put her cake down as she leaned over and covered her mouth with his, sucking his bottom lip. He cupped her face with his hands and she straddled him. In one quick motion his arms encir-cled her and he stood up, still holding her, and carried her into his bedroom. He placed her on the bed and she yanked his shirt from his pants and unbuttoned it as her hands ca-ressed his chiseled chest. He groaned as her fingertips rubbed his nipples and lay her on her back. His tongue was hot as he licked along her neck and down her collarbone as he slipped her dress over her head.

"You are so beautiful," he whispered as he stared at her body. He diligently removed the camisole she wore and ca-ressed her as he slipped her lace panties and stockings off. Once she was completely nude, he began kissing her, his lips leaving a warm trail from the top of her head, to the soles of her feet. She felt like she couldn't take it any more when he licked the insides of her ankles and began making his way back up her body. Camille reached her hand between his legs and placed the massive hardness in her hands. His nudity took her by surprise because she couldn't recall him stopping long enough to take his clothes off. For a second, she began to panic at his size. It won't fit. It's gonna be too big. She tried to think of what to do but was distracted by the pleasure of his tongue exploring the wetness of her center.

"Camille." Terrance kissed her again. "Are you sure about this?"

Camille could feel her legs shaking. She bit her own lip nervously, and told him, "Yes."

After putting on a condom, he gently placed himself between her legs and she gasped as he entered her. The pierc-
ing pain she felt was soon replaced by immense pleasure as
he slipped in and out of her hot moistness. Camille felt as if
she was climbing a mountain, going higher and higher, faster
and faster as her body met his with each stroke.

"Terrance," she moaned as she felt herself on the verge of
erupting. She knew from the novels she read and the talk
she'd heard over the years that this had to be what an orgasm
felt like.

"Cam," he groaned, moving faster and harder, beads of
sweat forming on his head. "You ready, baby?"

"Yes," she screamed and dug her nails into his shoulders.
She felt his body tense as he climaxed with her. His sweaty
body fell beside her and she panted as she tried to catch her
breath. "Damn, that was amazing."

"Damn, right." He smiled and kissed her.

*I finally did it. I did it. I'm no longer a virgin. It was the
right time and with the right person.* She couldn't have imag-
ined it being any better.

"Thank you," she told him.

"Cam," he said in the darkness. "I don't want you to have
any regrets about this."

"Now, why would I do that?" she rolled over on her stomach and asked. "It was perfect."

"I mean, it's just that . . ." he started.

"Terrance, I'm starting to feel like you're gonna be the one
to regret this," she said, frowning. "Was it bad? Do I suck in
bed?"

"Baby, no." He pulled her close to him. "It was great and
satisfying."

"You make it sound like beer." Her eyes widened. "Was it
less filling too?"

"Well, it did taste great," he said, laughing.

"Unbelievable." She pouted.

"No, I'm just kidding." He kissed her forehead. "It was magical."

"Will you stop playing and tell me."

"I'm being serious, Cam." His fingers ran through her hair. "It was truly magical."

Chapter 22

"Is there something you need to get off your chest?" Taryn asked Lincoln as she got ready for bed. He was sitting on the side of the bed, staring blankly at the television. He hadn't really said anything to her all evening. She hated tension and was determined to figure out what was going on with him.

"No, is there something you need to tell me?" he asked.

"If I had something to tell you, I would." she blinked. "Is there something you think I should tell you?"

"Taryn, I hate playing games as much as you do. If you wanna go ahead and do your thing, then I understand."

"What the hell are you talking about, Lincoln?"

"You and your lawyer. It's obvious he has a thing for you."

Taryn shook her head in amazement. "What? Please don't go there."

"I'm just saying. If you want to explore your options, I'm cool with that."

"Lincoln, please. If I didn't know any better, I would think you were jealous. First of all, Jimmy is married and even if I was interested in him, I have more self-respect than to deal

with a married man. Second, I had options just like you before we got into this relationship. But, it's you I want to be
with. If I didn't know any better, I would think you were jealous." She walked over and put her arms around his neck. He
looked up into her eyes and she smiled.

"No, I'm not jealous at all. It's just that sometimes, I think that
you deserve better than what I give. I mean, I don't know . . .
you're beautiful, successful, and intelligent and further down
the line, I don't want you to look back and think that you settled.
I got this chick lying about being pregnant by me and all these
other issues—"

"Lincoln, stop it. I know you're not flawless. I don't expect
you to be. You don't think I have issues of my own? I'm not
with you because you're perfect, I'm with you because I love
you, issues and all." She kissed him. As the words came from
her mouth, she realized how true they were. She had fallen in
love with Lincoln and was willing to deal with whatever issues
that came with him.

Something was wrong. Taryn's eyes flew open and she
shifted under the covers. Lincoln stirred beside her. She sat
up and saw that it was a little after four in the morning. She
didn't know what it was, but she had an eerie feeling.

"What's wrong, baby?" Lincoln murmured, rubbing her
thigh.

"I don't know. I feel weird," she whispered.

"Oh, really?" He snickered and his hand started traveling
further up her leg.

"Not like that, stupid." She swatted his hand away. "I'm
going to check on Yaya."

"She's probably asleep," he said, turning over.

Taryn slipped her feet into her slippers and wrapped her
robe around her. She was barely able to see in the dark hallway. She peeked into the guest bedroom, but the bed was
empty.

She noticed a light coming from under the bathroom door and knocked. "Yaya, are you in there?"

There was no answer and the door was locked. She could hear water running in the sink. She rattled the door, trying with all her might to get the lock to pop and open the door. God, please let me get in here, she prayed. She used both hands and turned the knob, forcing it to rotate with both her palms. The door opened with a pop. She found Yaya laying topless on the cold bathroom floor, her body in the fetal position. A horrible stench filled her nose and she almost gagged when she looked at the commode of what looked like thick, green pus.

"YAYA! YAYA!" Taryn screamed. She fell to Yaya's side and lifted her head. Her body was burning up and she was barely conscious.

"What the hell is wrong?" Lincoln came rushing in.

"I don't know." Taryn began crying uncontrollably. "I found her in here like this. Yaya, please, wake up. Lincoln, call the ambulance!"

"Fuck that!" Lincoln picked Yaya up off the floor. "Grab her some clothes. We'll get there faster than they can get here!"

Lincoln went into straight superhero mode. He wasted no time wrapping Yaya in a blanket and carrying her out to his SUV. Taryn pulled on a pair of sweats and grabbed Yaya's purse and phone and rushed out the house behind him. She jumped in the backseat, cradling Yaya's head in her lap as she called Quincy while they were en route. He told her he would meet them at the hospital.

"Yaya, baby, please be all right." She stroked her fevered face. Yaya began shivering and convulsing as she vomited more of the thick green stuff. Taryn began to panic even more. "Lincoln, she's dying! You gotta hurry up!"

"Awww, hell, I just got my seats shampooed," he moaned as he drove even faster. "Reach in that bag in the back and it should be a towel."

"I'm not thinking 'bout your damn seats!" Taryn screamed.

"I'm talking about for her mouth so she don't choke on that shit that's coming out her mouth instead of her ass!" he yelled back. "Get the damn towel!"

Taryn turned around and fumbled in the bag. There was a toothbrush, toothpaste, mouthwash, cologne, breath spray. *What the hell?* Finally, she found a towel and wiped Yaya's mouth. Within minutes, they were pulling up to the emergency room. Lincoln jumped out and ran to the door, once again grabbing Yaya and running inside. The doctors and nurses quickly grabbed Yaya and placed her on a gurney and whisked her to the back. *Lord, please let her be okay. She's my best friend and I can't lose her.*

"She can't die." Taryn shook her head and cried.

Lincoln hugged her tight. "She's not gonna die, baby. She's gonna be fine. I'm just glad you woke up when you did."

"Sir, is that your black Expedition by the door?" a nurse came and asked.

"Yeah," Lincoln said, nodding.

"We need for you to move it. It's parked in the ambulance bay," she said, smiling.

"No problem," Lincoln said. "Baby, I'ma be right back."

"Go ahead." Taryn sniffed and wiped her eyes. She turned to the nurse and asked, "Is she gonna be all right?"

"We're doing everything in our power to make sure she is," the nurse replied. "Are you her sister?"

"Her best friend," Taryn said.

"Is there a next of kin?" the nurse asked.

"Why? Is she dying? What's wrong?" Taryn's heart began pounding.

"No, we need these forms filled out, that's all," the nurse assured her.

"Her brother is on his way, but I'm sure I know more of her personal information than he does," Taryn told her.

"Taryn, where is she?" Quincy came running in. Paige was right behind him.

"They took her to the back." Taryn broke down again. "Q, it was horrible."

"It's okay, Taryn." Paige hugged her.

"Are you her brother?" the nurse asked Quincy.

"Yeah, can you tell me what's wrong with my sister?" Quincy demanded.

"The doctors are working on her right now. They're gonna run a series of tests and it'll be just a little while," she said. "In the meantime, you can help by filling these forms out."

Quincy took the forms and looked at them. "I don't know any of this stuff," he said sadly.

"That's what she said." The nurse took the forms and passed them to Taryn. "You can bring them to the desk when you finish. In the meantime, you all can wait in the room right over there."

They walked down the hall to the waiting room she directed them to. There were several people already seated inside. Some were watching the two small televisions hanging in the corners, other were nodding. The three of them sat in a set of empty seats against the far wall of the room. Taryn told them how she found Yaya in the bathroom and how quickly Lincoln took over the situation.

"Man, parking sucks in this place," Lincoln said, walking in at that moment. "Hey Q."

"What's up, Lincoln. Man, thanks for being there." Quincy stood and they quickly shook hands and embraced. "This is my girlfriend, Paige."

"Nice to meet you." Paige hugged him as well.

"Have they said anything yet?" he asked, taking Taryn's hand.

"Not yet." She shook her head. "I can't believe I didn't see how sick she was."

"It's not your fault," Paige told her.

"Yes, it is. She's been throwing up for months; complaining about her stomach. We thought she was being overdramatic." Taryn began crying again.

"Come on, T, you can't blame yourself." Lincoln rubbed her shoulders. "You know Yaya is too much of a diva to give up now."

Taryn filled out the forms and got Yaya's insurance card out of her wallet. Her eyes fell on a picture that they had taken several years ago. They looked so young and they were ready to conquer the world. Over the years they had fought, partied, traveled, laughed, cried, worked, vacationed, stopped speaking, made up, been sick, gotten well, and shared their dreams. *We need to take a new picture*, she thought, smiling at their big hair and even bigger gold earrings.

The sun was shining bright when they finally heard Qianna's name being called. They all walked over where a doctor was waiting to talk with them. Taryn's heart pounded and she held onto Lincoln's hand for dear life.

"Is she all right? What's going on?" Quincy asked. "I'm her brother."

"She's gonna be fine. We're prepping her for surgery now," the doctor advised them.

"Surgery? For what?" Quincy's voice got louder. Paige touched his shoulder and whispered something in his ear.

"We're going to have to remove her gall bladder. It's stopped functioning. That's why she's been having the stomach pains and constant vomiting. Her body hasn't been able to digest her food," he explained.

"Her gall bladder." Quincy seemed relieved.

"Thank God," Paige said.

"That really was crap coming outta her mouth." Lincoln frowned his face up.

"Can we see her?" Taryn asked.

"A couple of you can go back for a few minutes. She's

pretty doped up, but she's conscious," the doctor said. "The surgery should only take an hour."

"You two go ahead," Paige said. "Lincoln and I will go and get everyone some coffee."

"Yeah, that's a good idea," Lincoln said and gave Taryn a kiss. "Tell Yaya I'ma send her the detailing bill for my truck."

"I will." Taryn smiled. She and Quincy followed the doctor to the room where they found Yaya sleeping. An IV was in her arm and she was hooked up to a beeping monitor.

"Ya." Quincy touched his sister's forehead. She stirred under his touch and her eyes slowly opened. She looked like a little girl.

"It's us, sweetie." Taryn tried to smile as she wiped away the tears from her eyes.

"They say I gotta have surgery." Yaya's voice was weak.

"I know. They're taking out your gall bladder," Quincy said, nodding.

"Don't worry, it's all laparoscopic, girl. No scar," Taryn said, winking.

"My girl." Yaya held out her fist and Taryn gave her a pound.

"You two have got to be the vainest women of all time." Quincy shook his head.

"Hey, T, check this out." Yaya gestured at the hanging IV bag. "They gave me good drugs. A morphine drip, and all I have to do is push this button and it gives me more."

"Save some for me," Taryn leaned and whispered loudly.

"I got you." Yaya nodded.

"Well, Ms. Westbrooke, we need to get you upstairs," the doctor came in and announced. An orderly and a nurse began unhooking Yaya from the machine.

"Well, that's my cue," Yaya said, sighing. "T, do I need a touch-up? Dr. York here is married, but the anesthesiologist may be cute. You never know."

"You're good, Yaya. Your lashes are still hanging on from last month." Taryn reached and squeezed her hand.

"You know you always do the bomb lashes," Yaya told her. "That's why I keep you as my best friend."

"You two need to stop." Quincy was stunned at their friendly banter.

"Come on, Q, lighten up. Laughter is the best medicine. Right, Dr. York?" Yaya had a goofy grin on her face and Taryn knew the morphine was working well.

"That's right." Dr. York nodded. "We'll let you know when she's in recovery."

They began wheeling her out the room.

"I love you, Yaya," Quincy said, kissing his sister.

"I love you too Q; and you too T! Q and T! QT! My cuties," Yaya began to sing.

Quincy hugged Taryn close to him. "My sister is officially insane."

Paige and Lincoln were waiting with steaming cups of coffee when they got back. She was surprised that Fitz had yet to show up. Lincoln said he called him when he was parking the truck.

"How is she?" Paige asked.

"She's fine." Quincy took the coffee from her. "High, but fine."

"They gave her a morphine drip and she's a bit excited about it," Taryn added.

"Did you give her my message?" Lincoln smiled.

"No, and even if I did, she probably wouldn't have remembered, baby."

"Thanks, Paige." Taryn took the cup Paige was giving her. "Where's Ms. Myla?"

"She spent the night with my best friend Nina and her daughter, Jade," Paige answered. "I'm kinda glad I let her go because she was supposed to be under punishment. See how things work out."

"I guess it's back to waiting." Quincy sat down.

"I'm gonna run by her house and grab a few things so she'll have them when they put her in a room," Taryn told him.

"That's a good idea," Paige agreed. "You want me to go help?"

"I think we got it," Taryn said. "Thanks for being here, Paige. I know Yaya appreciates it."

"Please, she's family. Why wouldn't I be here?" Paige gave her a warm smile. Then she reached into her purse and tossed Lincoln her keys. "You guys go ahead and take my car. I got a feeling Lincoln probably needs to air his out before driving it this morning."

"Good call." Lincoln grinned. "I'm going to let my windows down right now."

"I like her," Taryn said as they scanned the parking lot for Paige's champagne-colored Benz.

"Yeah, she's cool."

"There it is," she said, pointing, and walked over to the car. Lincoln unlocked the doors and they got inside.

"Ahhhh, new car smell," he said, winking as he adjusted the seats and mirrors.

Looking at her watch and seeing that it was now after nine, she asked Lincoln, "Have you talked to Fitz?"

"Oh, yeah. Micha and Carver had a rough night, so he was up kinda late, but he said he would be here as soon as he got them settled," Lincoln said. She could tell he was really trying to cover for his brother, but he wasn't helping at all.

"Yeah, if he does show up, I'll let him know that Yaya had a rough night too. She spent most of it on the bathroom floor." Taryn rolled her eyes.

"Come on, T, I know you're mad, and you have a right to

be. But you said yourself that you didn't even realize Yaya was that sick." Lincoln glanced at her.

"That's bullshit, and you know it, Lincoln," she told him. "His ass should be here and you know it. And there's nothing you can say to change the fact that Yaya is in surgery and he still hasn't called to check on her, let alone showed up."

Chapter 23

I'm alive, was the first thought Yaya had when she felt herself waking up. She could tell by the faint smell of disinfectant, distant beeping noise and the feel of the blood-pressure cuff on her arm that she was in the hospital. She was still afraid to breathe too hard, thinking that she would once again be overcome with the excruciating pain that engulfed her on Saturday night. Her eyes slowly blinked open and she looked around. Taryn was asleep in the chair near her bed. *My girl is always here for me.* When she woke up earlier she was in a busy recovery area; now she was in a private room, but had no recollection of them moving her.

"Well, I damn sure haven't died and gone to heaven if you're here," she strained to say loud enough where she could be heard.

Taryn's eyes fluttered open and she smiled. "You know theres no way your behind is going to heaven anyway. How you feeling?"

"Groggy as hell. Is it nighttime?" She glanced toward the window.

"No, crazy girl. It's only three. I pulled the shades so we could sleep better."

Good call." Yaya nodded. "You've been here this whole time?"

"Of course, where the hell else was I supposed to be? You know if this wasn't the first face you saw when you woke up, you woulda swore I was the worst friend in the world."

"You damn right about that," Yaya agreed. "Did they say how long I was gonna have to be in here?"

"I think a couple of days." Taryn stood up. "I guess I'll go let everyone know you're finally awake."

"Who's all here?" Yaya tried to sit up, but her body ached. She grimaced in pain.

"Keep still, Yaya. You just got outta surgery, you need to take it easy." Taryn adjusted her pillow so she could be more comfortable. "Your brother and Paige are here. Lincoln, who, by the way, says you owe him because he's gonna have to get his car detailed where you threw up. Monya and Camille are here too. Your family."

Yaya blinked and hesitated, wondering if Taryn was saving Fitz's name for last or if she had purposely not said it. *She know she doesn't have to say his name because I already know he has to be out waiting with everyone else.* She looked down to see that she was still dressed in the wretched green-and-white hospital gown. She caught Taryn just as she was about to walk out the door. "T, wait a sec."

"What'cha need?"

Realizing she must look a hot mess, she told her, "I hope you don't plan on bringing anyone back in here with you."

"Hell yeah. They've been waiting all morning. You think I'm just gonna run out there and tell them you said 'Hi' like you're sending shout-outs?" Taryn looked at her like she was crazy.

"T, don't play." She rubbed her hands against her unkempt hair. "I need to take a shower and curl my hair first."

"You really have issues, Yaya."

"I know you brought me some decent pajamas, Taryn. Where are they?"

Taryn glanced over at the suitcase she had packed with Yaya's things. "Ya, you know I got you covered. But right now, these folks don't give a damn how you look right now. They're just glad you're alive. I'll be right back."

Yaya raked her fingers over her hair once again, trying to make it lay down as best as possible. She moistened her lips and made sure there was no crust in her eyes. By the time Taryn returned with everyone, she had managed to prop herself up and arrange the sheet to where it covered most of the ugly gown.

"Hey there."

"Hey, girl."

"How are you feeling?"

They all wore big smiles and hugged her, everyone speaking at once.

"I'm a little achy and groggy, but I'm good," she told them. She tried to act as if she didn't even notice her boyfriend's absence and focus on the people that did care enough about her to be there. "I probably look worse than I feel."

"If that's the case, you must feel wonderful, because you're looking fierce as usual." Monya snapped her fingers in a diva fashion.

"Only my sister can make hospital gear look high fashion," Quincy told them.

"True divas make anything look better." Camille struck a model pose.

"Why are you so dressed up?" Yaya asked, noticing the fierce red-and-black dress Camille was wearing and black stiletto heels. Strangely enough, she didn't have on any stockings.

Camille looked guilty as hell and nervously answered, "We'll talk later."

"After we talk," Paige said, smugly.

"And see, you were worried about how you looked," Taryn said to Yaya. "I told you."

"Thanks," she told them. "I really appreciate you all."

"Ahem, sorry to interrupt, but we need to run a few more tests," the nurse came in and told them a few minutes later.

"That's our cue to leave," Lincoln said.

"I hear I owe you a detailing job," Yaya said, smiling.

"Don't worry, I won't give you the bill until you're released." He leaned over and gave her a kiss on the cheek. "I know you're good for it."

They all gave their good-byes and left, with the exception of Taryn. She began taking Yaya's pajamas and toiletries out of the bag. Yaya knew she was trying to avoid stating the obvious.

"I'll help you take a shower after you finish your tests," she said.

"Did he at least call?" Yaya asked right before the nurse stuck a thermometer in her mouth.

Taryn turned and faced her. "Yes, he called, Yaya. He's called several times. We told him your surgery went fine and you were resting. I'm supposed to call as soon as you wake up."

"Don't bother." Yaya shook her head. "If he was that concerned, he would've been right here when I woke up." She pushed the button on her morphine pump and closed her eyes, allowing the medicine to take her off into a deep slumber.

Taryn spent the night in Yaya's room. Every time Yaya woke up, her best friend was right there.

"When are you going home?" she asked Monday morning.

"When you go home," Taryn said, readjusting herself in the chair that was now her permanent spot.

"T, you don't have to do this. Girl, you need to go and get some rest, spend some time with your man . . ."

"Don't worry, I am. I just wanna make sure you're all right," Taryn told her.

"I'm fine. You hooked me up with a shower, brushed my teeth and combed my hair. And I've got my good ol' drip here." She smiled and raised her eyebrows up and down. "What more do I need?"

"How about a kiss to make it all better?"

They turned to see Fitz standing in the doorway carrying a bouquet of flowers.

"Hey, Fitz. Uh, I'm gonna run to the cafeteria and get me some coffee." Taryn stood up and folded her blanket that she brought from home. "Either of you want anything?"

"Nope," Yaya answered, and began flipping through the channels on the small television.

"No thanks," Fitz told her. He placed the flowers on the stand where there were already three other bouquets and a mass of balloons. "Wow, seems like a lot of people want you to get well soon. Someone must be popular."

"Not popular enough," Yaya said without looking at him. *I've been in the hospital almost forty-eight hours and he is just now showing up. I don't wanna see him. I don't even know why he even bothered.*

"How you feel?" He reached over and touched her face. "You look great."

"It's the drugs," she said, shrugging.

"No, you're just beautiful." He smiled. "I know you're pissed because I'm just now getting here. But Lincoln told me it was already a rack of people here. I knew the doctors would be tripping about you needing your rest and Taryn told me you were sleep most of the time. But, Yaya, I called every hour and checked on you."

"Thanks," she told him. She wanted to tell him that so did

a million other people. Once word spread about her being in the hospital, both she and Taryn's phones had been ringing nonstop. *What the hell makes you think your calls are so special, Fitz?*

"Qianna, I'm sorry," he said, softly. "I love you and I don't want you to be mad."

She looked over at him, shaking her head. "Fitz, you knew I wasn't feeling well Saturday and you still found Micha more important than me."

"I was there for my son, Yaya. Why do you insist on making it be about Micha?"

"Because that's how I feel. You left me in the church to go and comfort her, not your son. He was still in the church when you went running behind his mother."

"All right, you're right about that. And I'm sorry. Yaya, Micha is more than my son's mother, she's my friend and when I saw her so upset, I went with my first instinct. In that moment, I didn't think before I acted. That was stupid," he confessed. "But my feelings for her don't go beyond that point. What she and I had was over a long time ago. I'm not in love with her; I'm in love with you."

Yaya didn't know what to say. She wanted to believe him, but didn't know if he was being truthful.

"Let me ask you a question," Fitz continued. "If someone close to you and Jason died, and you were at the funeral and saw him crying like that. What would your first instinct be?"

"Jason and I aren't friends," she told him.

"Well, think of an ex you are friends with," he said, shrugging.

For some reason, her thoughts turned to Diesel. She knew that if something happened to someone close to Diesel, she would be right there for him, the same way he would be for her. And the same way Fitz was for Micha.

"I guess I understand," she said slowly.

"Yaya, I do love you." He came closer to her.

"I love you too Fitz," she replied. He leaned over to kiss her but she raised her hand and stopped him. "And I probably would've forgiven you if you woulda came in here and told me that *yesterday*."

Chapter 24

"Thanks for calling After Effex, where before and after are never the same!"

"What are you doing, Camille Davis?"

"Studying for my skin-care test." Camille smiled. "What are you doing, Terrance Oxford?"

"About to go to work. You know I won't get home until around midnight. Will you be there when I get there?"

"I don't know," she told him. She had spent the last three nights there and although Paige wasn't making a big deal out of it, she knew she probably needed to slow things down and spend some time at home. It was so hard though. She loved staying with Terrance and the more she stayed, the more she enjoyed it. He cooked for her; they played video games, watched television. They even showered together after their intense, pleasurable lovemaking sessions. It was like she was a junkie and Terrance Oxford was her drug of choice. Although he hadn't directly come out and asked her to be his girlfriend, they did any and everything a couple would do. He didn't bring up where they stood in their relationship, so she didn't. Instead, she chose to just enjoy the time they spent together.

"Come on, I'll help you study for your skin test," he promised.

"You're lying," she told him. "You're not gonna help me study."

"I know all about skin. Haven't I showed you that?" he asked seductively. "I'm a great tutor."

She tried not to blush, but couldn't help it. "I bet you are. But, I don't know, Terrance."

"What's wrong? Are you tired of me?" he asked.

"No, not at all," she told him. She wasn't tired of him, she was just tired. With Yaya being out and Taryn taking care of her most of the time, most of the makeup and facial clients had to be called, canceled or rescheduled, with the exception of the basics that Camille was able to do. She also had midterms to prepare for.

"Then it's settled," Terrance replied. "I'll see you when I get home."

He hung up and she turned her attention back to the note cards she was studying before he called.

"Hey lovergirl, can you refill this acetone bottle for me right quick? And grab me another jar of acrylic?" Monya looked up from her client and asked.

"Ha ha ha." Camille said as she got up. "You're certainly a woman of many talents, Monya. A nail tech and a comedian, who knew?"

"It's nice to see young people in love these days," Monya called out as Camille grabbed the empty bottle from her station. She went into the storage room and filled it with acetone and found the jar of acrylic Monya needed. When she returned into the main area, there were two men dressed in suits, standing by the receptionist counter. A tall, slim black guy and a shorter, older Asian one.

"Can I help you?" Camille asked. She looked over at Monya who looked as clueless as she was.

"I'm Detective Wyn and this is Detective Jones. Are you Camille Davis?" The Asian man flashed his badge.

Camille's heart began pounding and flashbacks of her being arrested flooded her mind. *Oh hell no, not again. Jimmy said he was taking care of things so this wouldn't happen.*

"Uh, yes," she stammered.

"We have a couple of questions for you. Is there somewhere we can speak in private?" Detective Jones asked.

Again, Camille looked over at Monya, who said, "Use Taryn's office."

Camille led them into the office and offered them a seat. She wondered what they wanted with her. Her court date for the failure to appear and other charges wasn't even scheduled for another month.

"So, how can I help you?" She sat in Taryn's comfortable chair and tried to remain cool.

"We're looking into the missing person's case for Celeste Peterson. Were you aware that she's been missing for the past six days?" Detective Jones stared at her.

Camille was so relieved, that she almost started laughing out loud. "I know supposedly no one has heard from her for a few days. I wouldn't go so far as to call her missing."

"Have you had any contact with Ms. Peterson?" Detective Wyn asked.

Camille frowned at him. "No. Why would I have contact with her?"

"You don't seem too concerned about Ms. Peterson's disappearance, Ms. Davis. From your demeanor, I would even go so far as to say you're happy she's gone," Detective Jones commented.

"I would say that her supposedly being missing doesn't make me upset, sad, or even concerned. I really don't care one way or another," Camille told them. "Celeste Peterson has caused more than her fair share of problems and I can think of a lot of people who are actually happy that she's nowhere to be found."

"So, in other words, you really don't care for Ms. Peterson very much." Detective Wyn gave her a devious smile.

"Honestly, no, I don't. Can't stand her." Camille stared into his eyes and smiled back. She knew from watching years of *Law & Order* marathons how to handle herself with the cops and was determined not to think she was easily broken. She had dealt with them enough with her identity being stolen and they hadn't been any help nor seemed to care whatsoever. Now, having to talk to two detectives about a girl she had grown to hate was making her blood boil.

Detective Jones reached into his pocket and took out a small voice recorder and placed it on the desk. He hit the *play* button and turned the volume up. She frowned, wondering what was on it.

"Look, I asked you to leave. Why are you being so damn difficult?" she heard her own voice yelling.

"I'm not leaving until I see Taryn. This ain't got shit to do with you, so sit the fuck down somewhere and mind your damn business!" Celeste responded.

"You want me to sit down? You sit me down then, trick," the tape continued, *"What you jumping for, huh, heifer? Because you know I'll kill your ass if you don't get out my face. I mean that!"*

Camille was so mad, she couldn't speak. *That heifer came in here starting confusion on purpose. She wanted me to go off so she could get it on tape.* She wondered where the hell the police could have gotten the tape from since Celeste was supposedly missing.

Detective Jones cut the recorder off and sat back in his chair. "Well, I think you saying you can't stand her is an understatement."

"You have anything to say, Ms. Davis?" Once again, Detective Wyn wore the devious grin. He looked as if he wanted her to confess to something, he didn't care what it was.

"Anything else that needs to be said will be done in the presence of my attorney," she replied the moment she heard her voice on that tape, the police attempting to trick her into incriminating herself was a given.

"Taryn wants you to call her ASAP!" Monya said when the detectives were finally gone. "She called to warn you as soon as you went back into the office, but it was too late."

Camille went back into the office and dialed Taryn's number. She answered before the phone even had a chance to ring. "Hey Cam. What happened?"

"They think I had something to do with Celeste being missing. Remember the day she came in here and we almost had that fight? They got the whole thing on audio, Taryn," Camille told her.

"I know. They're talking to all of us. Me, you, Yaya, Lincoln. Apparently, Marlon's wife, Kasey, found the recorder in Celeste's room while she was going through Celeste's things and turned it in to the police. This whole thing is just crazy," Taryn said. "They're pulling phone records, text messages, the whole nine because her fat ass has probably gone off to some pathetic person's eating convention somewhere. I tell you this much, if she ain't laid up hurt somewhere now, she will be when I get finished with her."

"Not if I can get to her first," Camille responded.

"So, what did you tell them?"

"I told them I didn't like her and when they played the tape, I asked for my attorney."

"Good thinking. That was the right thing to do," Taryn told her.

"I'm over at Yaya's. You and Monya need to come here as soon as you all close the salon, okay?"

"I'll be right there," Camille agreed. "How is she doing?"

"She's fine. She's walking around a lot more. I think the detectives coming over here pissed her off and speeded up her recovery," Taryn said, laughing.

"You got that right," Yaya's voice yelled from the background.

"We'll see you when you get here," Taryn said and hung up. Camille then called Terrance to let him know that she wouldn't be staying with him tonight. With everything she had going on right now, his *tutoring* her for her test would definitely have to wait.

"I was just about to call you," Terrance told her. "Cam, you're not gonna believe what just happened to me."

"You're not gonna believe what just happened to me, either."

"I just got a call from Deon Carroll's agent. You know he just got traded last week. He's willing to do an in-depth interview for the *Tuff Love Report*." Terrance's voice was full of excitement.

"Are you serious? That's the bomb, Terrance. I'm so happy for you," she told him.

"I'm catching a red-eye out tonight. I guess I'm gonna have to *tutor* you when I get back," he said. "So, what happened to you?"

After hearing his wonderful news, she didn't feel the need to share with him the pandemonium of her own life. "It's not important."

Terrance getting an interview with someone of Deon Carroll's caliber had to be a dream come true and would probably boost his career even further. Deon Carroll hardly ever gave interviews, period, let alone to a small-time sports reporter like Terrance. To get a call out of the blue from Deon Carroll's agent was unbelievable. Either there was more to the story than what Terrance was telling her, or the man upstairs was definitely looking out for him.

Chapter 25

"And how is the patient today?" Diesel asked when Taryn got to the door. Thursday was the day that business at the salon began getting hectic and there was no way all their weekend clients could be serviced with both Taryn *and* Yaya being out. Taryn had to get back to work and when Diesel offered to sit with Yaya, Taryn didn't hesitate to say yes.

"I keep telling you I don't need a babysitter!" Yaya called from the sofa in her living room.

"She's still complaining as usual." Taryn smiled and let him in.

"Then things are back to normal," Diesel said, laughing. "What's up, Qianna boo?"

"You don't have to be here, Diesel. I keep telling y'all I don't need a babysitter," Yaya said, sighing.

Taryn knew she didn't need to be alone. She hadn't really said anything about Fitz, but she knew Yaya was despondent if not totally depressed about his not being there for her. Even Lincoln had to agree that the way his brother handled the whole situation was inappropriate and he could've been more supportive. *It was for the best and Yaya deserves better. If anyone can cheer her up and make her feel better, Diesel can.*

"I'm not here to babysit, Yaya. I'm here to keep you company," Diesel told her.

"What's in that bag?" Yaya pointed to the large leather bag he wore on his shoulder.

"My laptop." He put the bag on the coffee table and took out the small computer.

"You need a bag that big for your laptop?" She laughed.

"I'm a big man, and as you know, bigger is definitely better," he said, pulling a small folder out and passing it to her. "Besides, I keep files and paperwork in here too."

"What is this?" she asked, opening the folder and flipping through the contents.

"I got a couple of ideas, and I thought we could brainstorm." He smiled guiltily.

"You volunteered to keep me company so we could brainstorm, Diesel. And to think, I thought you really cared." Yaya frowned at him.

"I guess old habits really do die hard. Well, I can see you two will be getting along great as usual. You both have my numbers. Call me if you need anything," Taryn said, laughing as she headed out the door. "No fighting! And I'll be home by eight!"

It's time for our lives to get back to normal, and it's starting today!

"Hey, are you at work yet?"

"I'm on my way now," Taryn replied. There was something strange about the sound in Lincoln's voice. "What's wrong?"

"The police want me to come down to the station and answer questions about this crazy-ass girl Celeste," he told her.

"I thought they questioned you yesterday," Taryn asked, wondering why they were calling him back.

"They did, and I told them everything I knew. That Detective Wyn dude just called. I'm supposed to be at the station in an hour."

Taryn's heart began beating fast. She wondered what would give the police more reasons to question Lincoln, and at the station at that. "Lincoln, is there anything you're not telling me?"

"Taryn, I swear, I have told you from day one, I didn't have nothing and I mean NOTHING to do with that girl. I didn't sleep with her, I didn't get her pregnant, I didn't give her any STDs, and I didn't do nothing to make her ass disappear. Although at this point, I wish I did," he told her.

"I think we're all persons of interest in her disappearance, Lincoln." She tried to sound reassuring. "That's what the detectives told me."

"I'm a black man, T, which makes me a *suspect*. Get it right." He sounded deflated. "I gotta go find a lawyer. Have a good day at work. Love you and I'll call you later."

"Love you too. Lincoln," she said and hung up. She made a U-turn and headed in the opposite direction as she dialed the salon's number. "Monya, it's me. I'ma be there in about another hour. Can you handle things until then?"

"Mr. Grossman will be with you in a moment, Ms. Green. Would you like some coffee while you wait?" Jimmy's secretary asked.

"No, I'm fine." Taryn smiled and sat down in the posh lobby of his law firm. There were several other people already seated and waiting. She picked up an old issue of *Black Enterprise* and flipped through the pages. She looked at her watch and prayed that Jimmy would be able to help.

The door opened and a well-dressed white woman carrying an Italian leather briefcase came out. "That sounds wonderful, Jamison. I'll have my clients sign the contract and get it back to you immediately."

"Not a problem, Liz," Jamison said as he walked her out.

After they said their good-byes, he turned to Taryn and said, "Ms. Green, it's nice to see you again. You can follow me right into my office."

"Thank you, Mr. Grossman," Taryn said and walked with him.

Once inside, he motioned for her to take a seat in one of the stylish leather chairs he had facing his massive desk. The inside of his office was just as tastefully decorated on the inside as it was on the outside. She looked at all the awards, plaques, and accolades he had placed on shelves and hanging on the walls, including his distinguished law degree from Howard University.

"This is really nice." She nodded in approval.

"It's not as chic as yours, but it'll do," he said, smiling. "So, what's going on? What's happened now?"

"I don't like the tone of your voice. You make it sound as if I'm the one causing all of this mess, which I'm not," she said, frowning.

"I'm not saying that at all," he told her. "It's just that this whole missing Celeste fiasco is having a snowball effect and I gotta feeling it's just gonna get worse," he told her. "You're here first thing this morning and so, what's happened now?"

"Well, now, they have Lincoln down at the station, questioning him about Celeste," she said, affirming his presumption that something else had happened.

"Well, you knew he was a suspect," Jimmy told her.

"Person of interest," she corrected him.

"Yeah, right." Jimmy frowned. "So, Lincoln is at the station and?"

"I was wondering if you can maybe go down there or call and check . . ."

"Taryn, you can't be serious." Jimmy sat back and stared at her.

"What? Jimmy, you know you're the best attorney in this state, no better yet, this side of the country—"

"That's true, but I don't need for you to tell me that," he interrupted her. "Taryn, be realistic. I'm *your* attorney. My job is to take the focus off you so you don't get caught in the middle of this mess that for some reason, you keep getting deeper and deeper into. Not to mention, I'm also Camille's attorney in all of this too, remember. The fact that Lincoln is down at the station makes me feel relieved."

"How can you say that, Jimmy? Lincoln didn't have anything to do with this and you know it," Taryn snapped.

"No, I know that he *says* he didn't have anything to with it. When it gets down to it, Taryn, that's all that you know. From what I hear, they have text messages and voice mails of him and her going back and forth, some of them threatening. So, yeah, his being down there makes me relieved. Because that means for the time being, my clients aren't directly under the radar, he is."

Taryn tried to fight the tears that were forming, but she couldn't. They escaped her eyelids and she could feel them as they fell down her cheeks when she finally blinked. Questions began filling her head. *How the hell did Celeste get Lincoln's cell phone number in the first place and why the hell was he communicating with her when he claimed he barely knew her.* Jimmy reached into his desk and passed her a tissue.

"Thanks," she whispered.

"I'll make a call down to the station, Taryn. I'll even call a friend of mine to represent him for you. But I can't be his lawyer, Taryn. It's too much of a conflict of interest." Jimmy heaved a sigh. "Now stop crying!"

Taryn found herself smiling. Deep down, she knew that Jimmy was right and coming here to ask for his help was a long shot. She didn't get the answer from him she wanted, but she knew he would help Lincoln as best he could.

"Okay." She nodded.

"Now, I have to call my other client, Camille, because she got other issues to deal with this morning herself. I think we've got a break in this whole identity-theft thing and we're gonna get to the bottom of it. One things for sure, having After Effex as a client is gonna pay for my new Jag," he said, winking.

Taryn's cell phone began playing Jay-Z loudly and she quickly tried to grab it out her purse. "My bad. I thought it was on vibrate. But that's Camille's ring tone. She loves Jay-Z. Hey, Cam. I'm in Jimmy's office and he needs to talk to you. Hold on."

"What's up baby girl," he said when he took it from her. "I got a couple of urgent e-mails this morning that I need to discuss with you. Can you swing by the office? Midterm. Okay. Well, I can, but Taryn is sitting in my office right now. You want me to call you back?"

"I can step out. It's not a problem," Taryn told him.

"No, she says stay because she's gonna wind up telling you everything I say anyway," he said, laughing. "Let me pull them up right quick. Okay. We got charges on a Banktrust Visa card, which I'm assuming you don't even realize you have, right? I figured that. It must've slipped through the system some kinda way. I'm glad we put that alert on your Social. Now here's the crazy thing: the charges are fairly recent and some are in Westwood but there are a lot in Dunbar at restaurants and a Days Inn."

Taryn listened. Westwood was the city that Camille's mother and brother lived, forty-five minutes away and Dunbar was a fairly smaller city that was another hour drive from there.

"You don't know anyone in Dunbar, do you? What about Chelsea Women's Center, because there's a large charge made there. What? You're kidding!"

"What?" Taryn asked after she saw the expression on his face.

"She says her brother's wife is a nurse at Chelsea women's clinic. Where are you now, Camille? Taryn and I are on our way to pick you up." He hung the phone up and told Taryn, "Let's go. We're 'bout to get to the bottom of this right now!"

The normalcy that Taryn had declared would start today was nowhere to be found as they picked up Camille and headed to Dunbar. Jimmy drove his money-green Range Rover at full speed and they all stayed on their cells making calls the entire ride there. Taryn called Monya and Yaya and told them what was going on. Camille called Paige, her brother, and tried to reach Terrance, who was in LA somewhere. Jimmy called the authorities in Dunbar and Westwood and informed them of his findings.

When they finally arrived at the Days Inn, the officers had Celeste in handcuffs, reading her her rights and putting her in the back of the car.

"I'm going to kick her ass!" Camille yelled as soon as the truck stopped.

"Cam, wait!" Taryn yelled, but she had already jumped out.

"I got her." Jimmy hurried behind Camille. He tried to hold on to her as she screamed and yelled at Celeste, who had the nerve to be crying herself. Camille was so angry, she was trying to kick the police car. Finally, Jimmy was able to get her back to the car and wait as he went and talked with the other officers on the scene, including Detectives Jones and Wyn.

"Can someone please tell me what the hell is going on?" Marlon asked, rushing into the police station and to his sister's side. She was sitting in a waiting area along with Paige and Taryn.

"They just arrested Celeste and they're on their way to pick up your wife," Paige told him.

"My wife? What for?" Marlon snapped.

"Because the two of them stole my identity, ran up my credit and had this crazy scheme that for some reason, they actually thought they would get away with," Camille said, sniffing as she wiped the tears from her eyes.

"What?" Marlon was still dumbfounded.

"God, Marlon, you can't be this slow." Paige sighed. "Somehow, Celeste and Kasey got ahold of Camille's birth certificate and Social Security card. They got credit cards, utilities, bank accounts, the whole nine. The police have receipts, fake ID's with both their pictures and Camille's name, bills, you name it."

"Man, how in the world?" Marlon began rubbing his hands over his head. "How could they get ahold of your personal information? Where were you keeping that stuff, Cam?"

"Oh hell no, you're not gonna put this on her, Marlon. I'm not even gonna sit here and let you do that!" Paige jumped up.

"That's not what . . ."

"I don't give a damn what you meant! I just told you your trifling-ass wife stole your sister's identity and you wanna question her? Think again!"

"Okay, everyone needs to calm down," Taryn said, softly. "This isn't helping Camille."

"If I didn't know any better, I'd think Lucille probably gave them Camille's info." Paige took her seat.

"Don't go there, Paige," Marlon warned.

"She's right. The only person that had access to that stuff was you and Mama. You know she kept all that stuff in the lockbox. Did you take it?" Camille stared at her brother, realizing what Paige was saying made sense.

"Hell no, I didn't take it, Camille, you know better than that," Marlon told her.

"I rest my case," Paige said, sighing.

"Marlon! Marlon!"

They all turned to see Kasey being brought in wearing handcuffs and crying. Her hair was standing on top of her head and she looked possessed.

"You'd better hurry and go check on your wife because in about two seconds, I'm kicking her ass," Camille warned him.

"I think we'd better wait and see what the detectives have to say." Marlon shifted and then turned, walking in the direction of where they took Kasey. "I need to find out where the baby is."

"I'm starting to hate him too," Camille said.

"He's just Marlon." Paige put her hand on her shoulder. "You know that."

Soon, Jimmy came out. "Celeste just finished giving a statement. She told everything. She claims that they didn't do this to hurt you and planned to pay everything back. It started out as a way to get things for the baby, but things just got out of hand."

"That's bullshit," Camille answered.

"And what about the whole pregnancy lie?" Taryn asked.

"Well, it turns out that she wasn't pregnant before, but she is now. Somehow, Kasey helped her conceive using fertility drugs she was getting from a clinic she used to work at. Celeste was sleeping with various men at the hotel in an effort to get pregnant."

"So, she was whoring around to get knocked up? That's pathetic." Camille shook her head. "Did she say how they got my info?"

"No, she didn't say," Jimmy told her. "I'm going to need for you to make a statement in a little while."

Paige's cell phone began ringing. "It's my mother. I'll take this outside."

"I need to go talk with the prosecutor. I'll be back in a few minutes," Jimmy said. "Hey, it's almost over. You're about to get your life back."

"I hate her. I wish someone had killed her ass," Camille cried into Taryn's arms. "How dare she? How dare them?"

"It's okay, Camille," Taryn tried to comfort her. "We got her."

"They stole my name, Taryn. Celeste, that bitch Kasey and my own mother probably had something to do with it! Do you know my name was the only thing in life I had, Taryn. My good name. The name I was working hard to preserve and be proud of. The only thing I had and they took it and ruined it."

"That's not the only thing you have, Camille. And you still have a name to be proud of. There is only one Camille Davis and I don't give a damn how many people try and grind your name in the ground, you know you're someone that can hold her head up high and continue to be the success that you are. They can't take away your talent, your character, your pride, and they damn sure can't touch your faith if you don't let them."

Camille sat up and stared at Taryn. "My own mother, Taryn. She helped them plot and do this."

"Camille, anyone you let in your life will eventually hurt you in one way or another. The trick is finding out who's worth the pain. But remember, the ones that you think are worth the pain are the ones that hurt you the most, even your mother."

Later that evening, after a long, hot bath and she had climbed into bed, Camille called Terrance to tell him about what had happened.

"Man, I'm sorry, Cam. That's rough," he told her.

"I wish you were here," she said, sighing.

"Yeah, I feel you, but it sounds like Jimmy has everything under control," he said. Camille didn't understand what he meant and it certainly wasn't the reaction she hoped to hear. He had actually been kind of distant the past couple of days that she talked to him.

"When are you coming home?" she asked.

"Uh, a day or so. Look, I'm kinda in the middle of something right now. I'll call you when I get into town."

Before she could respond, he hung up. The hurt that she

felt seemed to radiate through her body. Here she had given this man her innocence and this was what she got in return. More than anything, at this moment, she needed him, and he couldn't even be there for her. She prayed that giving Terrance her heart wouldn't turn out to be a regret, nor would the fact that she gave him her virginity.

Chapter 26

"Hey."

Yaya looked up from the mail she was sorting at her desk. She was surprised to see Fitz standing in her doorway. "Hey."

"I was next door and they told me you were back at work," he said. "I thought I'd come by and see how you're feeling."

Why does it matter? Am I Micha now?

"I'm good. I've been back for a couple of days now," she told him. He was looking awkward just standing there so she said, "You can come in and sit down."

"Thanks," he told her. "It's a good thing you were sick. You missed all the Celeste excitement, huh?"

"I guess," she said, shrugging, "I'm just glad it's all over."

"Yeah, we all are. That was wild. She was straight psychotic."

"I can't believe how that trick Kasey was in on it the entire time and they made those fake STD results, now that was trifling," she agreed.

"How's Camille holding up?"

"She's really just been working a lot. We keep trying to get her to talk about it, but she just downplays the whole thing. I know it has to be hard on her because she suspects her mother was involved in the whole thing. They wrote bad checks, got cell phones, the whole nine using Camille's identity."

"Man," he said. He was quiet then asked, "How are you?"

"I already told you I'm fine." She looked at him strangely. "How are Micha and Carver?"

"Still healing," he told her. "I see that you and Diesel have the flyers out about the swing classes. They sound like fun."

She nodded. She had agreed with Diesel that holding swing classes on Monday nights would be a fun activity and a great promotional event for the club. He begged her to help teach and she reluctantly agreed.

"Yeah, we're calling them the Monday Nighters. That reminds me, do you have my laptop?"

"Aw, man, I do have it. I can bring it to you tomorrow," he said. "Maybe we can meet for dinner or drinks."

"I can just pick it up tonight if you're gonna be home." She didn't want to entertain the idea of doing anything with him. "It's not a problem."

"Oh, well, that's cool. You can swing by. I'll be home all night." He stood up. "I'm glad you're better and I'll check you later."

"Cool," she told him. "I would walk you out but it still hurts when I walk."

"I understand," he said. "Yaya, can I ask you something and you'll give me an honest answer?"

"Sure." She tried to prepare herself for whatever it was he was about to ask.

"Sonya is really concerned about Diesel. I know he's your friend, and she's told me that she thinks he's cheating." He stared at her.

"Huh?" She was confused because that was definitely not what she thought he was gonna ask.

"He's spending more and more time at the club. It's no secret that the brother does have a reputation. People have been talking and she's heard some things."

"So, she's basing her assumption on the fact that he's been working hard and has a reputation?" she asked, and then realized that this was something that she really didn't even need to get into. "I don't know what to say, Fitz. I mean, I know she's your neighbor and all, but it's none of my business."

"You're right. But, I guess I figured since you and him are friends, you could say something to him."

"Not any of my business," she repeated.

"Qianna, it's you that Sonya thinks he's cheating with."

"How did that go? Was it awkward?" Taryn didn't waste any time coming into the office when he was finally gone.

"No, I was polite and I almost didn't cuss him out."

"Almost?"

"It was all good until he tells me Sonya thinks Diesel is cheating with me," she told her. "Then I let him have it."

"Whoa," Taryn said, laughing.

"T, now you know." Yaya exhaled. She and Diesel were just friends. After the breakup with Jason and her short-lived relationship with Fitz, she realized that the whole person she had become years ago, somehow got lost in the shuffle. With everything else she had going on in her life, and all she was trying to achieve, she had no room in her top priorities for a man. What she did need in her life was a friend like Diesel to help keep her focused on her talents and encourage her to stay on top of her game.

"Yes, I know," Taryn agreed. "I have to wonder though, did Fitz ask you out?"

"Yes, I told him I needed my laptop and he wanted to meet me for dinner and bring it to me. I told him I would pick it up on the way home."

"Girl, you can barely drive. You want me to pick it up for you?"

"That's probably a better idea. At least thing it won't be a setup. Don't be surprised if you get there and he's hooked up a candlelight meal because he's expecting me and not you," she informed her.

"If that does happen, you know I'll call you with the quickness."

Taryn called Lincoln and let him know she had a quick stop to make and would be a few minutes late for the meeting. After the mystery of Celeste had been solved, Taryn decided she had a mystery of her own to solve. She confronted Lincoln about his disappearing acts and he confessed that he would sneak out to drink. He was an alcoholic. At first, she wasn't sure if she could handle any more of his issues. He told her that he wanted to seek help and would she support his effort. Taryn could hear Jimmy's voice in her head: *"Is he worth it?"* She knew that she was in love with him when she heard her heart answer *YES!*

"You want me to wait for you in the parking lot?" he asked.

"No, you go ahead inside. You can do this, Lincoln, and I'm gonna be there to help. I promise," she told him.

"Love you," he said.

"Love you too!" she replied. Her phone made a chirping noise and went dead. *Damn, I forgot to charge it up and my car charger is in Yaya's car.* She pulled into the lot of Fitz and Lincoln's condo and parked next to Fitz's station wagon. She walked up the steps and knocked on the door. There was no answer. *He's gotta be here, his car is out front.* She turned and walked back to her car. Just as she was about to turn out of the parking lot, another car turned inside. She recognized the driver and paused before she drove off. Taryn put the car in reverse, and turned around, this time parking two doors down. She watched as the woman got out and walked up the same steps as she just did. Taryn got out the car and walked to get a closer look. Just as she suspected, the woman knocked on Fitz's door. Suddenly it opened and he stepped out, smiling widely as he took her into his arms and kissed Micha passionately.

Taryn shook her head in disappointment. She didn't know how she'd be able to tell Yaya. Breaking the news to her best friend that her man indeed was cheating with his ex was not something she looked forward to, but she had to do it.

"I got my midterm grades," Camille said to Terrance when he walked into the salon. He called her the night before and she had gone over to his house. They didn't make love, they didn't even kiss. They sat back, ordered Chinese food and watched movies. It was like old times, when they first started hanging out together.

"And what did you get?" Terrance asked.

"All A's," she sang.

"I'm so proud of you," he told her.

"Proud enough to take me to the Melting Pot?" She bat her eyelashes at him.

"Yeah, but not tonight. I got invited to a reception at the Sports Hall of Fame and I got an interview set up with this guy in Memphis who is probably gonna be the first draft pick this year," he said, groaning. "I'm on my way to the airport now."

Camille was disappointed. They had barely been spending any time together these days. Somehow, he had turned into an instant celebrity and was traveling more than Yaya. He had only been home one night and he claimed to be so tired that he wasn't up for company. At the time when she needed him the most, he wasn't there.

"When are you coming back?" she stepped back and asked.

"Monday afternoon," he said. "We can do something then, I promise. I gotta run, boo."

"Okay," she said. He leaned in and kissed her and before she could catch herself, she told him, "I love you, Terrance."

"You are a special person, Camille." He touched her cheek and walked away. That wasn't the answer she wanted and she didn't know how to react. She felt as if she was reaching out, trying to grab Terrance and bring him back to the place where they were when they first made love, but he was getting farther and farther away from her. She loved him and now, she questioned whether he truly loved her in return.

Epilogue

"A'ight peeps, look at what my man sent me before it even hits the stands." Diesel waltzed into the salon carrying a manila envelope. He had become a familiar face in the salon since his breakup with Sonya. Taryn believed that although they weren't romantically involved, he and Yaya were finding comfort in one another in their healing process. Their platonic friendship was needed by each of them.

"It better not be what I think it is!" Yaya squealed. "Give it here! Give it here!"

"Let me see it," Taryn added. They both rushed to snatch the envelope, but he was too quick. "Be nice. We will look at it together."

"Fine," Yaya told him. They calmed down and patiently watched him slip the glossy magazine out of the envelope. They had been waiting on edge for the *True Diva* issue with Geneva Johnson on the cover to arrive. Her eyes stared at the big and bold words. She swore her heart stopped beating when she realized what the cover truly said.

"Oh my God," she heard Taryn say, and realized her partner had noticed the same thing so it had to be real and not a dream.

FEELING GOOD IN THE HOOD: ONE SALON'S SUCCESS AT BRINGING BEAUTY TO THE STREET the headline read and featured the four of them posing in front, wearing their fierce denim jackets. They looked hot, they looked glamorous, and they looked damn good! They looked so good, that they outshone Geneva Johnson who was standing beside them.

Taryn and Yaya began screaming and everyone ran to see what they were seeing. It was the proudest moment of Yaya's life. They had all been though so much, endured, and conquered and in the end, they were a success. She and Taryn began hugging each other and cried tears of joy.

"Damn, y'all ain't even read the article," Diesel teased. When they regained their composure, they were able to read the article, which quoted beauty tips from each of them, several shots of Geneva being pampered, and highlighted the salon's services.

"The photographer told me he was gonna hook us up, but I never expected this," Taryn told them.

Camille looked down at the photo of herself with her name printed beside it: "Camille Davis is the rising star in the salon, a professional, pleasant young woman who has a promising career ahead of her," she read to herself. Taryn was right. No matter what Celeste, Kasey, and her mother tried to do, they couldn't tarnish her good name.

"You know we gotta celebrate, right?" Monya told them. "I think drinks at State Street's are in order."

"Cool," they quickly agreed.

"You hear that, Camille? No flaking out at the last minute," Taryn warned her. She had been in a funk because of Terrance traveling so much and it was time for her to come out of it.

"Sure," Camille said and continued looking through the

magazine. She stopped when she got to the Hot Couples section.

"Golf phenomenon Geneva Johnson had a new beau on her arm since her recent breakup with Deon Carroll. Geneva and sports journalist Terrance Oxford have been inseparable since they met at an exclusive interview he did. According to Geneva, known for blabbing bedroom secrets, *"Terrance can go more than the eighteen rounds I need."* The photo under the article of the two of them kissing made her sick to her stomach. She had been played for a fool. Better yet, she played herself for a fool. Trusted a man, given all she had, knowing deep in the back of her mind that he really hadn't made a commitment to her. She had played with fire, and gotten burned.

"The ones that you think are worth the pain are the ones that hurt you the most," she repeated Taryn's words. Camille was determined not to be hurt again.

"Ladies, I'd like to make a toast." Yaya raised her glass. Taryn, Monya, and Camille all looked at her. They were at State Street's, celebrating their being on the cover of *True Diva* and sharing a much needed girls night out. Camille had been hesitant to join them, but they pretty much told her if she didn't come, she was fired.

"I think a toast is in order." Taryn nodded to her best friend.

"To the success of the salon, the integrity of hard work and dedication, to enduring the drama and maintaining the sisterhood through it all. I love you all. To my girls!" Yaya said, smiling.

"To my girls." Taryn and Monya held their glasses to hers. They looked at Camille, who stared.

"Uh, Cam, we're waiting," Monya told her.

The words Yaya said echoed in her head and she reflected

on them. The truth in what she said rang true and she realized as she looked at each of them that they had all endured
drama—not just herself—been successful and they were a
sisterhood. Instead of having a pity party, she embraced the
feeling of family that surrounded her. She didn't know how
they did it, but she was determined to learn the secret to
their always being able to come out on top, even when they
seemed to hit bottom. It was a good lesson to learn.